A TEXT BOOK OF

COMPUTER GRAPHICS

FOR
SEMESTER – II

SECOND YEAR DEGREE COURSE IN
COMPUTER ENGINEERING

Strictly According to New Revised Credit System Syllabus
of Savitribai Phule Pune University
(w.e.f June 2016)

Mrs. PRAJAKTA S. KULKARNI
ME (IT)
Assistant Professor,
Information Technology Deptt.,
RMD Sinhgad School of Engineering
Warje, Pune.

Mrs. PALLAVI P. AHIRE
M.E. (Comp. Engg.)
Assistant Professor,
Information Technology Deptt.,
Sinhgad Institute of Technology
Lonavala, Pune

NIRALI
PRAKASHAN
ADVANCEMENT OF KNOWLEDGE

N3577

COMPUTER GRAPHICS (SE COMPUTER)   ISBN 978-93-86353-21-4

First Edition : **January 2017**

© : **Authors**

Published By :   Polyplate

NIRALI PRAKASHAN

Abhyudaya Pragati, 1312, Shivaji Nagar,
Off J.M. Road, Pune – 411005
Tel - (020) 25512336/37/39, Fax - (020) 25511379
Email : niralipune@pragationline.com

☞ DISTRIBUTION CENTRES

PUNE

Nirali Prakashan : 119, Budhwar Peth, Jogeshwari Mandir Lane, Pune 411002, Maharashtra
Tel : (020) 2445 2044, 66022708, Fax : (020) 2445 1538
Email : bookorder@pragationline.com, niralilocal@pragationline.com

Nirali Prakashan : S. No. 28/27, Dhyari, Near Pari Company, Pune 411041
Tel : (020) 24690204 Fax : (020) 24690316
Email : dhyari@pragationline.com, bookorder@pragationline.com

MUMBAI

Nirali Prakashan : 385, S.V.P. Road, Rasdhara Co-op. Hsg. Society Ltd.,
Girgaum, Mumbai 400004, Maharashtra
Tel : (022) 2385 6339 / 2386 9976, Fax : (022) 2386 9976
Email : niralimumbai@pragationline.com

☞ DISTRIBUTION BRANCHES

JALGAON

Nirali Prakashan : 34, V. V. Golani Market, Navi Peth, Jalgaon 425001,
Maharashtra, Tel : (0257) 222 0395, Mob : 94234 91860

KOLHAPUR

Nirali Prakashan : New Mahadvar Road, Kedar Plaza, 1st Floor Opp. IDBI Bank
Kolhapur 416 012, Maharashtra. Mob : 9850046155

NAGPUR

Pratibha Book Distributors : Above Maratha Mandir, Shop No. 3, First Floor,
Rani Jhanshi Square, Sitabuldi, Nagpur 440012, Maharashtra
Tel : (0712) 254 7129

DELHI

Nirali Prakashan : 4593/21, Basement, Aggarwal Lane 15, Ansari Road, Daryaganj
Near Times of India Building, New Delhi 110002
Mob : 08505972553

BENGALURU

Pragati Book House : House No. 1, Sanjeevappa Lane, Avenue Road Cross,
Opp. Rice Church, Bengaluru – 560002.
Tel : (080) 64513344, 64513355,Mob : 9880582331, 9845021552
Email:bharatsavla@yahoo.com

CHENNAI

Pragati Books : 9/1, Montieth Road, Behind Taas Mahal, Egmore,
Chennai 600008 Tamil Nadu, Tel : (044) 6518 3535,
Mob : 94440 01782 / 98450 21552 / 98805 82331,
Email : bharatsavla@yahoo.com

niralipune@pragationline.com | www.pragationline.com

Also find us on  **www.facebook.com/niralibooks**

PREFACE

It gives us great pleasure in publishing this text book on "**Computer Graphics**" for the students of Second Year Degree Course in Computer Engineering. This book is strictly written according to **New Revised Credit System Syllabus** of Savitribai Phule Pune University (2015 Pattern).

As per the policy of the University, Engineering Syllabi is revised every five years. Last revision was in the year 2012. New revision is coming little earlier, as university has introduced **Online System of Examination** from year 2012.

As per the **New Credit System**, the **Online Examinations** Phase-I will be conducted based on First & Second Units and Phase II on Third & Fourth Units. The **Online** examinations will have objective types of questions with multiple choices. End Sem. Theory Examination will be based on all the six units and that will be conducted in traditional way and the Theory Course will have 4 credits.

It is our objective to keep the presentation systematic, consistent, intensive and clear presentation of concept through explanatory notes and figures. So we are sure that this book will cater for all your needs for this subject.

Main feature of this book is, **Complete Coverage** of the New Credit System Syllabus with large number of **Worked (Solved) Examples and Exercises.**

We have given Separate Book of Multiple Choice Questions (MCQ's) which will be very useful to the students especially for Online Examinations.

We take this opportunity to express our sincere thanks to Shri. Dineshbhai Furia, Shri. Jignesh Furia, Mrs. Nirali Verma and Shri. M. P. Munde and entire team of Nirali Prakashan namely Mrs. Deepali Lachake (Co-ordinator), who really have taken keen interest and untiring efforts in publishing this text.

The advice and suggestions of our esteemed readers to improve the text are most welcomed, and will be highly appreciated.

Vinayak Chaturthi

Pune   **Authors**

SYLLABUS

Unit I : Graphics Primitives and Scan Conversion   **09 Hours**

Concepts, applications of computer graphics, pixel, frame buffer, resolution, aspect ratio.

Plotting Primitives: Scan conversions, lines, line segments, vectors, pixels and frame buffers, vector generation

Scan Conversion: Line and line segments, qualities of good line drawing algorithms,

line drawing algorithms: Digital Differential Analyzer (DDA), Bresenham and parallel line algorithms, Line styles: thick, dotted and dashed. Circle drawing algorithm: DDA, Bresenham. Character generating methods: stroke and bitmap method.

Display Files: display file structure, algorithms and display file interpreter. Primitive operations on display file.

Unit II : Polygons and Clipping Algorithms 09 Hours

Introduction to polygon, types: convex, concave and complex. Representation of polygon, Inside test, polygon filling algorithms – flood fill, seed fill, scan line fill and filling with patterns.

Windowing and clipping: viewing transformations, 2-D clipping: Cohen – Sutherland algorithm, Polygon clipping: Sutherland Hodgeman algorithm, generalized clipping.

Unit III : 2-D, 3-D Transformations and Projections   **09 Hours**

2-D transformations: introduction, matrices, Translation, scaling, rotation, homogeneous coordinates and matrix representation, translation, coordinate transformation, rotation about an arbitrary point, inverse and shear transformation.

3-D transformations: introduction, 3-D geometry, primitives, 3-D transformations and matrix representation, rotation about an arbitrary axis, 3-D viewing transformations, 3-D Clipping

Projections : Parallel (Oblique: Cavalier, Cabinet and orthographic: isometric, diametric, trimetric) and Perspective (Vanishing Points – 1 point, 2 point and 3 point)

Unit IV – Segment and Animation   **09 Hours**

Segment: Introduction, Segment table, Segment creation, closing, deleting and renaming, Visibility. Animation: Introduction, Design of animation sequences, Animation languages, Keyframe, Morphing, Motion specification.

Colour models and applications: Properties of Light, CIE chromaticity Diagram, RGB, HSV, CMY, YIQ, colour Selection and applications.

Unit V – Shading, and Hidden Surfaces   **09 Hours**

Illumination Models: Light Sources, Ambient Light, Diffuse reflection, Specular Reflection, and the Phong model, Combined diffuse and Specular reflections with multiple light sources, warn model, Shading Algorithms: Halftone, Gauraud and Phong Shading. Hidden Surfaces Introduction, Back face detection and removal, Algorithms: Depth buffer (z), Depth sorts (Painter), Area subdivision (Warnock), BSP tree, and Scan line.

Unit VI : Curves and Fractals   **09 Hours**

Curves: Introduction, Interpolation and Approximation, Blending function, B-Spline curve, Bezier curve, Fractals: Introduction, Classification, Applications, Fractal generation: snowflake, Triadic curve, Hilbert curve. Gaming: Introduction, Gaming platform (NVIDIA, i8060 etc.), Advances in Gaming, Graphics Tools: Introduction, Interactive graphics tool: OpenGL

CONTENTS

GRAPHICS PRIMITIVES AND SCAN CONVERSION

1.1 INTRODUCTION TO COMPUTER GRAPHICS

1.1.1 Basic Elements of Graphics

Pixel : It refers a point on the screen. It is also known as pel and is shortened form of picture element.

Frame Buffer : Frame buffer also known as refresh buffer is the memory area that holds the set of intensity values for all the screen points.

Point : A point marks a position in space. In pure geometric terms, a point is a pair of x, y coordinates.

Line : A line is an infinite series of points. A line is the connection between two points, or it is the path of a moving point.

Plane : A plane is a flat surface extending in height and width. A plane is the path of a moving line; it is a line with breadth.

Aspect Ratio : The ratio of the width to the height of an image or screen is called aspect ratio.

Resolution : Resolution is the number of pixels (individual points of color) contained on a display monitor, expressed in terms of the number of pixels on the horizontal axis and the number on the vertical axis. The sharpness of the image on a display depends on the resolution and the size of the monitor.

Persistence : Persistence is the time to which the phosphors in the cathode ray tubes emit light until the next electrons is fired. It is actually a measure of time taken by the emitted light from screen to decay one tenth of its original intensity. Higher persistence phosphors are used to display complex images.

1.1.2 Applications of Computer Graphics

- **Computer-Aided Design for Engineering and Architectural Systems etc.**

  Objects maybe displayed in a wireframe outline form. Multi-window environment is also favored for producing various zooming scales and views. Animations are useful for testing performance.

- **Presentation Graphics**

  To produce illustrations which summarize various kinds of data. Except 2D, 3D graphics are good tools for reporting more complex data.

- **Computer Art**

  Painting packages are available. With cordless, pressure-sensitive stylus, artists can produce electronic paintings which simulate different brush strokes, brush widths, and colors. Photorealistic techniques, morphing and animations are very useful in commercial art. For films, 24 frames per second are required. For video monitor, 30 frames per second are required.

- **Entertainment**

  Motion pictures, Music videos, and TV shows, Computer games.

- **Education and Training**

  Training with computer-generated models of specialized systems such as the training of ship captains and aircraft pilots.

- **Visualization**

  For analyzing scientific, engineering, medical and business data or behavior. Converting data to visual form can help to understand mass volume of data very efficiently.

- **Image Processing**

  Image processing is to apply techniques to modify or interpret existing pictures. It is widely used in medical applications.

- **Graphical User Interface**

  Multiple window, icons, menus allow a computer setup to be utilized more efficiently.

1.1.3 Advantages of Computer Graphics

- A high quality graphics displays of personal computer provide one of the most natural means of communicating with a computer.

- It has an ability to show moving pictures, and thus it is possible to produce animations with computer graphics.

- Computer graphics use can also control the animation by adjusting the speed, the portion of the total scene in view, the geometric relationship of the objects in the scene to one another, the amount of detail shown and so on.

- The computer graphics also provides facility called update dynamics. With update dynamics it is possible to change the color, shape or other properties of the objects being viewed.

- The interactive graphics can now provide audio feedback along with the graphical feedbacks to make the simulated environment even more realistic.

1.1.4 Classification of Computer Graphics

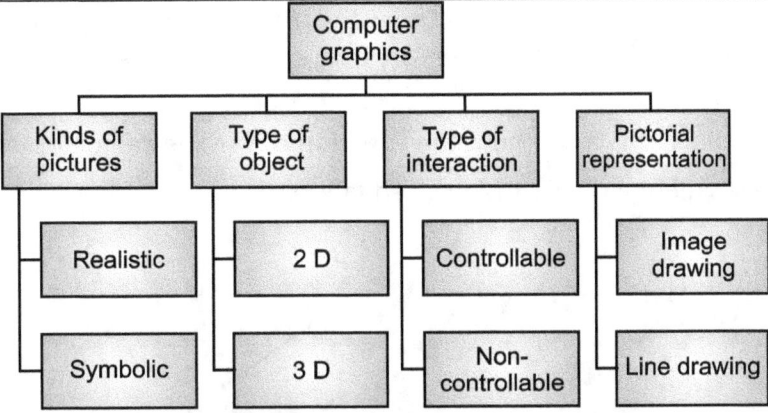

Fig. 1.1 : Classification of computer graphics

1.2 PLOTTING PRIMITIVES

A picture is completely specified by the set of intensities for the pixel positions in the display.

Shapes and colors of the objects can be described internally with pixel arrays into the frame buffer or with the set of the basic geometric – structure such as straight line segments and polygon color areas. To describe structure of basic object is referred to as output primitives.

Each output primitive is specified with input coordinate data and other information about the way that objects is to be displayed. Additional output primitives that can be used to constant a picture include circles and other conic sections, quadric surfaces, spline curves and surfaces, polygon floor areas and character string.

1.2.1 Scan Conversions

Scan conversion or scan converting rate is a video processing technique for changing the vertical / horizontal scan frequency of video signal for different purposes and applications. The device which performs this conversion is called a scan converter.

The process of scan conversion can be accomplished in four ways :

- Real Time Scan Conversion.
- Run Length Encoding.
- Cell Encoding.
- Using Frame Buffer.

1.2.2 Line Segment

- A line segment is a part of a line that is bounded by two distinct end points.
- A line segment is a piece, or part, of a line in geometry.

- A line segment is represented by end points on each end of the line segment.

- A line in geometry is represented by a line with arrows at each end. A line segment and a line are different because a line goes on forever while a line segment has a distinct beginning and end.

- From the end points of line segment the equation of the line can be obtained

- Points on line segment always satisfy the equation of line.

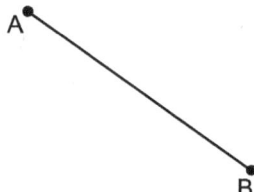

Fig. 1.2 : Line segment

1.2.2.1 Midpoint of Line Segment

- The point halfway between the end points of a line segment is called the midpoint. A midpoint divides a line segment into two equal segments.

- If the line segments are vertical or horizontal, you may find the midpoint by simply dividing the length of the segment by 2.

- If (x_1, x_2) and (y_1, y_2) are two end points of line segment, then mid point (x_m, y_m) is calculated by

$$(x_m, y_m) = \left(\frac{x_1 + x_2}{2}, \frac{y_1 + y_2}{2} \right)$$

1.2.2.2 Length of Line Segment

When we need to find the length (distance) of a segment such as AB we simply count the distance from point A to point B.

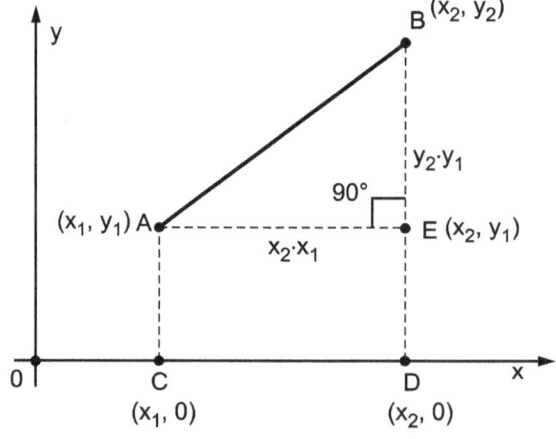

Fig. 1.3

Let (x_1, y_1) and (x_2, y_2) are two end points of line segment, construct a right triangle as shown in Fig. 1.3. By Pythagoras theorem we can calculate the length of AB. Length of AE is calculated by (x_2-x_1) , similarly the length of EB is $(y_2 - y_1)$

$$\text{Length of AB} = [(x_2-x_1)^2 + (y_2- y_1)^2]^{1/2}$$

1.2.3 Vectors

- A vector is a quantity having direction as well as magnitude, especially as determining the position of one point in space relative to another.

- A vector has magnitude (size) and direction :

- Two vectors are the same if they have the same magnitude and direction.

- A vector which has a magnitude of one is called unit vector.

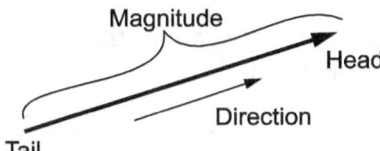

Fig. 1.4

- The length of the line shows its magnitude and the arrowhead points in the direction see Fig. 1.4.

Addition and Subtraction of Vectors

To add or subtract two vectors whose components are known, we simply add or subtract the components i.e. x parts and y parts. Therefore, if

$$v = (X_1, Y_1) \text{ and } w = (X_2, Y_2) \text{ we have :}$$

- $v - w = (X_1 - X_2, Y_1 - Y_2)$

- $v + w = (X_1 + X_2, Y_1 + Y_2)$

- Addition of vectors is commutative i.e. $a + b = b + a$, as well as associative i.e. $(a + b) + c = a + (b + c)$.

Multiplication of Vectors

- If vector is multiplied by a number, then multiplication is performed by multiplying each component of a vector by a number.

  Let $V(X_1, Y_1)$ is multiplied by a number n then,

  $$n.V = n.[X_1, Y_1] = [n.X_1, n.Y_1]$$

- The result of multiplication changes the magnitude of the vector but preserves the direction.

1.2.4 Pixels and Frame Buffers

Pixel :

- It refers a point on the screen. It is also known as pixel and is shortened form of 'picture element.

- A pixel is the smallest piece of information in an image.

- Pixels are normally arranged in a regular 2D grid, and are often represented using dots or squares.

- The intensity of each pixel is variable; in color systems, each pixel has typically three or four components such as red, green, and blue, or cyan, magenta, yellow, and black.

Frame Buffer :

- Frame buffer also known as refresh buffer is the memory area that holds the set of intensity values for all the screen points.

- Each screen pixel corresponds to a particular entry in a 2D array residing in memory. This memory is called a frame buffer or a bit map.

- The number of rows in the frame buffer equals to the number of raster lines on the display screen.

- The number of columns in this array equals to the number of pixels on each raster line.

- The term pixel is also used to describe the row and the column location in the frame buffer array that corresponds to the screen location. A 512x512 display screen requires 262144 pixel memory locations.

- Whenever we wish to display a pixel on the screen, a specific value is placed into the corresponding memory location in the frame buffer array.

- Each screen pixel's location and corresponding memory's location in the frame buffer is accessed by nonnegative integer coordinate pair (x, y).

- The x value refers to the column, the y value to the row position.

Types of Frame Buffer :

1. Black and White Frame Buffer

If the frame buffer stores one bit pixel information, thus single bit plane can be store only two values 0 and 1, thus it can yield black and white display

2. N-Bit Plane Gray Level Frame Buffer

The binary value i.e. 0 or 1 frame each of the N-bit plane is stored in the register, which is interpreted as an intensity level between 0 and 2^N where 0 represents dark and 2^N represents full intensity.

3. **Color and 3-Bit Planes**

A simple color frame buffer is implemented with 3-bit planes, one for each primary order. The bit plane drives an individual color gun for each of the three primary colors in color video.

Vector Generation

The process of "turning on" the pixels for a line segment is called vector generation. Suppose the end points of the segment are known, then how to decide changing intensity pixels. There are two approaches to this problem.

1. DDA i.e. Digital Differential Analyzer.

2. Bresenham's Algorithm.

1. Vector generation principle/ DDA i.e. Digital Differential Analyzer.

Consider Positive slope

(i) Slope is m< = 1

$$M = \frac{y_2 - y_1}{x_2 - x_1}$$

$$X_2 = x_1 + 1$$

$$y_2 = y_1 + m$$

So a unit change in x along x axis changes y by m which is constant

(ii) Slope is m > 1

i.e. Increment in y will make greater than 1 on unit increment in x, which is not valid, so we interchange the roles of x and y

$$\Delta y = 1$$

Calculate each successive x value as follows

$$X_2 = x_1 + \frac{1}{m}$$

Now consider negative slope

All the above assumption are based on that the line is processed from left to right, if this convention is reversed then the line is proceeding from right to left

Then we have

$$\Delta x = -1 \qquad\qquad y_2 = y_1 - m$$

When slope is greater than 1 (m > 1) we have $\Delta y = -1$ and $X_2 = x_1 - \frac{1}{m}$

1.3 QUALITIES OF GOOD LINE DRAWING ALGORITHMS

- Lines should appear straight - no jaggies Discretization problem Horizontal, vertical and diagonals easy others difficult.
- Lines should terminate accurately Discretization Cumulative round-off : e.g. octagon.
- Lines should have constant density dots/line length equal spacing of dots.
- Line density should be independent of line length or angle.
- Lines should be drawn rapidly efficient algorithms.

1.4 LINE DRAWING ALGORITHM

1.4.1 DDA Line Drawing Algorithm

The digital differential analyzer is a scan-conversion line algorithm based on calculating either dy or dx. We sample the line at unit intervals in one coordinate and determine corresponding integer values nearest to the line path for the other coordinate.

Algorithm :

Step 1 : Read the end points of the line (x_1, y_1) and (x_2, y_2) such that they are not equal.

Step 2 : If abs $(x_2 - x_1) \geq$ abs $(y_2 - y_1)$.

      then   length = abs $(x_2 - x_1)$

      else   length = abs $(y_2 - y_1)$

Step 3 : Initialize Δx or Δy to be equal to one raster unit.

$$\Delta x = (x_2 - x_1)/length$$

$$\Delta y = (y_2 - y_1)/length$$

Step 4 :   Round the values. Sign function is used to make the algorithm work on all quadrants.

$$x = x_1 + 0.5 \; sign \, (\Delta x)$$

$$y = y_1 + 0.5 \; sign \, (\Delta y)$$

Step 5 : Plot (x,y)

Step 6 : for(int i=1; i <= length; i++)

```
    {
    x = x + Δx
    y = y + Δy
                plot (integer (x), integer (y))
    }
end
```

Note : The sign function is used which return 1, 0, −1 for the argument as greater than zero, equal to zero and less than zero respectively.

Advantages of DDA

- The logic is easy to understand.

- The integer arithmetic is involved.

- It is a faster method for calculating pixel position.

- It is the simplest algorithm and does not require special skills for implementation.

Disadvantages of DDA

- Floating point arithmetic in DDA algorithm is still time-consuming.

- Division logic is needed, which switches it towards hardware logic.

- Floor integer values are used in place of normal integer values, which may give different values.

- The algorithm is orientation dependent. Hence end point accuracy is poor.

SOLVED EXAMPLES

Example 1.1 : Rasterize a line from (0, 0) to (8, 4) using DDA algorithm.

Solution : The end points of line are (0, 0) and (8, 4).

By evaluating the steps of DDA we have,

$$X_1 = 0 \qquad y_1 = 0$$
$$X_2 = 8 \qquad y_2 = 4$$

If abs $(x_2 - x_1) \geq$ abs $(y_2 - y_1)$.

$$\text{then} \qquad \text{length} = \text{abs } (x_2 - x_1)$$
$$\text{else} \qquad \text{length} = \text{abs } (y_2 - y_1)$$

∴ abs $(x_2 - x_1) = (8 - 0) = 8$ and abs $(y_2 - y_1) = (4 - 0) = 4$

As $\quad$ abs $(x_2 - x_1) >$ abs $(y_2 - y_1)$ $\quad$ therefore

$$\text{Length} = \text{abs } (x_2 - x_1) = 8$$

Now, $$\Delta x = (x_2 - x_1)/\text{length}$$
$$= [(8-0)/8] = 1$$
$$\Delta y = (y_2 - y_1)/\text{length}$$
$$= [(4-0)/8] = 0.5$$
$$x = x_1 + 0.5 \text{ sign } (\Delta x)$$
$$= 0+0.5 \text{ sign } (1)$$
$$= 0.5$$

$$y = y_1 + 0.5 \text{ sign } (\Delta y)$$
$$= 0 + 0.5 \text{ sign } (1.5)$$
$$= 0.5$$

Tabulating the result for each iteration we get,

i	x	y	Plot
	0.5	0.5	(0,0)
1	1.5	1	(1,1)
2	2.5	1.5	(2,1)
3	3.5	2	(3,2)
4	4.5	2.5	(4,2)
5	5.5	3	(5,3)
6	6.5	3.5	(6,3)
7	7.5	4	(7,4)
8	8.5	4.5	(8,4)

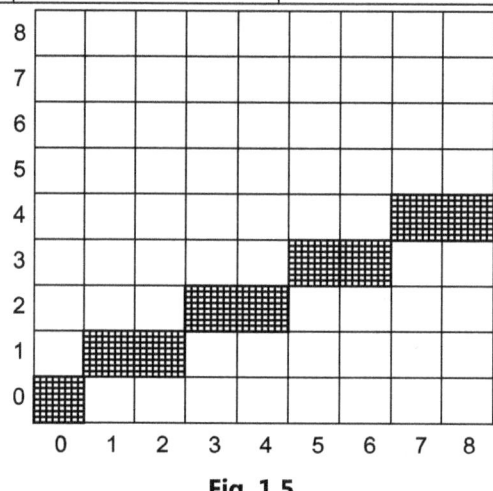

Fig. 1.5

Example 1.2 : Interpret Digital differential analyzer (DDA) algorithm to find which are the pixels turned on for the line segment between (3,4) and (9,8).

Solution : The end points of line are (3, 4) and (9, 8).

By evaluating the steps of DDA we have

$$X_1 = 3 \quad y_1 = 4$$
$$X_2 = 9 \quad y_2 = 8$$

If abs $(x_2 - x_1) \geq$ abs $(y_2 - y_1)$,

then	length	= abs $(x_2 - x_1)$
else	length	= abs $(y_2 - y_1)$

$\therefore$ abs $(x_2 - x_1)$ = $(9 - 3)$ = 6 and abs $(y_2 - y_1)$ = $(8 - 4)$ = 4

As   abs $(x_2 - x_1)$ > abs $(y_2 - y_1)$ therefore

Length = abs $(x_2 - x_1)$ = 6

Now,

$$\Delta x = (x_2 - x_1)/length$$
$$= [(9-3)/6] = 1$$
$$\Delta y = (y_2 - y_1)/length = [(8-4)/6] = 0.6$$
$$x = x_1 + 0.5 \, sign \, (\Delta x)$$
$$= 3 + 0.5 \, sign \, (1)$$
$$= 3.5$$
$$y = y_1 + 0.5 \, sign \, (\Delta y)$$
$$= 4 + 0.5 \, sign \, (0.6)$$
$$= 4.5$$

Tabulating the result for each iteration we get,

i	x	y	Plot
	3.5	4.5	(3,4)
1	4.5	5.1	(4,5)
2	5.5	5.7	(5,5)
3	6.5	6.3	(6,6)
4	7.5	6.9	(7,6)
5	8.5	7.5	(8,7)
6	9.5	8.1	(9,8)

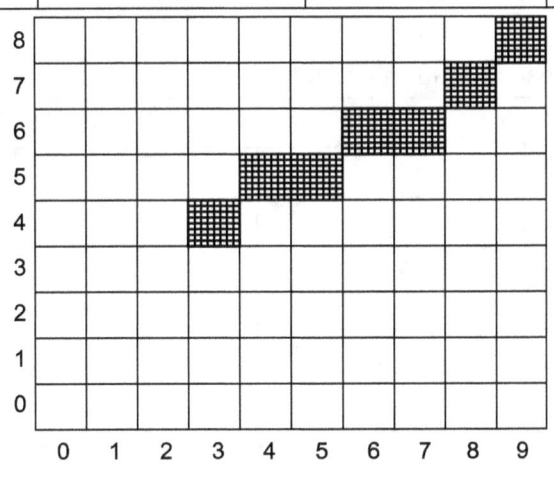

Fig. 1.6

Example 1.3 : Explain DDA line drawing algorithm. Consider a line segment from A(2, 1) to B(7, 8) Use DDA line drawing algorithm to rasterize this line.

Solution : For DDA line drawing algorithm explanation refer section no 1.4.1.

The end points of line are (2, 1) and (7, 8).

By evaluating the steps of DDA we have

$$X_1 = 2 \quad y_1 = 1$$
$$X_2 = 7 \quad y_2 = 8$$

If abs $(x_2 - x_1) \geq$ abs $(y_2 - y_1)$,

       then   length $=$ abs $(x_2 - x_1)$

       else   length $=$ abs $(y_2 - y_1)$

$\therefore$ abs $(x_2 - x_1) = (7 - 2) = 5$ and abs $(y_2 - y_1) = (8 - 1) = 7$

  As   abs $(y_2 - y_1) >$ abs $(x_2 - x_1)$ therefore

              Length $=$ abs $(y_2 - y_1)$ $= 7$

Now, $\Delta x = (x_2 - x_1)/\text{length}$

                  $= [(7-2)/7] = 0.7$

                 $\Delta y = (y_2 - y_1)/\text{length}$

                  $= [(8-1)/7] = 1$

                 $x = x_1 + 0.5 \text{ sign } (\Delta x)$

                  $= 2 + 0.5 \text{ sign } (0.7)$

                  $= 2.5$

                 $y = y_1 + 0.5 \text{ sign } (\Delta y)$

                  $= 1 + 0.5 \text{ sign } (1)$

                  $= 1.5$

Tabulating the result for each iteration we get,

i	x	y	Plot
	2.5	1.5	(2,1)
1	3.2	2.5	(3,2)
2	3.9	3.5	(3,3)
3	4.6	4.5	(4,4)
4	5.3	5.5	(5,5)
5	6	6.5	(6,6)
6	6.7	7.5	(6,7)

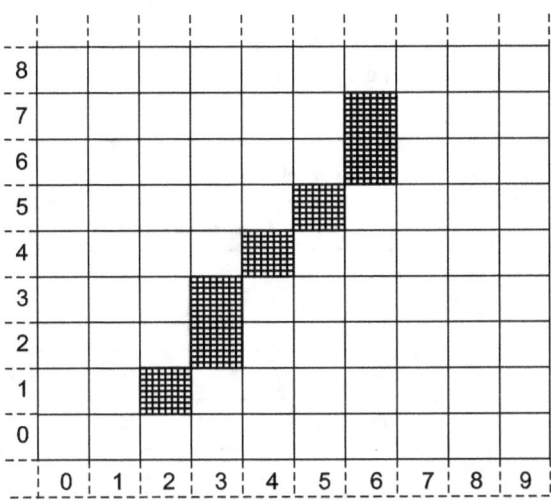

Fig. 1.7

Example 1.4 : Explain DDA line generation algorithm. Rasterize the line segment with starting point as A(1, 0) and end point as B(5, 7).

Solution : For DDA line drawing algorithm explanation refer section no 1.4.1

The end points of line are (1, 0) and (5, 7).

By evaluating the steps of DDA we have

$$X_1 = 1 \quad y_1 = 0$$
$$X_2 = 5 \quad y_2 = 7$$

If $\text{abs}(x_2 - x_1) \geq \text{abs}(y_2 - y_1)$,

then $\text{length} = \text{abs}(x_2 - x_1)$

else $\text{length} = \text{abs}(y_2 - y_1)$

$\therefore$ $\text{abs}(x_2 - x_1) = (5 - 1) = 4$ and $\text{abs}(y_2 - y_1) = (7 - 0) = 7$

As $\text{abs}(y_2 - y_1) > \text{abs}(x_2 - x_1)$ therefore

$$\text{Length} = \text{abs}(y_2 - y_1) = 7$$

Now, $\Delta x = (x_2 - x_1)/\text{length}$

$$= [(5-1)/7] = 0.5$$

$$\Delta y = (y_2 - y_1)/\text{length}$$

$$= [(7-0)/7] = 1$$

$$x = x_1 + 0.5 \, \text{sign}(\Delta x)$$

$$= 1 + 0.5 \, \text{sign}(0.5)$$

$$= 1.5$$

$$y = y_1 + 0.5 \text{ sign } (\Delta y)$$
$$= 0 + 0.5 \text{ sign } (1)$$
$$= 0.5$$

Tabulating the result for each iteration we get,

i	x	y	Plot
	1.5	0.5	(1,0)
1	2	1.5	(2,1)
2	2.5	2.5	(2,2)
3	3	3.5	(3,3)
4	3.5	4.5	(3,4)
5	4	5.5	(4,5)
6	4.5	6.5	(4,6)

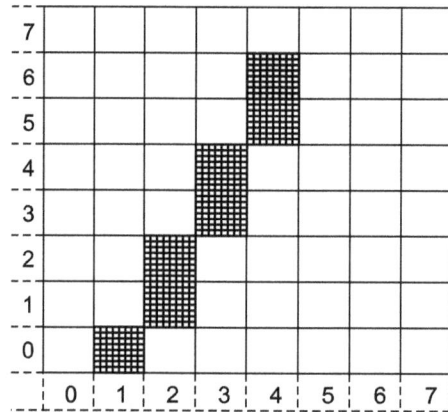

Fig. 1.8

Example 1.5 : Explain DDA line drawing algorithm. Consider a line segment from A(0,0) to B(4,6). Use DDA line drawing algorithm to rasterize the line.

Solution : For DDA line drawing algorithm explanation refer section no 1.4.1

The end points of line are (0, 0) and (4, 6).

By evaluating the steps of DDA we have,

$$X_1 = 0 \quad y_1 = 0$$
$$X_2 = 4 \quad y_2 = 6$$

If $\text{abs } (x_2 - x_1) \geq \text{abs } (y_2 - y_1).$

   then $\text{length} = \text{abs } (x_2 - x_1)$

else   length = abs $(y_2 - y_1)$

$\therefore$ abs $(x_2 - x_1)$ = (4-0) = 4 and abs $(y_2 - y_1)$ = (6-0) =6

As   abs $(y_2 - y_1)$ > abs $(x_2 - x_1)$ therefore

Length = abs $(y_2 - y_1)$ = 6

Now, Δx = $(x_2 - x_1)$/length

= [(4-0)/6] = 0.6

Δy = $(y_2 - y_1)$/length

= [(6-0)/6] = 1

x = x_1 + 0.5 sign (Δx)

= 0 +0.5 sign (0.6)

= 0.5

y = y_1 + 0.5 sign (Δy)

= 0 + 0.5 sign (1)

= 0.5

Tabulating the result for each iteration we get,

i	x	y	Plot
	0.5	0.5	(0,0)
1	1.1	1.5	(1,1)
2	1.7	2.5	(1,2)
3	2.3	3.5	(2,3)
4	2.9	4.5	(2,4)
5	3.5	5.5	(3,5)
6	4.1	6.5	(4,6)

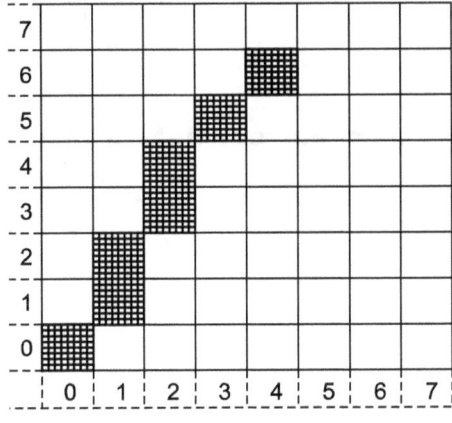

Fig. 1.9

1.4.2 Bresenham Line Drawing Algorithm

- The Bresenham algorithm is another incremental scan conversion algorithm. The big advantage of this algorithm is that, it uses only integer calculations. Moving across the x axis in unit intervals and at each step choose between two different y coordinates.

- Bresenham algorithm uses only integer calculations such as addition, subtraction and multiplication by 2 which the computer can perform rapidly. Thus, it is an efficient method for scan converting the straight line.

- The basic principle is that, to select an optimum raster location to present a straight line. The algorithm always increments either x or y value by one unit depending on the slope of the line.

- The increment in the other variable is determined by examining the distance between the actual line location and the nearest pixel. This distance is called the Decision Variable or error represented as e. If e >= 0, it implies that the pixel above the line is closes to the true value. if e <=0, it implies the pixel below the line is closer to the true value.

- Thus by checking the sign of the error term, it is possible to determine the better pixel to represent the line path.

Algorithm

Step 1 : Initialize variable

The line end points are (x_1, y_1) and (x_2, y_2), assumed these are not equal.

$$x = x_1, \quad y = y_1$$
$$\Delta x = abs(x_2 - x_1) \quad s_1 = sign(x_2 - x_1)$$
$$\Delta y = abs(y_2 - y_1) \quad s_2 = sign(y_2 - y_1)$$

Sign function returns -1 , 0, 1 as its argument is <0, =0, >0 respectively

Step 2 : Interchange

    If Δy > Δx then

    Δx and Δy and set Interchange = 1

Else Interchange = 0

Step 3 : Initialise error $\bar{e}$ to compensate for non-zero intercept.

$$\bar{e} = 2 * \Delta y - \Delta x$$

Step 4 : For i = 1 to Δx

      Plot (x, y)

While ($\bar{e}$ >=0)

If(Interchange=1) then,

$$x = x + s_1$$

else

$$y = y + s_2$$

End If

$$\bar{e} = \bar{e} - 2\Delta x$$

End While

If (Interchange=1) then

$$y = y + s_2$$

else

$$x = x + s_1$$

End if

$$\bar{e} = \bar{e} + 2\Delta y$$

i++

Step 5 : END

Example 1.6 : Interpret Bresenham's algorithm to find which are pixel are turned on for the line segment between (1,2) and (7,6).

Solution :

Step 1 : Initialise variable

The line end points are (1,2) and (7,6)

$$x_1 = 1, \quad y_1 = 2$$
$$x_2 = 7, \quad y_2 = 6$$
$$x = y_1 = 1, \; y = y_1 = 2$$
$$\Delta x = abs(x_2 - x_1)$$
$$= abs(7\text{-}1) = 6$$
$$\Delta y = abs(y_2 - y_1)$$
$$= abs(6\text{-}2) = 4$$
$$s_1 = sign(x_2 - x_1) = 1 \quad as\ (6{>}0)$$
$$s_2 = sign(y_2 - y_1) = 1 \quad as\ (4{>}0)$$

Step 2 : Interchange as , $\Delta y < \Delta x$

Interchange Δx and Δy and set Interchange =0

Tabulating the result for each iteration

i	x	y	$\bar{e}$	plot
	1	2	2	(1,2)
1	2	3	8	(2,3)
2	3	4	4	(3,4)
3	4	5	0	(4,5)
4	5	6	-4	(5,6)
5	6	6	4	(6,6)
6	7	7	0	(7,7)

Example 1.7 : Consider the line from (5,5) to (13,9). Use the Bresenham's algorithm to rasterize the line.

Solution :

Step (i) : The line end points are (5,5) and (13,9)

Initialise Variable

$$x = x_1, \quad y = y_1$$
$$x = 5, \quad y = 5$$
$$\Delta x = abs(x_2 - x_1)$$
$$= abs(13 - 5) = 8$$
$$\Delta y = abs(y_2 - y_1)$$
$$= abs(9-5) = 4$$
$$s_1 = sign(x_2 - x_1) = 1 \qquad as\ (8>0)$$
$$s_2 = sign(y_2 - y_1) = 1 \qquad as\ (4>0)$$

Step (ii) : as , $\Delta y < \Delta x$

Interchange Δx and Δy and set Interchange = 0

Tabulating the result for each iteration

i	x	y	$\bar{e}$	Plot
	5	5	0	(5,5)
1	6	6	-8	(6,6)
2	7	6	0	(7,6)
3	8	7	-8	(8,7)
4	9	7	0	(9,7)
5	10	8	-8	(10,8)
6	11	9	-16	(11,9)
7	12	9	-8	(12,9)
8	13	9	0	(13,9)

1.5 LINE STYLES

It is a type of primitive. Many display devices offer a selection of line styles. Lines may be continuous, or they may be dashed or dotted. The user is also able to select the color of the line or its intensity or thickness. Sometimes, it is desirable to change the line style in the middle of the display process. Thus, a display file command is used to change the line style. When the interpreter encounters such a command, the line style is changed and all subsequent lines are drawn in this new style. The display-file commands are composed of three-parts, the opcode and the two operands for the x and y co-ordinates. A special opcode is used to indicate the change of line style (color or intensity).

1.6 CIRCLE DRAWING ALGORITHMS

- Drawing a circle on the screen is a little complex than drawing a line. There are popular algorithms for generating a circle – DDA circle algorithm, bresenham's algorithm and Midpoint Circle Algorithm.

- These algorithms are based on the idea of determining the subsequent points required to draw the circle.

- A circle is a symmetrical Figure. It has eight way symmetry as shown in Fig. 1.10.

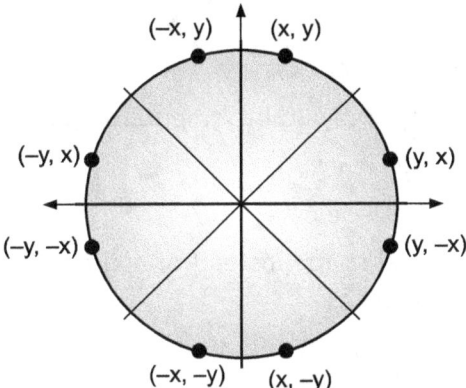

Fig. 1.10 : Symmetry of circle

The equation for a circle is :

$$X^2 + Y^2 = r^2$$

where

r is the radius of the circle

So, we can write a simple circle drawing algorithm by solving the equation for y at unit x intervals using :

$$Y = \pm \sqrt{r^2 - X^2}$$

1.6.1 DDA Circle Drawing Algorithm

The Equation of Circle is

$$X^2 + Y^2 = r^2$$

Hence , the circle equation in the form of differential equation

$$2x \, dx + 2yd \, y = 0$$

$$x \, dx + y \, dy = 0$$

$$\therefore \qquad y \, dy = - x \, dx$$

Therefore , The differential equation of a circle with center as origin is

$$\frac{dy}{dx} = \frac{-x}{y}$$

From above equation we can construct a circle by using x value and y value incremental values Δx and Δy as,

$$\Delta x = \varepsilon y \text{ and}$$

$$\Delta y = - \varepsilon x$$

Where,

$$\varepsilon = 2^{-n}$$

$2^{n-1} \le r \le 2^n$ and r is radius of the circle.

Thus, we can get next pixel by applying incremental steps

$$x_{n+1} = x_n + \varepsilon \, y_n$$

$$y_{n+1} = y_n - \varepsilon \, x_n$$

But, above equations gives a spiral shape instead of a circle. To make it a circle we need to do one correction in above equation as,

$$x_{n+1} = x_n + \varepsilon \, y_n$$

$$y_{n+1} = y_n - \varepsilon \, x_{n+1}$$

Algorithm :

Step 1 : Read radius of circle (r) and calculate value of ε (epsilon).

Step 2 : $\qquad\qquad x = 0$

$$y = r$$

Step 3 : $\qquad\qquad x_1 = x$

$$y_1 = y$$

Step 4 : do

{

$$X_2 = x_1 + \varepsilon\, y_1$$

$$Y_2 = y_1 - \varepsilon\, x_2$$

plot (x_2, y_2)

}

While $((y_1 - y) < \varepsilon \,||\, (x - x_1) > \varepsilon)$ //condition is for , whether current point is starting point

Step 5 : Stop.

1.6.2 Bresenham Circle Drawing Algorithm

- Jack E. Bresenham invented this algorithm in 1962. The objective was to optimize the graphic algorithms for basic objects, in a time when computers were not as powerful as they are today.

- This algorithm is called as incremental, because the position of the next pixel is calculated on the basis of the last plotted pixel, instead of just calculating the pixels from a global formula. Such logic is faster for computers to work on and allows plotting circles without trigonometry.

- The algorithm use only integers, and that's where the strength is floating point calculations slow down the processors.

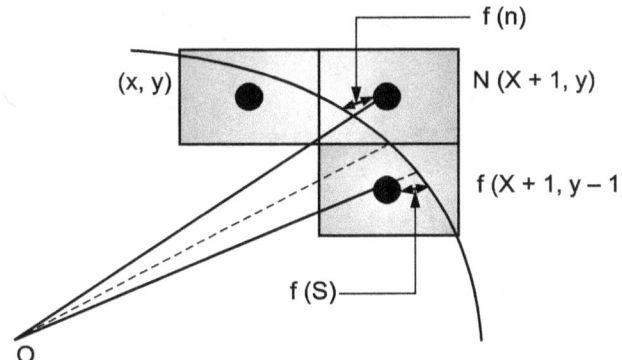

Fig. 1.11 : Bresenham circle drawing

- At any point (x,y), we have two choices – to choose the pixel on east of it, i.e. N(x+1,y) or the south-east pixel S(x+1,y-1). To choose the pixel, we determine the errors involved with both N and S which are f(N) and f(S) respectively and which ever gives the lesser error, we choose that pixel.

Let d = f(N) + f(S), where d can be called as "decision parameter",

if d<=0, then, N(x+1,y) is to be chosen as next pixel

and if d>0, then, S(x+1,y-1) is to be chosen as next pixel;

- After performing derivations and putting the values of f(N) and f(S) in equation of circle, we get the value of decision parameter as

for $\qquad$ d < 0; $\qquad$ d = d + 4x + 6

for $\qquad$ d> = 0; $\qquad$ d = d + 4 (x − y) + 10

Algorithm

Step 1 : Read radius (r) of circle.

Step 2 : initialize decision variable d=3-2r

Step 3 : x = 0 and y = r

Step 4 : do

```
        {
            Plot(x,y)
            x = x + 1
            if (d<0)
                {    d = d+ 4x + 6
                }
            else if (d≥0)
                {
                    y = y - 1
                    d= d+ 4 (x - y) + 10
                }
        }
}
```

while(x<y)

Step 5 : Plot pixels in all octants as

Plot (x, y)

Plot (y, x)

Plot (-y, x)

Plot (-x, y)

Plot (-x, -y)

Plot (-y, -x)

Plot (y, -x)

Plot (x, -y)

Step 6 : Stop.

1.6.3 Midpoint Circle Algorithm

Equation for Decision Parameter of Midpoint Circle Algorithm :

- A circle is defined as a set of points that are all at a given distance r from a center positioned at (X_c, Y_c).

- This is represented mathematically by the equation,

$$(x - x_c)^2 + (y - y_c)^2 = r^2 \qquad \text{... (1.1)}$$

- Using equation (1.1) we can calculate the value of y for each given value of x as

$$y = y_c \pm \sqrt{r^2 - (X_c - X)^2} \qquad \text{... (1.2)}$$

Thus one could calculate different pairs by giving step increments to x and calculating the corresponding value of y. But this approach involves considerable computation at each step and also the resulting circle has its pixels sparsely plotted for areas with higher values of the slope of the curve.

Midpoint circle algorithm uses an alternative approach, where in the pixel positions along the circle are determined on the basis of incremental calculations of a decision parameter.

Let,

$$f(x, y) = (x - x_c)^2 + (y - y_c)^2 - r^2 \qquad \text{... (1.3)}$$

Thus, $f(x, y) = 0$ represents the equation of a circle.

Further, we know from coordinate geometry, that for any point, the following holds :

1. $f(x, y) = 0 \rightarrow$ The point lies on the circle.

2. $f(x, y) < 0 \rightarrow$ The point lies within the circle.

3. $f(x, y) > 0 \rightarrow$ The point lies outside the circle.

- In midpoint circle algorithm, the decision parameter at the kth step is circle function evaluated using the coordinates of the midpoint of the two pixel centres which are the next possible pixel position to be plotted.

Let us assume that we are giving unit increments to x in the plotting process and determining the y position using this algorithm. Assuming we have just plotted the kth pixel at (X_k, Y_k), we next need to determine whether the pixel at the position (X_{k+1}, Y_k) or the one at (X_{k+1}, Y_{k-1}) is closer to the circle.

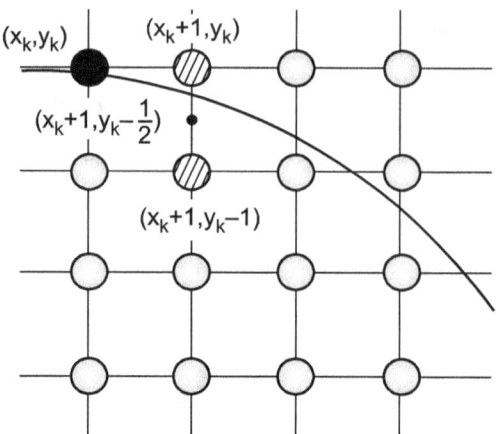

Fig. 1.12 : Decision parameter for mid point circle

Our decision parameter p_k at the kth step is the circle function evaluated at the midpoint of these two pixels.

The coordinates of the midpoint of these two pixels are $(X_k+1, Y_k-1/2)$.

Thus p_k

$$p_k = f\left(x_k + 1, y_k - \frac{1}{2}\right) = (x_k + 1)^2 + \left(y_k - \frac{1}{2}\right)^2 - r^2 \qquad \ldots (1.4)$$

Successive decision parameters are obtained using incremental calculations, thus avoiding a lot of computation at each step. We obtain a recursive expression for the next decision parameter i.e. at the $k+1^{th}$ step, in the following manner.

Using Equation (1.4), at the $k+1^{th}$ step, we have :

$$p_k = f\left(x_k + 1, y_k - \frac{1}{2}\right) = (x_k + 1)^2 + \left(y_k - \frac{1}{2}\right)^2 - r^2$$

$$p_{k+1} = f\left(x_{k+1} + 1, y_{k+1} - \frac{1}{2}\right) = (x_{k+1} + 1)^2 + \left(y_{k+1} - \frac{1}{2}\right)^2 - r^2$$

Or, $$p_{k+1} = (x_k + 1 + 1)^2 + \left(y_{k+1} - \frac{1}{2}\right)^2 - r^2$$

Or, $$p_{k+1} = (x_k + 2)^2 + \left(y_{k+1} - \frac{1}{2}\right)^2 - r^2 \qquad \ldots (1.5)$$

Equation (1.5) and (1.4) gives,

$$p_{k+1} - p_k = (x_k + 2)^2 - (x_k + 1)^2 + \left(y_{k+1} - \frac{1}{2}\right)^2 - \left(y_k - \frac{1}{2}\right)^2 - r^2 + r^2$$

or, $$p_{k+1} = p_k + (2x_k + 3).1 + (y_{k+1} + y_k - 1)(y_{k+1} - y_k) \qquad \ldots (1.6)$$

Now, if $p_k <\ = 0$, then the midpoint of the two possible pixels lies within the circle, thus north pixel is nearer to the theoretical circle. Hence, $Y_{k+1} = Y_k$. Substituing this value of in equation (1.6), we have

$$p_{k+1} = p_k + (2x_k + 3) + (y_k + y_k - 1)(y_k - y_k)$$

or, $$p_{k+1} = p_k + (2x_k + 3)$$

If $p_k > 0$ then the midpoint of the two possible pixels lies outside the circle, thus south pixel is nearer to the theorectical circle. Hence, $Y_{k+1} = Y_k - 1$. Substituting this value of in Equation (1.6), we have

$$p_{k+1} = p_k + (2x_k + 3) + (y_k - 1 + y_k - 1)(y_k - y_k - 1)$$

or, $$p_{k+1} = p_k + 2(x_k - y_k) + 5$$

For the boundry condition, we have x=0, y=r. Substituting these values in (1.4), we have

$$p_0 = (0 + 1)^2 + \left(r - \frac{1}{2}\right)^2 - r^2$$

$$= 1 + r^2 + \frac{1}{4} - r - r^2 = \frac{5}{4} - r$$

For integer values of pixel coordinates, we can approximate $P_0 = 1 - r$,

Thus we have,

If $p_k \leq 0$; $Y_{k+1} = Y_k$

and $p_{k+1} = p_k + (2x_k + 3)$

If $pk > 0$; $Y_{k+1} = Y_k - 1$

and $p_{k+1} = p_k + 2(x_k - y_k) + 5$

Also, $p_o = 1 - r$

Advantage :

- The midpoint method for deriving efficient scan-conversion algorithms to draw geometric curves on raster displays in described. The method is general and is used to transform the nonparametric equation $f(x,y) = 0$, which describes the curve, into an algorithms that draws the curve.

Disadvantage :

- Time consumption is high.

- The distance between the pixels is not equal so we won't get smooth circle.

Eight Way Symmetry

In the mid-point circle algorithm we use eight way symmetry so only ever calculate the points for the top right eighth of a circle, and then use symmetry to get the rest of the points. Assume that we have just plotted point (x_k, y_k). The next point is a choice between (x_{k+1}, y_k) and (x_{k+1}, y_{k-1}). We would like to choose the point that is nearest to the actual circle.

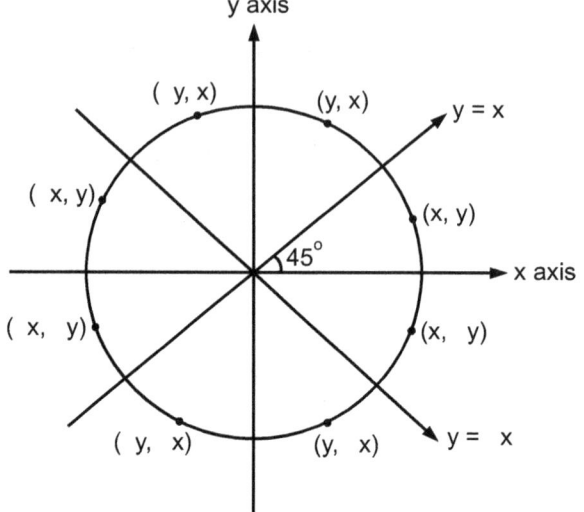

Fig. 1.13 : Eight way symmetry of circle

Algorithm

Step 1 : Set X = 0 and Y = R

Step 2 : Set P= 1–R

Step 3 : While (X < Y)

        plot(X, Y)

        If (P< 0) Then

                X = X + 1

                Y = Y

                P = P+ 2X + 1

            Else

                X = x+1

                Y = Y –1

                P = P+ 2(X –Y)+ 1

    End of While

Step 4 : Plot pixel (x, y) and also plot pixels in remaining seven octants as,

            Plot (y, x)

            Plot (-y, x)

Plot (-x, y)

Plot (-x, -y)

Plot (-y, -x)

Plot (y, -x)

Plot (x, -y)

Step 5 : Stop

1.7 CHARACTER GENERATION

Computer graphics involves display of picture, lines and other graphics like designs. These picture and graph will belongs to some data. Some information and instruction should be given to the user about this data. This is possible with the help of text display.

Since text consists of string of characters. so a character is a basic unit of text.

There are three methods for character generation. These are :

- Stroke Method
- Bitmap Method
- Starbust Method

1.7.1 Stroke Principle

Stroke method is based on natural method of text written by human being. In this method graph is drawing in the form of line by line.

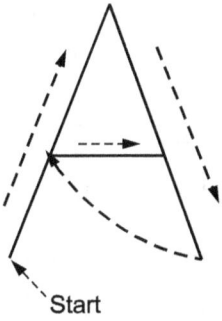

Fig. 1.14 : Stroke method

This method uses small line segments to generate a character. The small series of line segments are drawn like a stroke of pen to form a character. Refer Fig. 1.14. We can build our own stroke method character generator by calls to the line drawing algorithm. Here it is necessary to decide which line segments are needed for each character and then drawing these segments using line drawing algorithm.

1.7.2 Starbust Principle

Starbust method is used in a particular pattern where only 24 strokes are defined for character generation. Refer Fig. 1.15.

In this method a fix pattern of line segments are used to generate characters. There are 24 line segments. Out of these 24 line segments, segments required to display for particular character are highlighted. This method of character generation is called starbust method because of its characteristic appearance.

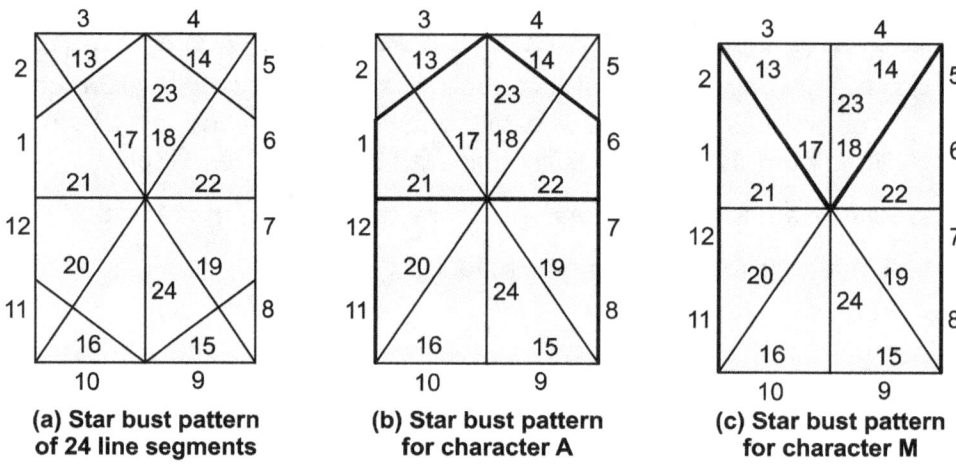

(a) Star bust pattern of 24 line segments   (b) Star bust pattern for character A   (c) Star bust pattern for character M

Fig. 1.15 : Starbust method

The patterns for particular characters are stored in the form of 24 bit code, each bit representing one line segment. The bit is set to one to highlight the line segment; otherwise it is set to zero. For example, 24-bit code for Character A is 0011 0000 0011 1100 1110 0001 and for character M is 0000 0011 0000 1100 1111 0011.

1.7.3 Bit Map Method

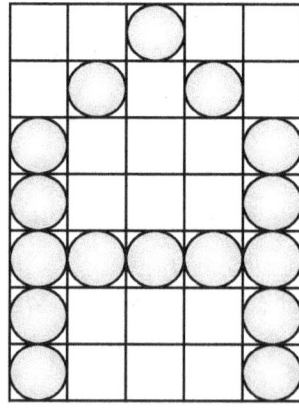

Fig. 1.16 : Bitmap method

- The third method for character generation is the bitmap method. It is also called dot matrix because in this method characters are represented by an array of dots in the matrix form.
- It is a two dimensional array having columns and rows. A 5×7 array is commonly used to represent characters. However 7×9 and 9×13 arrays are also used. Refer Fig. 1.16.
- Higher resolution devices such as inkjet printer or laser printer may use character arrays that are over 100×100. Each dot in the matrix is a pixel.
- The character is placed on the screen by copying pixel values from the character array into some portion of the screen's frame buffer. The value of the pixel controls the intensity of the pixel.
- In bit map method, when the dots is stored in the form of array the value 1 in array represent the characters i.e where the dots appear we represent that position with numerical value 1 and the value where dots are not present is represented by 0 in array.

1. Aliasing and Anti-Aliasing Techniques

- In computer graphics, the process by which smooth curves and other lines become jagged because the resolution of the graphics device or file is not high enough to represent a smooth curve. Smoothing and antialiasing techniques can reduce the effect of aliasing.
- The errors caused by aliasing are called artefacts. Common aliasing artefacts include jagged profiles, disappearing or improperly rendered fine detail, and disintegrating textures.
- Antialiasing is a software technique for diminishing *jaggies* - stairstep-like lines that should be smooth. Jaggies occur because the output device, the monitor or printer, doesn't have a high enough resolution to represent a smooth line.
- Antialiasing reduces the prominence of jaggies by surrounding the stairsteps with intermediate shades of gray (for gray-scaling devices) or color (for color devices). Although this reduces the jagged appearance of the lines, it also makes them fuzzier.
- The process of mapping a continuous function to a discrete one is called sampling
- The process of mapping a discrete function to a continuous one is called reconstruction

2. Antialiasing Techniques

1. Super sampling
2. Area sampling
   - Unweighted
   - Weighted

1. Supersampling

- Supersampling or postfiltering is the process by which aliasing effects in graphics are reduced by increasing the frequency of the sampling grid and then averaging the results down.

- This process means calculating a virtual image at a higher spatial resolution than the frame store resolution and then averaging down to the final resolution. It is called postfiltering as the filtering is carried out after sampling.

Supersampling is Basically a Three Stage Process :

- A continuous image I(x,y) is sampled at n times the final resolution. The image is calculated at n times the frame resolution. This is a virtual image.

- The virtual image is then lowpass filtered.

- The filtered image is then resampled at the final frame resolution.

- Divide each pixel into smaller grid of sub-pixels and count number of smaller sample point crossings.

- Use Bresenham's algorithm on sub-pixels to count these crossings n sub-divisions mean at most n sub-pixel crossings mean n + 1 intensities.

Advantages of Supersampling

- When a line is considered to have non-zero width then, additional pixels can be included (with low intensity); for example, pixel (1,3) in Fig. 1.16 might be included with low intensity.

- Also, with a color display a line that crosses several color regions we can average sub pixel intensities to get a blended color.

For example, given a blue line that encloses 4 sub pixels and 10 background green pixels, of its 4 x 4 sub pixels we can average the color to be (4 blue + 10 green) /16 if sum of subpixel weights is 16 so each subpixel counts for 1/16th of its weight

Supersampling Methods

1. Straight line segment
2. Supersampling considering finite line width
3. Supersampling with pixel weighing mask

1. Straight Line Segment

- Supersampling for gray scale display of straight line segment, we divide each pixel into number of subpixels and count the number of subpixels that are along the line path.

- The intensity level of each subpixel is then set to a value that is proportional to this subpixel count.

- In Fig. 1.17 each pixel is divided into nine equal square pixels, and shaded region shows the subpixel that would be selected by Bresenham's algorithm.

- This scheme provides for three intensity settings above zero; similarly sixteen subpixels gives us four intensity levels above zero; twenty five subpixels gives us five levels and so on.

- The advantage of this method is that the number of possible intensity level for each pixel is equal to total number of sub pixels within the pixel area.

- If we have color display, we can extend the method to take background color into account.

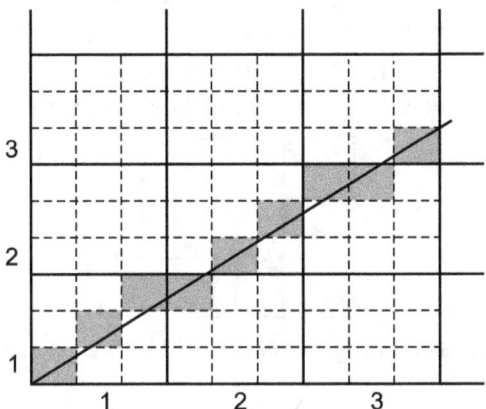

Fig. 1.17 : Super sampling of subpixel position

2. Supersampling Considering Finite Line Width

- We can represent the line with finite width by positioning the polygon boundary parallel to the line path and each pixel can now be set to one of the nine possible brightness levels above zero.

- The advantage of finite line width is that , the total line intensity is distributed over more pixels. Refer Fig. 1.18.

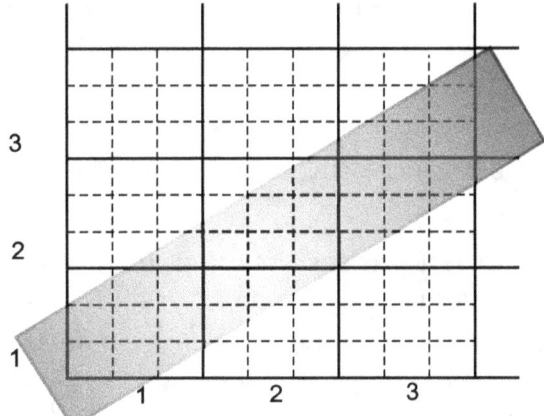

Fig. 1.18 : Supersampling with finite line width

3. Supersampling with Pixel Weighing Mask

- Supersampling algorithm is often implemented by giving more weight to subpixels near the center of pixel area, so these subpixels are more important in determining overall intensity of a pixel.

- For 3 × 3 pixel subdivision we have to consider weighting scheme.
- The center subpixel here is weighted four times that of the corner subpixels and twice that of remaining subpixels.
- The intensities calculated for each grid of nine subpixels would then be averaged so that the center subpixel is weighted by a factor of ¼; the top, bottom and side subpixels are weighted by a factor of 1/8; and the corner subpixels are each weighted by a factor of 1/16; similar mask can be set for larger subpixel grid. Refer Fig. 1.19.

1	2	1
2	4	2
1	2	1

Fig. 1.19 : Weighing mask for grid of 3 by 3 subpixels

Pixel Phasing

- Pixel phasing is used to anti-alias object.
- Pixel phasing is an anti-aliasing method where the stair-steps along line path or object boundary are removed or smoothed out by moving the electron beam to an exact position determined by the object geometry.
- Some hardware systems (CRT) have ability to pin-point sub-pixel location. A full pixel still gets drawn but as needed, the pixel can be shifted closer to the line path.
- Pixel phasing systems were designed so that electron beam can be shifted by 1/4 , 1/2 or 3/4 of a pixel diameter to plot points closer to the true path of a line or an object edge.

2. Area Sampling

Setting intensity proportional to amount of area covered.

The intensity decreases as the distance between the pixel and the edge increases.

Unweighted Area Sampling

- In this method the next closest pixels are selected. The intensity of pixel is proportional to the amount of line area occupied by the pixel.
- Equal areas contribute equal intensity, regardless of distance between the pixel's regardless of distance between the pixel's center and the area; only the total amount of overlapped area matters.

Weighted Area Sampling

- In this method, the intensity of the pixel is dependent on the line area occupied and the distance of the area from the pixel's center.
- Equal areas contribute unequally. A smaller area closer to the pixel center has a greater influence than does one at greater distance.

1.8 DISPLAY FILE

1.8.1 Display File Structure

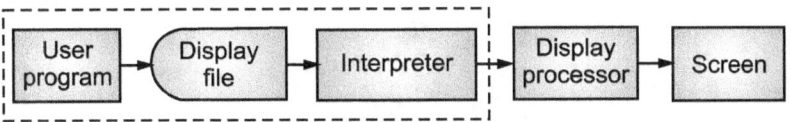

Fig. 1.20 : Display file structure

- The file used to store the commands necessary for drawing the line segments is called display file.

- The Fig. 1.20 shows the structure of display file, which contains series of commands Each display file command contains two fields, an operation code(opcode) and operands .

- Opcode identifies the commands such as line draw, move cursors, etc and the operands provide the co-ordinate of a point to process the commands.

- An application program is input and stored in the system memory along with a graphics package.

- Graphics commands in the application program are translated by the graphics package into a display file stored in the system memory.

The display file structure contains display file instructions which can be stored in one dimensional array as DF_OP(Display file operand), DF_X (Display file X value), DF_Y (Display file Y Value)

Table 1.1 : Display File Structure

DF_OP Array	DF_X Array	DF_Y Array
.	.	.
.	.	.
1	10	10
2	10	80
1	50	10
2	50	80
1	10	40
2	50	40
.	.	.
.	.	.

Command 1 : (1, 10,10)

Moves the current cursor position to point (10, 10)

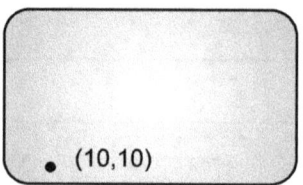

Fig. 1.21

Command 2 : (2, 10, 80)

Draws line between point (10, 10) and (10, 80)

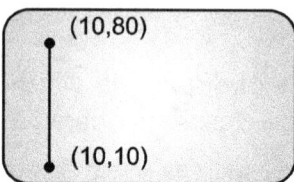

Fig. 1.22

Command 3 : (1, 50, 10)

Moves the current cursor position to point (50, 10)

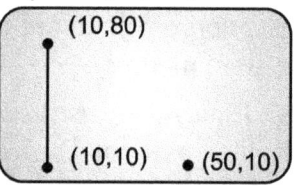

Fig. 1.23

Command 4 : (2, 50, 80)

Draws line between point (50, 10) and (50, 80)

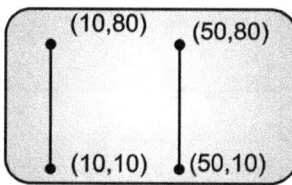

Fig. 1.24

Command 5 : (1, 10, 40)

Moves the current cursor position to point (10, 40)

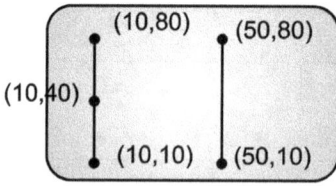

Fig. 1.25

Command 6 : (2, 50, 40)

Draws line between point (10, 40) and (50, 40)

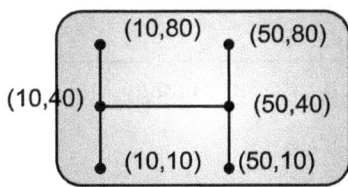

Fig. 1.26

1.8.2 Algorithms and Display File Interpreter

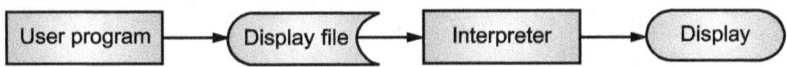

Fig. 1.27 : Display file and interpreter

- The program which converts these commands into actual picture is called the display file Interpreter. It is an interface between the graphics representation in the display file and display device.

- Every instruction possess a MOVE, LINE or PLOT commands. As shown in above Fig. 1.27 the interpreter executes the instruction and the output will be a visual image.

- The display processor is connected to the display device, processes and manages the display process.

- In some graphical system the task of display file interpreter is performed by using a separate computer or CPU. Hence, it acts as an interface between the graphics user program and a display service, which is known as display processor.

- The display device and its interpreter can be thought of as a machine on which any standard program can run. The display file instructions are actually saved in a file for later display or for transfer to another machine. Such files are called as metafiles.

- The advantage of using interpreter is that saving raw image takes much less storage than saving the picture itself.

1.8.3 Primitive Operations on Display File

- Move a cursor to specific location (x,y)

- Draw a Line up to a specific location(x,y)

The primitive instructions stored in metafile called as display file.

One of the way to store opcode and operands of series of commands is to use separate arrays, one for opcode, one for x-coordinate and one for y-co-ordinate of the operand. It is also necessary to assign meanings to the possible opcode before we can proceed to interpret them.

COMMAND	OPCODE
MOVE	1
LINE	2

Algorithm for entering the polygon into the display file.

Algorithm :

1. Read AX and AY of length N

2. i = 0

    DF_OP[i] N

    DF_x[i]

    AX[i]

    DF_y[i]

    AY[i]

    i←i+1

3. do

    {

    DF_OP[i]←2

    DF_x[i]←AX[i]

    DF_y[i]←AY[i]

    i←i +1

    }

    While (i< N)

4. DF_OP[i]←2

    DF_x[i]←AX[0]

    DF_y[i]←AY[0]

5. Stop.

Other Display File Structure

Array Structure

First we used simple array structure but it is not much efficient. If we want to perform delete operation in display file, then we have to move all succeeding instruction i.e if display file is too large , a lot of processing is required to recover small amount of storage

Advantages of Array Structure

*   Because of simple structure, easy to use.
*   Modification is easy.
*   Not require additional fields.

Disadvantages of Array Structure

- More number of arrays required.

- Deletion of any instruction requires lot of processing.

- There is limitation on size of array.

(a) Linked List

In link list instructions are not arranged sequentially; rather new field has been added to the instruction called link pointer which gives location of the next instruction.

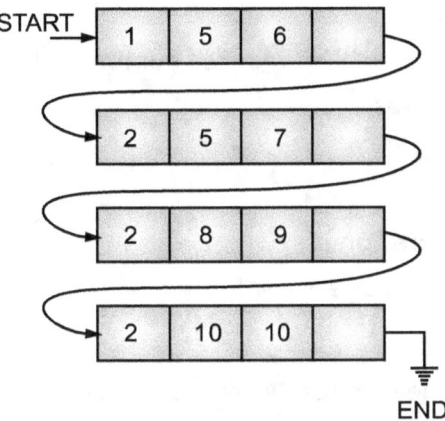

Fig. 1.28 : Link list

Advantages of Linked List Structure:

- Deletion and insertion of instruction is easy.

- Dynamic processing is possible.

Disadvantages of Linked List Structure:

- Require more storage space because of additional field.

- Only sequential access is possible, random access is not possible.

(b) Paging Scheme

- Paging scheme is combination of array and linked list structure.

- Display file is organized into a number of small arrays called as pages. The pages are linked such that it forms a linked list of pages.

- Each segment starts at the beginning of a page. If segment ends before the page boundary, the remaining page is not used.

- Instruction access is same as the array structure.

- When the end of page is reached, a link is followed to find the next page refer Fig. 1.29.

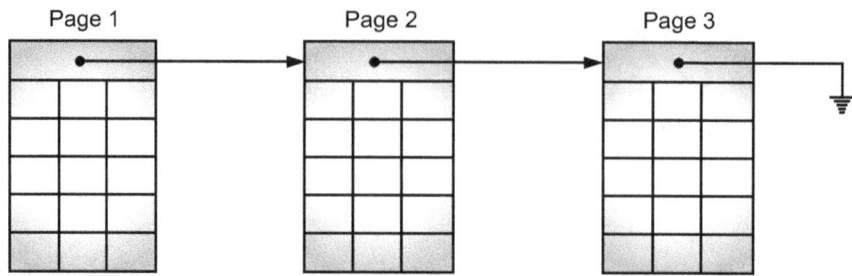

Fig. 1.29 : Paging scheme for display file

Advantages

- As the instruction in page available it reduces number of links.
- Deletion of any segment is easy.
- Deleted pages can be reused.

Disadvantages

- Accessing instruction is more complex.
- Storage space is waste when page is not full.

1.8.4 Raster Scan Display

- In a raster- scan system, the electron beam is swept across the screen, one row at a time from top to bottom. As the electron beam moves across each row, the beam intensity is turned on and off to create a pattern of illuminated spots.

- Picture definition is stored in memory area called the refresh buffer or frame buffer. This memory area holds the set of intensity values for all the screen points. Stored intensity values are then retrieved from the refresh buffer and " painted" on the screen one row (scan line) at a time.

- At the end of each scan line, the electron beam returns to the left side of the screen to begin displaying the next scan line. The return to the left of the screen, after refreshing each scan line, is called the horizontal retrace of the electron beam refer Fig. 1.30.

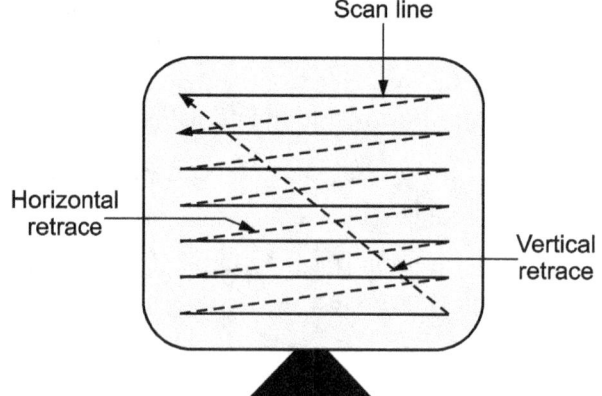

Fig. 1.30 : Raster scan display

- And at the end of each frame (displayed in 1/80th to 1/60th of a second), the electron beam returns (vertical retrace)to the top left corner of the screen to begin the next frame.
- The capability of this system to store intensity values for pixel makes it well suited for the realistic display of scenes contain shadow and color pattern.

1.8.5 Random / Vector / Calligraphic Scan Displays

- In this technique, the electron beam is directed only to the part of the screen where the picture is to be drawn rather than scanning from left to right and top to bottom as in raster scan. It is also called vector display, stroke-writing display, or calligraphic display.

- Picture definition is stored as a set of line-drawing commands in an area of memory referred to as the refresh display file.

- To display a specified picture, the system cycles through the set of commands in the display file, drawing each component line in turn. After all the line-drawing commands are processed, the system cycles back to the first line command in the list.

- These systems are designed for line-drawing and can't display realistic shaded scenes. Mathematical functions are used to draw an image. Refer Fig. 1.31.

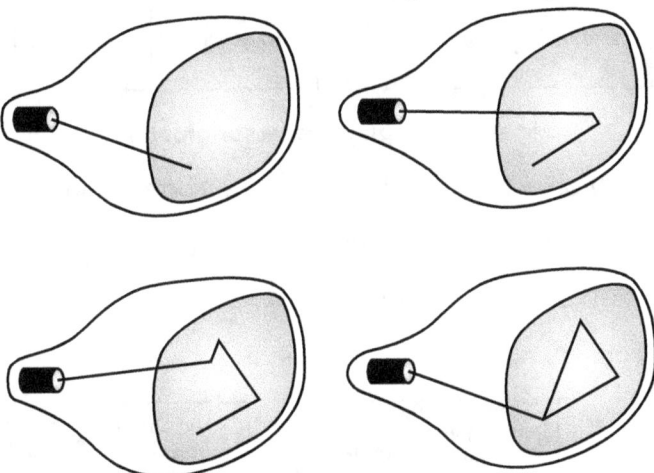

Fig. 1.31 : Random scan display

1.8.6 Display Processor

- The display processor is used to convert digital information from the CPU into analog value needed by the display device.
- Display processors are also designed to perform a number of additional operations. These functions include generating various line styles (dashed, dotted, or solid), displaying color areas, and performing certain transformations and manipulations on displayed objects. Also, display processors are typically designed to interface with interactive input devices, such as a mouse.

- A major task of the display processor is digitizing a picture definition given in an application program into a set of pixel-intensity values for storage in the frame buffer. Refer Fig. 1.32.

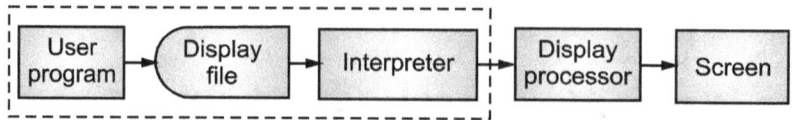

Fig. 1.32 : Display processor

- An application program is input and stored in the system memory along with a graphics package. Graphics commands in the application program are translated by the graphics package into a display file stored in the system memory. This display file is then accessed by the display processor to refresh the screen. The display processor cycles through each command in the display file program once during every refresh cycle. Sometimes the display processor in a random-scan system is referred to as a display processing unit or a graphics controller.

Display Processors Pipeline

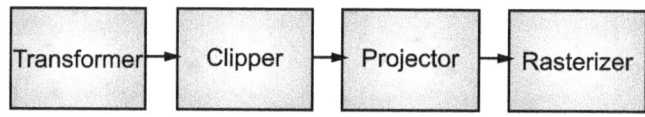

Fig. 1.33 : Display processor pipeline

- **Transformer :** Modify object such that viewed from correct angle.

- **Clipper :** Clips primitives to screen window.

- **Projector :** Project 3-D scene to 2-D image.

- **Rasterizer :** Scan convert, anti-aliasing operations.

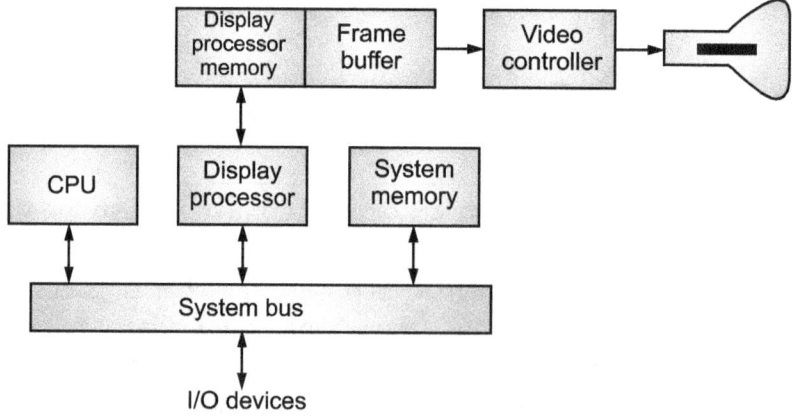

Fig. 1.34 : Display file system

- In some graphics system, a separate computer is used to interpret the commands in the display file. Such computer is called as a display processor. Display processor access display file and it cycles through each command in the display file once during every refresh cycle.
- This display file is then accessed by the display processor to refresh the screen.
- Sometimes the display processor in a random-scan system is referred to as a display processing unit or a graphics controller.

EXERCISE

1. What is mean by Computer Graphics?
2. Why the name DDA is given for line drawing algorithm?
3. What are the disadvantages of DDA Algorithm?
4. Define (1) Line (2) Line segment (3) Vector
5. What is the need of Bresenham's Circle drawing algorithm?
6. What is the difference between DDA Circle generation algorithm and Bresenham's circle generation algorithm?
7. What is the need of DDA circle generation algorithm?
8. What is scan conversion?
9. Write the properties of video display devices?
10. What is rasterization?
11. Name any four input devices.
12. Write the two techniques for producing color displays with a CRT?
13. What is vertical retrace of the electron beam?
14. Short notes on video controller?
15. What is bitmap?
16. Differentiate plasma panel display and thin film electro luminescent display?
17. What is resolution?
18. What is horizontal retrace of the electron beam?
19. Explain following terms with suitable example :
    (i)   Pixels
    (ii) Resolution
    (iii) Frame buffer.   **[Apr. 2013, 6 Marks]**
20. Describe Frame buffer display in computer graphics.   **[June 2015, 4 Marks]**

21. Explain the following :
    (i)   Frame buffer
    (ii) Resolution
    (iii) Aspect ratio   **[Dec. 2013, 6 Marks]**

22. Explain following terms with suitable example
    (i)   Pixels
    (ii) Resolution
    (iii) Frame buffer   **[Dec. 2013, 6 Marks]**

23. Write short notes on : Persistence, Resolution, Aspect ratio.   **[June 2015, 4 Marks]**

24. What is computer graphics ? State the applications of computer graphics.
                                                                [Dec. 2014, 6 Marks]

25. Write and explain any four state of the applications of computer graphics.
                                                                [May 2016, 4 Marks]

26. Explain Bresenham's circle drawing algorithm in detail. Also explain error factor with derivations   **[Apr. 2013, 12 Marks]**

27. Explain Bresenhams circle drawing algorithm with mathematical treatment. Explain significance of Δ, δ, δ'

28. Explain Bresenham's circle drawing algorithm with mathematical derivation.
                                                                [May, 6 Marks]

29. Explain significance of error term in Bresebham's circle drawing algorithm. Explain its mathematical derivations.   **[May 2016, 8 Marks]**

30. What is error factor in Bresenham's circle drawing algorithm? Write Bresenham's circle drawing algorithm.   **[Dec. 2015, 8 Marks]**

31. Explain Bresenham's Line drawing algorithm.   **[June 2015, 4 Marks]**

32. Explain the various character generation methods **[April 2013, Dec. 2013, 6 Marks]**

33. Explain display file and its structure.   **[June 2015, 4 marks]**

34. Explain in brief :   **[Dec. 2015, 4 Marks]**
    (i)   Raster scan display
    (ii) TIFF file format

35. Explain the TIFF image file format with block diagram. **[May 2014, 6 Marks]**

36. Define Persistence, Random scan and Raster scan displays? Explain functioning of flat panel display.   **[May 2014, 6 Marks]**

37. Explain TIFF file organization with block diagram.   **[Dec. 2014, 6 Marks]**

UNIVERSITY QUESTIONS

1. What is antialiasing? Explain any two antialiasing.   **[Apr. 2013, 6 marks]**

2. What is antialiasing? Explain any two antialiasing techniques.

   [Dec. 2013, Dec. 2014, 6 Marks]

3. Write short notes on :   **[May 2016, 6 Marks]**

   (i)   Frame Buffer

   (ii) Display Devices

   (iii) Character Generation Methods.

4. Find out points for line segment having end points $(0, 0)$ $(-8, -4)$ using DDA line drawing algoritm.   **[Dec. 2015, 6 Marks] Refer 1.1**

5. Using DDA algorithm find out which pixels would be turned on for the line with end points $(1, 1)$ to $(5, 3)$.   **[June 2015, 4 Marks]**

6. Consider the line from $(0,0)$ to $(6,6)$ Bresenham's algorithm to rasterize this line.

   [April 2013, 6 Marks]

7. Consider the line from $(0,0)$ to $(6,6)$ Bresenhams algorithm to rasterize this line.

   [Dec. 2013, 6 Marks]

8. Explain Bresenham's line algorithm and find out which pixels would be turned on for the line with end points $(5, 2)$ to $(8, 4)$ using the same.   **[Dec. 2014, 6 Marks]**

9. A write Bresenham's line drawing algorithm. Compare pixel values for line $P(0, 0)$ $Q(6, 6)$.   **[May 2016, 6 Marks]**

10. Write Bresenham's line algorithm and find out which pixel would be turned on for the line with end points $(2, 2)$ to $(6, 5)$ using the same.   **[May 2014, 6 Marks]**

11. Explain following terms with suitable example :

    (i)   Pixels

    (ii) Resolution

    (iii) Frame buffer.   **[Apr. 2013, 6 Marks]**

12. Describe Frame buffer display in computer graphics.   **[June 2015, 4 Marks]**

13. Explain the following :

    (i)   Frame buffer

    (ii) Resolution

    (iii) Aspect ratio   **[Dec. 2013 6 Marks]**

14. Explain following terms with suitable example
    (i) Pixels
    (ii) Resolution
    (iii) Frame buffer   **[Dec. 2013, 6 Marks]**

15. Write short notes on : Persistence, Resolution, Aspect ratio.   **[June 2015, 4 Marks]**

16. Write and explain any four state of the applications of Computer Graphics.
                                                              [May 2016, 4 Marks]

17. Explain Bresenham's circle drawing algorithm in detail. Also explain error factor with derivations.   **[Apr. 2013, 12 Marks]**

18. Explain Bresenham's circle drawing algorithm with mathematical treatment. Explain significance of Δ, δ, δ'.

19. Explain Bresenham's circle drawing algorithm with mathematical derivation.
                                                              [May, 6 Marks]

20. Explain significance of error term in Bresebham's circle drawing algorithm. Explain its mathematical derivations.   **[May 2016, 8 Marks]**

21. What is error factor in Bresenham's circle drawing algorithm? Write Bresenham's circle drawing algorithm.   **[Dec. 2015, 8 Marks]**

22. Explain Bresenham's Line drawing algorithm.   **[June 2015, 4 Marks]**

23. Explain the various character generation methods.   **[Apr. 2013, Dec. 2013, 6 Marks]**

24. Explain display file and its structure.   **[June 2015, 4 Marks]**

25. Explain in brief :   **[Dec. 2015, 4 Marks]**
    (i) Raster scan display
    (ii) TIFF file format

26. Explain the TIFF image file format with block diagram.   **[May 2014, 6 Marks]**

27. Define Persistence, Random scan and Raster scan displays? Explain functioning of flat panel display.   **[May 2014, 6 Marks]**

28. Explain TIFF file organization with block diagram.   **[Dec. 2014, 6 Marks]**

POLYGONS AND CLIPPING ALGORITHMS

2.1 POLYGON INTRODUCTION

Polygon : A polygon is a plane figure that is bounded by a finite chain of straight line segments closing in a loop to form a closed chain or circuit. These segments are called its edges or sides, and the points where two edges meet are the polygon's vertices.

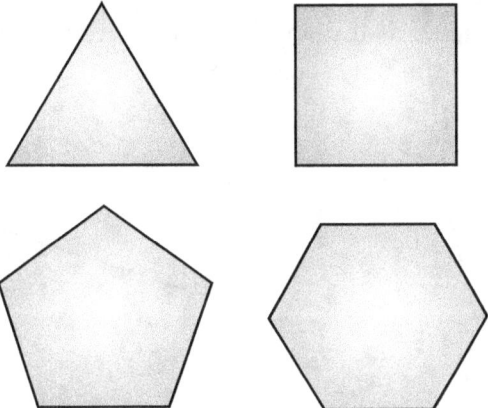

Fig. 2.1 : Polygon

2.1.1 Types of Polygon

There are two types of polygon :

1. Convex Polygon

2. Concave Polygon

3. Complex Polygon

1. Convex Polygon :

A convex polygon is defined as a polygon with all its interior angles less than 180°. This means that all the vertices of the polygon will point outwards, away from the interior of the shape.

In convex polygon the line joining any two interior points of the polygon lies completely inside the polygon.

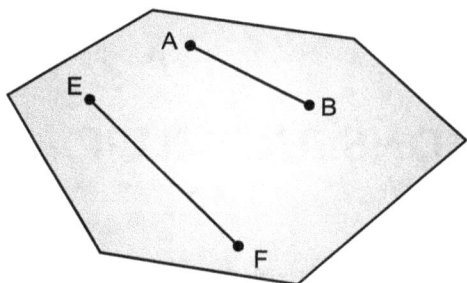

Fig. 2.2 : Convex polygon

2. Concave Polygon :

A polygon that has one or more interior angles greater than 180°

A concave polygon must have at least four sides.

A polygon is said to be concave if the line joining any two interior points of the polygon does not lie completely within the polygon.

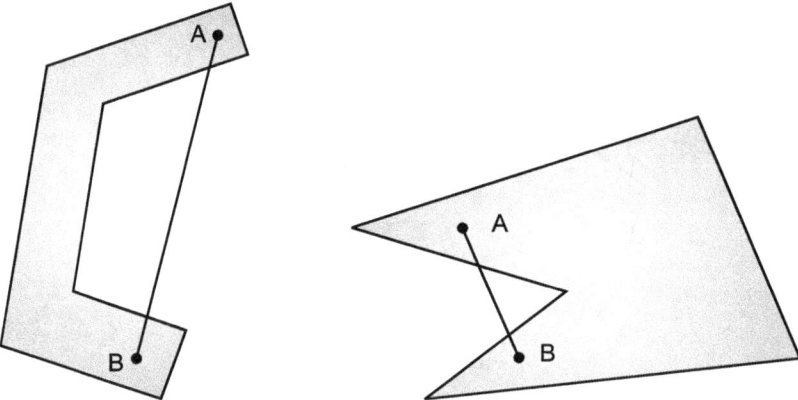

Fig. 2.3 : Concave polygon

3. Complex Polygon :

A complex polygon intersects itself! Many rules about polygons don't work when it is complex.

Fig. 2.4 : Complex polygoan

- In computer graphics, a complex polygon is a polygon which has a boundary comprising discrete circuits, such as a polygon with a hole in it.

- Self-intersecting polygons are also sometimes included among the complex polygons. Vertices are only counted at the ends of edges, not where edges intersect in space.

- A formula relating an integral over a bounded region to a closed line integral may still apply when the "inside-out" parts of the region are counted negatively.

- Moving around the polygon, the total amount one "turns" at the vertices can be any integer times 360°, e.g. 720° for a pentagram and 0° for an angular "eight".

2.1.2 Representation of Polygon

There are three ways to represent the polygon in graphics system.

1. Polygon drawing primitive approach

2. Trapezoid primitive approach

3. Line and point approach

Some graphics devices support polygon drawing approach, where directly basic polygon shapes are drawn. So here one polygon is saved as one unit.

Some graphics devices support trapezoid primitive approach, where a polygon is represented as a set of trapezoids. Trapezoids are formed from two scan lines and two line segments as shown in following Fig. 2.5.

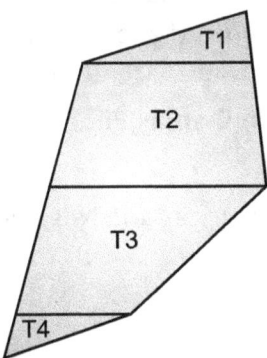

Fig. 2.5 : Trapezoid primitive approach

In line and point approach polygons are represented by series of lines and points. This series is considered as a single unit and is stored in display file. Display file stores the series in following format.

OP	x	y

Where,   OP = Number of operand which specifies command.

                          x, y = Co-ordinates of a point (vertex of polygon)

Following Fig. 2.6 shows a polygon and its representation using lines and points in a display file.

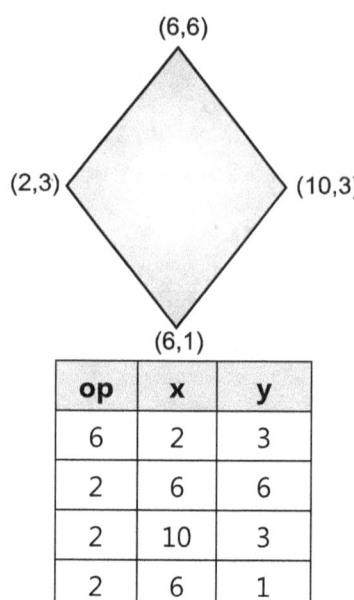

op	x	y
6	2	3
2	6	6
2	10	3
2	6	1

Fig. 2.6 : Representation of polygon using display file

2.1.3 Entering Polygon in Display File

Let us see, how to enter polygon command and data into the display file, the information of polygon can be entered by using following algorithm

Algorithm for Entering a Polygon in Display File

Step 1 : Read PX and PY of length N.

[PX and PY are arrays containing vertices and N is number of sides of polygon]

Step 2 : i=0

DF_OP [i] <– N

DF_x [i] <–PX [i]

DF_y [i] <–PY [i]

i<–i+1

Step 3 : do

DF_OP[i] <–2

DF_x [i] <– PX [i]

DF_y[i] <– PY [i]

i<–i+1

}

While (i<N)

Step 4 : DF_OP [i] <– 2

    DF_x [i] <–PX [0]

    DF_y [i] <–PY [0]

Step 5 : Stop

2.2 POLYGON INSIDE TEST

This method is also known as **counting number method**. While filling a polygon, we often need to identify whether particular point is inside the polygon or outside it. Basically there are two methods by which we can identify whether particular point is inside of polygon or outside of polygon.

- Odd-Even rule

- Nonzero winding number rule

2.2.1 Even-Odd Method

One simple way of finding whether the point is inside or outside of polygon is to test how many times a ray or line segment, starting from the point and going in any fixed direction, intersects the edges of the polygon. If the point is on the outside of the polygon the ray or line segment will intersect its edge an even number of times. If the point is on the inside of the polygon then it will intersect the edge an odd number of times. Unfortunately, this method won't work if the point is on the edge of the polygon.

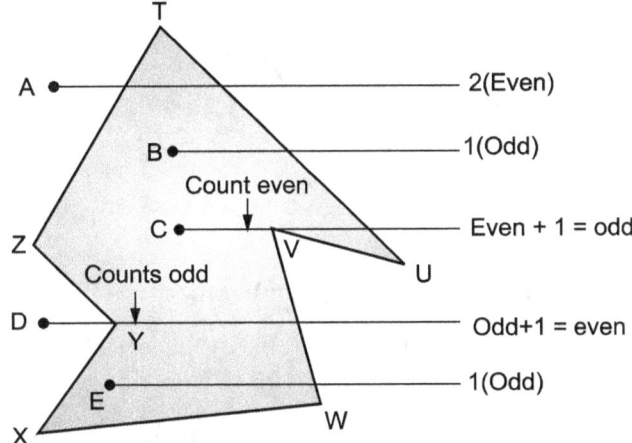

Fig. 2.7 : Even odd method

The above Fig. 2.7 shows the line segment or ray intersection with polygon boundary. If there are odd numbers of intersection, then the point is inside else it is outside of polygon boundary.

If the intersection point is vertex of polygon then, if the other end points of the two segments which meets at this vertex lie on same side of constructed line then point is taken as having even number of intersections. If they lie on the opposite side of constructed line then point is counted to have a single intersection.

- In above Fig. 2.6 polygon TUVWXYZ, point 'A' has total two intersection hence the point is outside.

- Point 'B' has only one means odd intersection hence the point is inside.

- In Fig. 2.7 point 'C' and 'D' are special cases as the intersection point is vertex.

- As the segment VW and VU lie on same side of ray then intersection point i.e. 'V' is count as even. So even + 1 (intersection) =odd; hence 'C' is inside of polygon.

- Similarly vertex 'Y' is intersection point and segment ZY and YX lie opposite side of ray hence intersection point i.e. 'Y' is count as odd. so odd + 1 (intersection) =even; hence point is outside of polygon.

2.2.2 Winding Number Method

Another method for inside test of polygon is the winding number method. Consider a piece of elastic between point in question and a point on polygon boundary, refer Fig. 2.8 below. Consider that elastic is tied to point in question and other end of elastic is sliding along the boundary of the polygon until it has made one complete rotation; then observe that how many times the elastic has wound around point in question. If it gets wounded at least once, then point is inside; and if there is no winding at all then the point is outside.

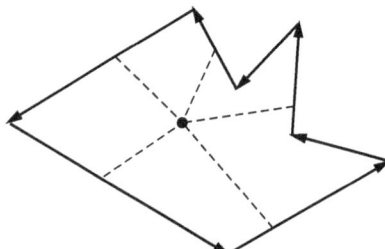

Fig. 2.8 : Winding number method

- Like even odd method, in winding number method we have to create line segment which joins outside point of a polygon and point in question.

- Here instead of counting intersections we have to assign direction number to each boundary which crosses the line segment.

- The edge starting below the line segment, crosses the segment and ends above the line segment ; assign direction number as -1, and the edge starting above the line segment , crosses the segment and ends below the line segment; assign direction number refer Fig. 2.9.

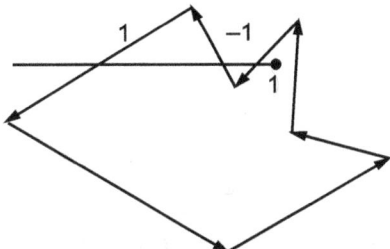

Fig. 2.9 : Winding number method

- After assigning direction number, calculate the sum of direction number; if the sum is non zero means point in question is inside , and if the sum is zero that means point in question is outside.

    In Fig. 2.9 the sum is (1-1+1=1) nonzero hence the point in question is inside.

2.3 POLYGON FILLING METHODS

The processes of coloring the area of polygon is called polygon filling. The techniques which are used to fill a polygon are generally divided into two categories :

1. Seed Fill
2. Scan line polygon filling

2.3.1 Seed Fill

The seed fill algorithm consider one of the pixel positions inside the polygon to be filled. This pixel is inside the region and set to polygon value. This pixel is referred as **seed pixel**. Then the algorithm tries to find the all other adjacent pixels interior to the polygon and subsequently color them. Then one of the adjacent pixels will become the new seed pixel. Then the algorithm is repeated till all inside pixels are get filled by color.

There are two types of seed fill algorithms.

1. Boundary Fill Algorithm
2. Flood Fill Algorithm

1. Boundary Fill

- Boundary Fill is algorithm used for the purpose of coloring figures in computer graphics. Boundary fill fills the chosen area with a color until the given colored boundary is found. This algorithm is also recursive in nature as the function returns when the pixel to be colored is the boundary color or is already the fill color.

- If the boundary is specified in a single color, the fill algorithm proceeds outward pixel-by-pixel until the boundary color is encountered. This is called boundary fill algorithm

Algorithm

Step 1 : The boundary fill procedure accepts the input as coordinates of an interior point (x, y), a fill color, and a boundary color.

Step 2 : Starting from (x, y)which is seed pixel, the procedure tests the neighboring positions to determine whether they are boundary color.

Step 3 : If not, they are painted with the fill color, and the neighbors are tested.

Step 4 : This process continues until all pixels up to the boundary color for the area have been tested.

- There are two methods for filling the pixel and find the neighbor pixel

    (1) 4- connected

    (2) 8-connected

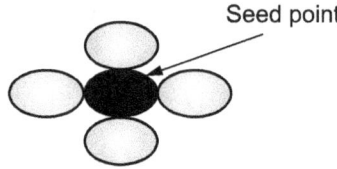

Fig. 2.10 : Four connected method   Fig. 2.11 : Eight connected method

1. 4- Connected Method

In this method 4-connected pixels are used as shown in the Fig. 2.10. The fill operation can proceed above, below, right, and left side of the current pixels and this process will continue until we get a boundary with different color.

Pseudo code for 4 connected boundary fill

Four_Fill (x, y, fill_col, bound_color)

if (curr_pixel_color != bound_color) and (curr_pixel_color != fill_col) then set_pixel(x, y, fill_col)

Four_Fill (x+1, y, fill_col, bound_col);

Four_Fill (x-1, y, fill_col, bound_col);

Four_Fill (x, y+1, fill_col, bound_col);

Four_Fill(x, y-1, fill_col, bound_col);

end;

(2) 8- Connected Method

In this method 8-connected pixels are used as shown in the Fig. 2.11. The fill operation can proceed above, below, right and left side as well as through diagonal pixels of the current pixels. This process will continue until we find a boundary with different color.

2. Flood Fill

- The purpose of Flood Fill is to color an entire area of connected pixels with the same color.

- Similarly boundary fill algorithm, we start with seed pixel, seed pixel is examined for specified interior color instead of boundary color.

- Flood fill algorithm is useful when, area does not have single boundary color.

- Once again, this algorithm relies on the Four-connect or Eight-connect method of filling in the pixels. But instead of looking for the boundary color, it is looking for all adjacent pixels that are a part of the interior.

Pseudo Code for Flood Fill Algorithm

Flood-fill (node, old-color, replacement-color) :

1. If the color of *node* is not equal to *old-color*, return.

2. Set the color of *node* to *replacement-color*.

3. Perform **Flood-fill** (one step to the left of *node, old-color, replacement-color*).

    - Perform **Flood-fill** (one step to the right of *node, old-color, replacement-color*).

    - Perform **Flood-fill** (one step to the top of *node, old-color, replacement-color*).

    - Perform **Flood-fill** (one step to the bottom of *node, old-color, replacement-color*).

4. Return.

2.3.2 Scan Line Polygon Filling

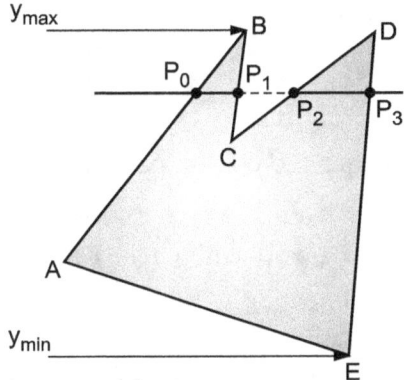

Fig. 2.12 : Scan line polygon filling

This algorithm works by intersecting scan line with polygon boundary and fills the polygon between pairs of intersections.

The following steps show how this algorithm works.

Step 1 : Find out the y_{min} and y_{max} from the given polygon.

Step 2 : ScanLine intersects with each edge of the polygon from y_{min} to y_{max}. i.e. scan line moves from y_{min} to y_{max}. Name each intersection point of the polygon. As per the Fig. 2.12 shown above, they are named as P_0, P_1, P_2, P_3.

Step 3 : Sort the intersection point in the ascending order of X coordinate i.e. (P_0, P_1), (P_1, P_2), and (P_2, P_3).

Step 4 : Fill all those pair of coordinates that are inside polygons and ignore the alternate pairs i.e. in above case P_0 to P_1 and P_2 to P_3 get fill by color, as these pixels are inside of polygon. Scan line fill algorithm ignores P_1 to P_2 as these pixels are outside of the polygon.

Characteristics of Scan Line Polygon Filling :

- It fills horizontal pixels across the line i.e. X axis.
- It avoids the stacking of neighboring pixels.
- It is used in orthogonal projection.
- It is non-recursive algorithm.
- Used for filling of polygon.
- Solved the problem of hidden.

2.3.3 Filling with Patterns

To fill an area with a pattern there are two modes

1. Transparent mode :

    Perform WritePixel() with foreground color if pattern = 1

    inhibit WritePixel() if pattern = 0

2. Opaque mode :

    Perform WritePixel() with foreground color if pattern = 1

    Perform WritePixel() with background color if pattern = 0

- The pattern is "anchored" at :

    Left most polygon vertex (doesn't work with circles)

    Screen origin (fast, seamless connection)

- Patterns are defined as small M by N bitmaps.
- Assume that the Pattern [0, 0] pixel is coincident with the screen origin, we can write a pattern in transparent mode with the following code :

```
if pattern
[ x mod M , y mod n ]
then
WritePixel
(x,y,color);
```

Note : In opaque mode, a whole row can be copied at once.

Pattern Filling Without Repeated Scan Conversion

- Scan convert a primitive first into a rectangular work area, then write each pixel to the appropriate place in the canvas.

- Twice as much work but good for primitives that are scan-converted repeatedly (e.g. characters).

- Don't have to worry about clipping.

- Use copyPixel() (or BitBlt()) for faster speed (drawing the entire rectangle encompassing the primitive at once).

- Problem with objects with "holes" when writing in opaque mode.

2.4 WINDOWING

2.4.1 Concept of Window and Viewport

- The space in which objects are described is called world coordinate.

- World coordinates used Cartesian XY coordinate system used in mathematics.

Window

- Defining a window in these world coordinate called "world window" or simply "window" in computer graphics

- The world "window" specifies which part of the world should be drawn, the part inside the window should be drawn and outside the window should be clipped.

- "Window" refers to the area in "world space" or "world coordinates" that you want to project onto the screen.

- The window is often centered around the origin.

Viewport

A viewport defines in normalized coordinates (u, v). A viewport is rectangular area on the display device where the image of the data appears. The viewport is an area (typically rectangular) expressed in rendering-device-specific coordinates, e.g. pixels for screen coordinates, in which the objects of interest are going to be rendered. The objects inside the world window appear automatically at proper sizes and locations inside the viewport.

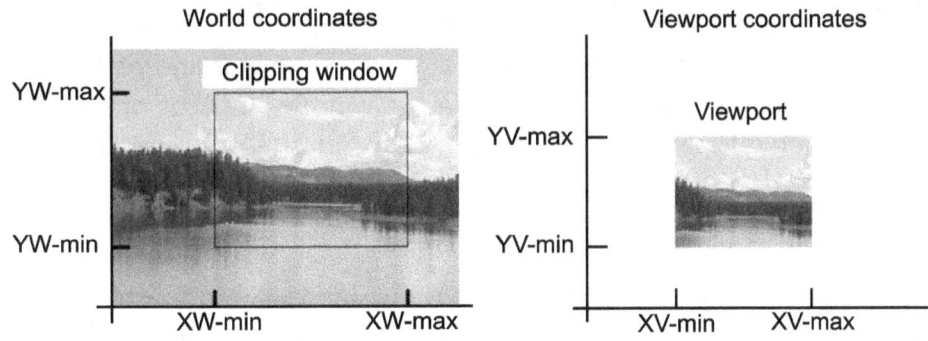

Fig. 2.13 : Window and viewport

2.4.2 Viewing Transformations

Moving objects from their 3D locations to their positions in a 2D view called viewing transformation.

Need to transform points from "world" view (window) to the screen view (viewport).

- Maintain relative placement of points (usually).

- Can be done with a translate-scale-translate sequence.

The window-to-viewport transform is

1. **Translate** lower-left corner of window to origin.

$$t_x = -x_{min} \text{ and } t_y = -y_{min}$$

2. **Scale** width and height of window to match viewport's.

$$s_x = \frac{u_{max} - u_{min}}{x_{max} - x_{min}} \text{ and } s_y = \frac{v_{max} - v_{min}}{y_{max} - y_{min}}$$

3. **Translate** corner at origin to lower-left corner in viewport.

$$t_x = u_{min} \text{ and } t_y = v_{min}$$

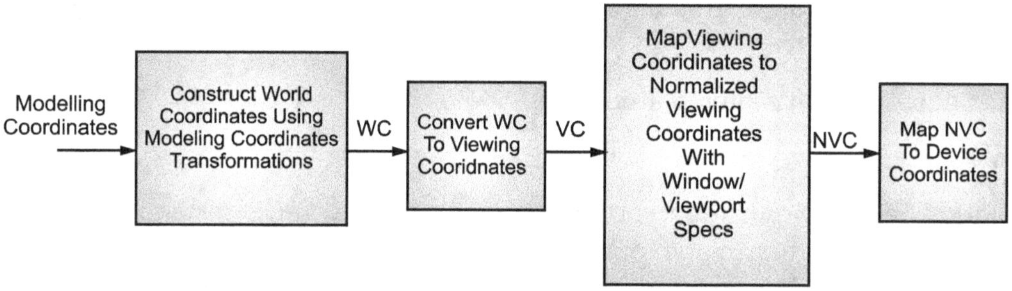

Fig. 2.14 : Translating world coordinate to device coordinate

2.5 LINE CLIPPING

- When a window is "placed" on the world, only certain objects and parts of objects can be seen. Points and lines which are outside the window are "cut off" from view. This process of "cutting off" parts of the image of the world is called Clipping.

- In clipping, we examine each line to determine whether or not it is completely inside the window, completely outside the window, or crosses a window boundary.

- **If inside** the window, **the line is displayed**. If **outside** the window, the lines and points are **not displayed**. If **a line crosses** the boundary, we must determine the point of intersection and **display only the part which lies inside the window**. Refer Fig. 2.15.

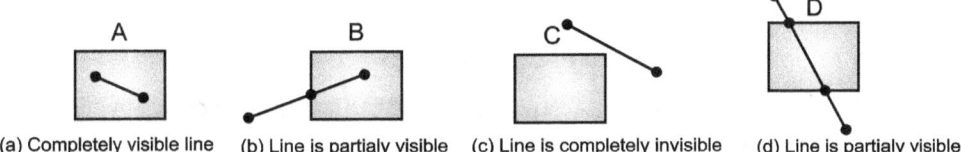

(a) Completely visible line   (b) Line is partialy visible   (c) Line is completely invisible   (d) Line is partialy visible

Fig. 2.15

2.5.1 Cohen Sutherland Method

- The Cohen-Sutherland line clipping algorithm quickly detects and dispenses with two common and trivial cases. To clip a line, we need to consider only its endpoints. If both endpoints of a line lie inside the window, the entire line lies inside the window. It is trivially accepted and needs no clipping. On the other hand, if both endpoints of a line lie entirely to one side of the window, the line must lie entirely outside of the window. It is trivially rejected and needs to be neither clipped nor displayed.

- According to cohen Sutherland method, the window is divided in total 9 regions.

- Cohen Sutherland uses 4-bits of code. These 4 bits represent the Top, Bottom, Right, and Left of the region as shown in the following Fig. 2.16.

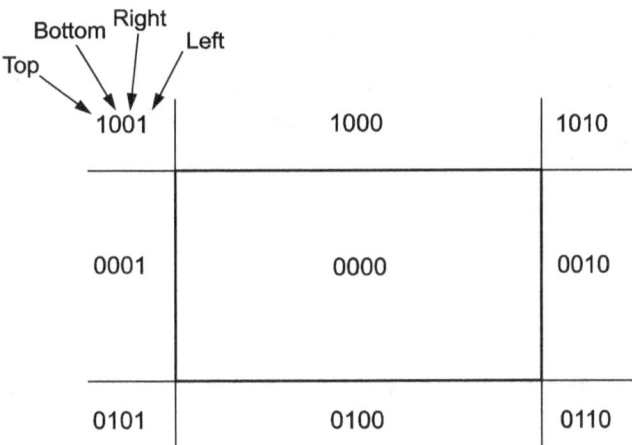

Fig. 2.16 : Cohen sutherland region codes

There are three possibilities for the line :

- Line can be completely inside the window (This line will be completely removed from the region).

- Line can be completely outside the window (This line will be completely removed from the region).

- Line can be partially inside the window (We will find intersection point and draw only that portion of line that is inside region).

Algorithm

Step 1 : Assign a region code for each end points.

Step 2 : If both end points have a region code **0000** then accept this line.(i.e. Line is completely visible)

Step 3 : If any one end point or both end points are not 0000 then, perform the logical **AND** operation for both region codes or for both end points.

Step 3.1 : If the result is not **0000,** then reject the line completely.(i.e. the line is completely outside)

Step 3.2 : Else clip the line.

Step 3.2.1 : select the endpoints of the line that is outside the window.

Step 3.2.2 : Find the intersection point at the window boundary (base on region code).

Step 3.2.3 : Replace endpoint with the intersection point and update the region code.

Step 3.2.4 : Repeat step 2 until we find a clipped line either trivially accepted or trivially rejected.

Step 4 : Repeat step 1 for other lines.

Finding out Intersection Point

Intersection points with a clipping boundary can be calculated using the slope-intercept form of the line equation. For a line with end points coordinates (x_1, y_1) and (x_2, y_2), they coordinate of the intersection point with a vertical boundary can be obtained with the calculation,

$$y = y_1 + m(x-x_1)$$

where the x value is set either to xw_{min}, or to xw_{max} and the slope of the line is calculated

as $m = (y_2 - y_1)/(x_2 - x_1)$

Similarly, if we are looking for the intersection with a horizontal boundary, the x coordinate can be calculated as

$$x = x_1 + \frac{y - y_1}{m}$$

with y set either to yw_{min}, or to yw_{max}

SOLVED EXAMPLES

Example 2.1 : Explain the process of polygon clipping using Sutherland Hodgeman Method. What are the intersecting point for line P_1 joining (-1,0) and (4,5) and line P_2 (3,1) and (6,2) if clipped against a window bounded by line x=0, y=0 and x=5,y=3.

Solution : For Sutherland Hodgman Method refer 2.6.1.

The window with given line segment will look like this,

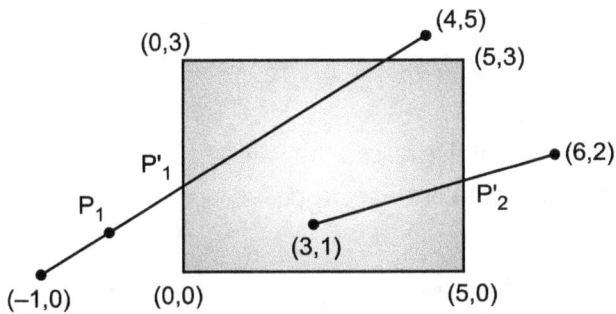

Fig. 2.17

To find P'_1 and P'_2, first we have to find slope m

$$m_1 = \frac{y_2 - y_1}{x_2 - x_1}$$

$$= \frac{5 - 0}{4 - (-1)}$$

$$= \frac{5}{5} = 1$$

$$m_2 = \frac{y_2 - y_1}{x_2 - x_1}$$

$$= \frac{2 - 1}{6 - 3} = \frac{1}{3}$$

$$= 0.33$$

For vertical line intersection, x intersection will be XW_{min}

hence $x_{int} = 0$

For y intersection

$$y_{int} = y_1 + m (x - x_1)$$

Where   x value $= 0$

$$= 0 + 1 (0 - (-1))$$

$$= 0 + 1$$

$$= 1$$

Hence for line P_1 the vertical intersection P'_1 is (0, 1).

Similarly,

For horizontal line intersection y intersection will be y_{max}

$$y_{int} = 3$$

For x intersection

$$x_{int} = x_1 + \frac{y - y_1}{m}$$

where, $y = Y_{wmax} = (-1) + \dfrac{(3-0)}{1}$

$\qquad\qquad\qquad\qquad\qquad\qquad = 2$

Hence for line P'_1 the horizontal intersection will be (2, 3).

For line P_2 there is no horizontal intersection.

For vertical intersection

$\qquad\qquad\qquad\qquad x_{int} = X_{wmax}$

$\qquad\qquad\qquad\qquad x_{int} = 5$

For Y intersection $y_{int} = y_1 + m(x - x_1) = 1 + (0.3)(5-1)$

$\qquad\qquad\qquad\qquad\qquad = 1 + 1.2$

$\qquad\qquad\qquad\qquad\qquad = 2.2$

Hence for line P_2 the vertical intersection point is (5, 2.2).

Example 2.2 : Consider the clipping window and the lines shown in below Fig. 2.17 find the region codes for each end point and identify whether the line is completely visible, partially visible or completely invisible.

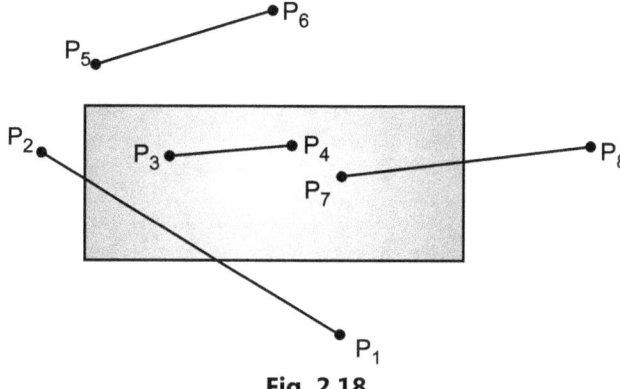

Fig. 2.18

Solution :

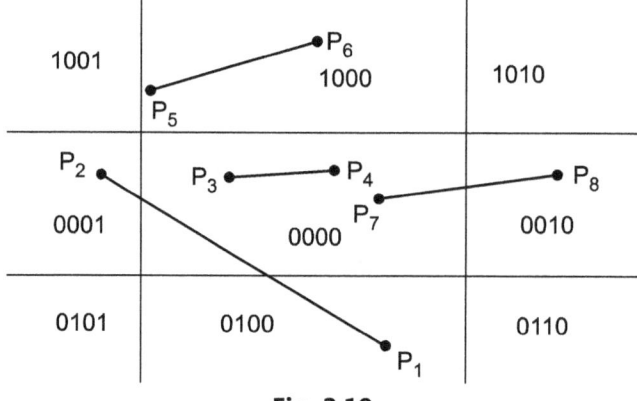

Fig. 2.19

The above Fig. 2.19 shows clipping window with region codes, the end points are ANDed to identify visibility.

Line	End Points		AND Result	Visibility
P1P2	0100	0001	0000	Partially Visible
P3P4	0000	0000	0000	Completely visible
P5P6	1000	1000	1000	Completely Invisible
P7P8	0000	0010	0000	Partially Visible

2.5.2 Mid Point Subdivision Method

- To avoid the computation of intersection of lines with window boundary the mid-point subdivision algorithm is developed.
- In this algorithm, the line which is partially visible is subdivided into two equal parts. Then, the two segments are tested for visibility. If both of them can not be rejected then continue with each half until the intersection with the window edge is found or the length of divided segments becomes as small as it can be treated as a point. Then the visibility of the point is then checked to determine whether it is inside or outside the window.

Algorithm

Step 1 : Assign a region code for each end points.

Step 2 : If both end points have a region code **0000** then accept this line.(i.e. Line is completely visible)

Step 3 : If any one end point or both end points are not **0000** then, perform the logical **AND** operation for both region codes or for both end points.

Step 3.1 : If the result is not **0000,** then reject the line completely.(i.e. the line is completely outside)

Step 3.2 : If step 2 and 3.1 both are not satisfied, line is partially visible.

Step 4 : Divide partially visible line segments to equal parts and repeat steps 3 through 5 for both sub divided line segments until you get completely visible and completely invisible line segments.

Step 5 : Stop.

2.6 POLYGON CLIPPING

- To clip polygons, we need to modify the line-clipping algorithm discussed in the previous section. A polygon boundary processed with a line clipper may be displayed as a series of unconnected line segments refer Fig. 2.20 and 2.21 depending on the orientation of the polygon to the clipping window.
- What we really want to display is a bounded area after clipping,
- Thus only line clipping algorithm will not work for polygon clipping as it generates disconnected edges of polygon as shown in Fig. 2.21.

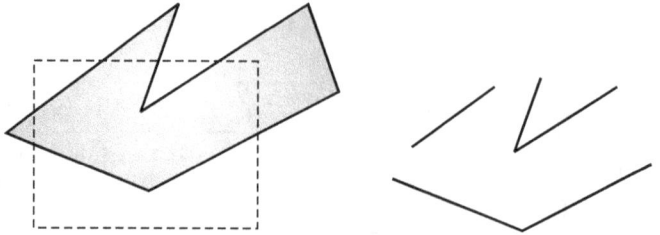

Fig. 2.20 : Before clipping   **Fig. 2.21 : After clipping**

2.6.1 Sutherland Hodgman Method for Clipping Method

- We can correctly clip a polygon by processing the polygon boundary as a whole against each window edge. This could be accomplished by processing all polygon vertices against each clip rectangle boundary in turn.

- Beginning with the initial set of polygon vertices, we can first clip the polygon against the left boundary to produce a new sequence of vertices. The new set of vertices can then passed to a right boundary clipper, a bottom boundary clipper, and a top boundary clipper, as in Fig. 2.23.

- At each step, a new sequence of output vertices is generated and passed to the next window boundary clipper.

The Sutherland- Hodgman's algorithm clips the original polygon against the simple window edge for obtaining intermediate polygon, by generating list of vertices. It then re-enters the procedure with intermediate polygon, which was generated in previous step and next window edge in the way, when it re-entered with last window edge it generates the list of vertices, which gives a clipped polygon.

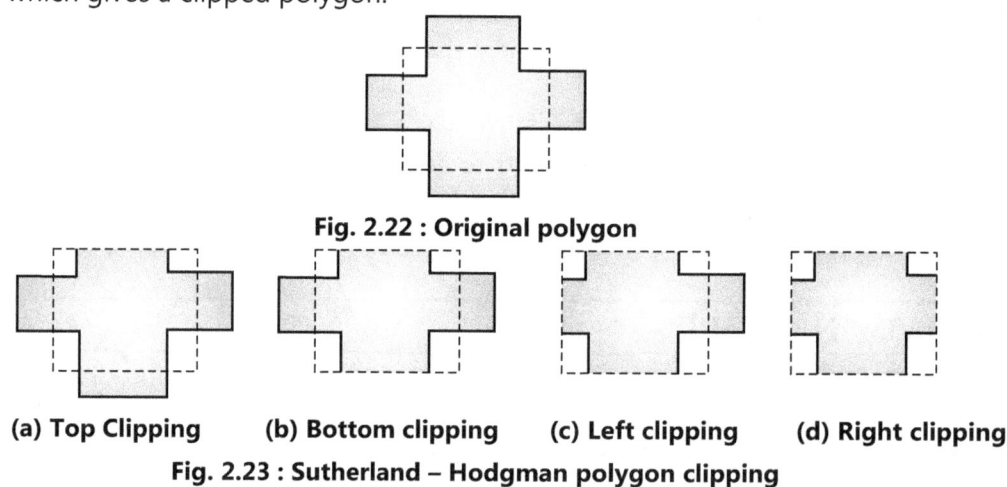

Fig. 2.22 : Original polygon

(a) Top Clipping   **(b) Bottom clipping**   **(c) Left clipping**   **(d) Right clipping**

Fig. 2.23 : Sutherland – Hodgman polygon clipping

There are four possible cases when processing vertices in sequence around the perimeter of a polygon. As each pair of adjacent polygon vertices is passed to a window boundary clipper, we make the following tests :

- If the first vertex is outside the window boundary and the second vertex is inside, both the intersection point of the polygon edge with the window boundary and the second vertex is added to the output vertex list.

- If both input vertices are inside the window boundary, only the second vertex is added to the output vertex list.

- If the first vertex is inside the window boundary and the second vertex is outside, only the edge intersection with the window boundary is added to the output vertex list.

- If both input vertices are outside the window boundary, nothing is added to the output list. These four cases are illustrated in Fig. 2.24 for successive pairs of polygon vertices. Once all vertices have been processed for one clip window boundary, the output list of vertices is clipped against the next window boundary.

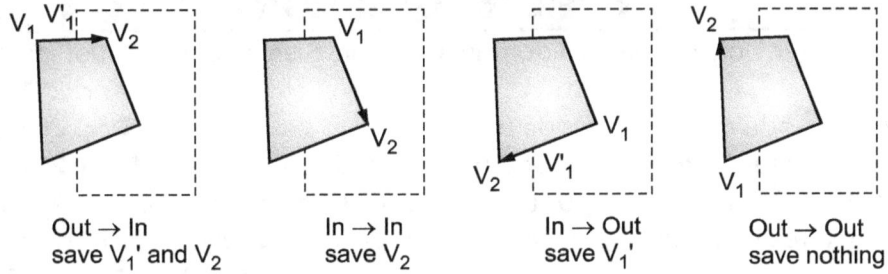

Out → In   In → In   In → Out   Out → Out
save V_1' and V_2 save V_2 save V_1' save nothing

Fig. 2.24 : Processing of edges against left window boundary

Limitation :

- It requires separate clipping routine, one for each boundary of the clipping window.

2.7 GENERALIZED CLIPPING

All the clipping routines are more or less identical. They differ only in the test for determining whether a point is inside of window or outside of window and through their parameters, information about boundary is passed. These routines will be entered four times. Every time with a different boundary specified by its parameters. The routine is generalized so that it can clip along any line including horizontal and vertical boundaries. This can clip along rectangular windows parallel to the axis along the arbitrary lines i.e. window sides may be at any angles. The algorithm is a recursive language that can be used to clip along an arbitrary convex plane.

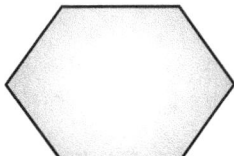

Fig. 2.25 : Windows with eight clipping points

EXERCISE

1. What is polygon and Polyline?
2. What are the different types of polygon?
3. Which are the various approaches used to represent polygon?
4. Represent the polygon using display file structure?
5. Write down the different methods for testing a pixel inside of polygon?
6. Which are the different methods used for filling polygon?
7. Explain boundary fill method for polygon?
8. What is mean by Seed pixel and what is mean by four connected region and eight connected region?
9. Compare Seed fill, edge fill method and flood fill ?
10. What is the need of scan line algorithm?

UNIVERSITY QUESTIONS

1. Enlist any three polygon filling algorithms. Explain even-odd method of inside test.
   [Apr. 2013, 8 Marks]
2. Explain even-odd method of inside test.   **[Dec. 2015, 3 Marks]**
3. What is inside test? Explain even odd method in detail.   **[May 2016, 6 Marks]**
4. Explain the different methods for testing a pixel inside a polygon.**[Dec. 2014, 5 Marks]**
5. Enlist any three methods of polygon filling. Explain how polygon is filled with pattern.
   [Apr. 2013, Dec. 2013, 8 Marks]
6. Enlist any three methods of polygon filling algorithms. Explain even-odd method of inside test.   **[Dec. 2015, 8 Marks]**
7. What is meant by Coherence and how it can increase the efficiency of scan line polygon filling.   **[June 2015, 4 Marks]**
8. Write algorithm to fill the polygon area using flood fill method.   **[June 2015, 4 Marks]**
9. Write flood fill algorithm.   **[Dec. 2015, 3 Marks]**
10. Explain scanline algorithm with example.   **[May 2014, 6 Marks]**
11. Describe 3D viewing transformations.   **[Apr. 2013, Dec. 2013, 8 Marks]**
12. Explain concept of viewing parameters with an example.   **[June 2015, 4 Marks]**
13. Explain Cohen-Sutherland outcode algorithm with example.
    [Apr. 2013, Dec. 2013, 8 Marks]
14. Write and explain Cohen-Sutherland line clipping algorithm.   **[Dec. 2015, 8 Marks]**
15. Write Cohen-Sutherland line clipping algorithm.   **[June 2015, 4 Marks]**
16. Write and explain with an example Cohen-Sutherland line clipping algorithm.
    [May 2016, 6 Marks]
17. Explain Sutherland-Hodgman clipping algorithm with example.   **[Dec. 2014, 6 Marks]**
18. Explain Sutherland-Hodgman clipping algorithm with example.   **[May 2014, 6 Marks]**

◈ ◈ ◈

2-D, 3-D TRANSFORMATIONS AND PROJECTIONS

3.1 2D GEOMETRIC TRANSFORMATIONS

3.1.1 Translation

The process of changing the position of an object is called as translation. The object is translated in straight line path from one position to another.

For example, consider point P(x, y) where x, y are the co-ordinates of original position. The point is translated to new position P'(x', y')

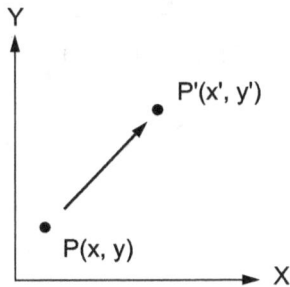

Fig. 3.1 : Translation

Here the point P has been shifted by t_x units in X-direction similarly in t_y units in Y-direction. where t_x, t_y be the quantities by which the point P has to be shifted in x and y-direction respectively.

$$x' = x + t_x \qquad \qquad \ldots (3.1)$$

$$y' = y + t_y \qquad \qquad \ldots (3.2)$$

$$P = \begin{bmatrix} x \\ y \end{bmatrix} \quad P' = \begin{bmatrix} x' \\ y' \end{bmatrix} \quad T = \begin{bmatrix} t_x \\ t_y \end{bmatrix}$$

$$\therefore \qquad P = P + T \qquad \qquad \ldots (3.3)$$

The pair t_x, t_y is called translation vector.

SOLVED EXAMPLES

Examples 3.1 : Translate the polygon with co-ordinates A(2, 3), B(5, 9)and C(8, 9) by 6 units in x- direction and 3 units in y-direction.   **[Oct 2010 4 Marks]**

Solution : From Equation 3

$$P' = P + T$$

$$A' = A + T$$

$$A' = \begin{bmatrix} 2 \\ 3 \end{bmatrix} + \begin{bmatrix} 6 \\ 3 \end{bmatrix} = \begin{bmatrix} 8 \\ 6 \end{bmatrix}$$

$$B' = \begin{bmatrix} 5 \\ 9 \end{bmatrix} + \begin{bmatrix} 6 \\ 3 \end{bmatrix} = \begin{bmatrix} 11 \\ 12 \end{bmatrix}$$

$$C' = \begin{bmatrix} 8 \\ 9 \end{bmatrix} + \begin{bmatrix} 6 \\ 3 \end{bmatrix} = \begin{bmatrix} 14 \\ 12 \end{bmatrix}$$

Thus the co-ordinates of triangle with new position will be A'(8, 6), B'(11, 12), C'(14, 12).

Example 3.2 : Translate the polygon A(5, 7), B(7, 11) and C(12, 15) by 4 units in x-direction and 6 units in y-direction.   **[April 2012, 4 Marks]**

Solution : From Equation 3

$$P' = P + T$$

$$A' = A + T$$

$$A' = \begin{bmatrix} 5 \\ 7 \end{bmatrix} + \begin{bmatrix} 4 \\ 6 \end{bmatrix} = \begin{bmatrix} 9 \\ 13 \end{bmatrix}$$

$$B' = \begin{bmatrix} 7 \\ 11 \end{bmatrix} + \begin{bmatrix} 4 \\ 6 \end{bmatrix} = \begin{bmatrix} 11 \\ 17 \end{bmatrix}$$

$$C' = \begin{bmatrix} 12 \\ 15 \end{bmatrix} + \begin{bmatrix} 4 \\ 6 \end{bmatrix} = \begin{bmatrix} 16 \\ 21 \end{bmatrix}$$

Thus the co-ordinates of triangle with new position will be A'(9, 13), B'(11, 17), C'(16, 21).

3.1.2 Scaling

This transformation is used to changes the size of an object. For example, consider point P(x, y). This point is to be scaled to P' (x', y'). Then the x scaling factor isS_x and y scaling factor is S_y for the x and y co-ordinates respectively.

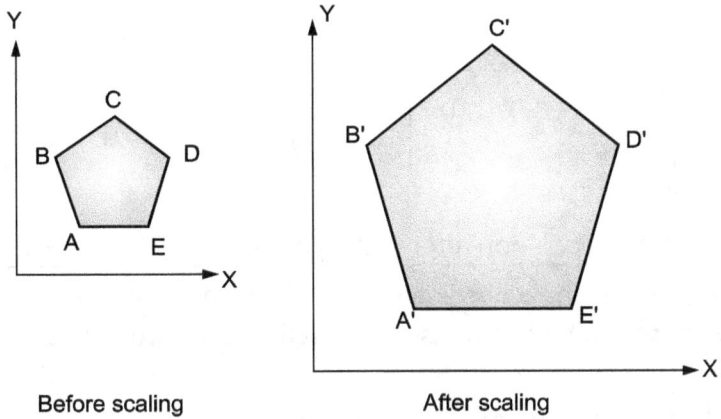

Before scaling   After scaling

Fig. 3.2 : Scaling

To obtain the scaled object point i.e. the new point the original point i.e. old point co-ordinates is to be multiplied by the scaling factors as :

$$x' = S_x \cdot x$$

$$y' = S_y \cdot y$$

$$\begin{bmatrix} x' \\ y' \end{bmatrix} = \begin{bmatrix} x \\ y \end{bmatrix} \begin{bmatrix} S_x & 0 \\ 0 & S_y \end{bmatrix}$$

$$\therefore \qquad P' = P \cdot S$$

$S_x > 1$,   Increase in size

$S_x < 1$,   Reduction in size

$S_x = 1$,   Uniform scaling

$S_x < 1$,   Reduction in size

$S_x = 1$,   Uniform scaling

Example 3.3 : Scale the polygon with coordinates A(2,5), B(7,10) and C(10,2) by 3 units in X direction and 4 units in y direction.   **[Oct. 2010, 6 Marks]**

Solution : The scaling matrix will be,

$$S = \begin{bmatrix} 3 & 0 \\ 0 & 4 \end{bmatrix}$$

The given coordinates of polygon in matrix form :

$$\begin{matrix} A \\ B \\ C \end{matrix} \begin{bmatrix} 2 & 5 \\ 7 & 10 \\ 10 & 2 \end{bmatrix}$$

$$A' \begin{bmatrix} x_1' & y_1' \\ B' & \\ x_2' & y_2' \\ C' & \\ x_3' & y_3' \end{bmatrix} = \begin{bmatrix} 2 & 5 \\ 7 & 10 \\ 10 & 2 \end{bmatrix} \begin{bmatrix} 3 & 0 \\ 0 & 4 \end{bmatrix} = \begin{bmatrix} 6 & 20 \\ 21 & 40 \\ 30 & 8 \end{bmatrix}$$

Therefore the coordinates of polygon after scaling are A'(6,20), B'(21,40), C'(30,8).

Example 3.4 : Find out the final coordinates of a figure bounded by the coordinates (1,1), (3,4), (5,7), (10,3) when scaled by two units in X direction and three units in Y direction.

[May 2015, 6 Marks]

Solution : The scaling matrix will be,

$$S = \begin{bmatrix} 2 & 0 \\ 0 & 3 \end{bmatrix}$$

The given coordinates of polygon in matrix form :

$$\begin{matrix} A \\ B \\ C \end{matrix} \begin{bmatrix} 1 & 1 \\ 3 & 4 \\ 5 & 7 \\ 10 & 3 \end{bmatrix}$$

$$\therefore \quad \begin{matrix} A' \\ B' \\ C' \\ D' \end{matrix} \begin{bmatrix} x_1' & y_1' \\ x_2' & y_2' \\ x_3' & y_3' \\ x_4' & y_4' \end{bmatrix} = \begin{matrix} A \\ B \\ C \end{matrix} \begin{bmatrix} 1 & 1 \\ 3 & 4 \\ 5 & 7 \\ 10 & 3 \end{bmatrix} \begin{bmatrix} 3 & 0 \\ 0 & 4 \end{bmatrix}$$

$$= \begin{bmatrix} 3 & 4 \\ 9 & 16 \\ 15 & 28 \\ 30 & 12 \end{bmatrix}$$

Therefore the coordinates of polygon after scaling are A'(3, 4), B'(9, 16), C'(15, 28),D'(30, 12).

3.1.3 Rotation

The transformation in which an object is rotated along the circular path is called rotation of an object about origin. In this case the object can be rotated by a given angle in either clockwise or anticlockwise direction.

Consider point P(x, y). Let the angle of rotation be θ°.

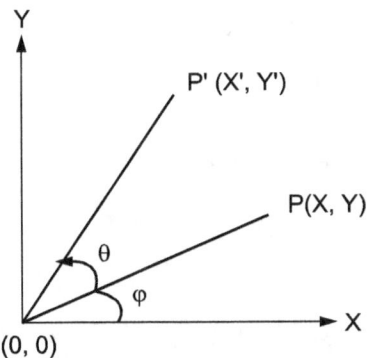

Fig. 3.3 : Rotation

The original coordinates of points is given as

$\therefore$ $x = r\cos \phi$

                                        $y = r \sin \phi$ ... (3.4)

we can express the transformed coordinates in terms of angles θ and φ as

                        $x' = r \cos (\phi + \theta) = r \cos \phi \cos \theta - r \sin \phi \sin \theta$

                        $y' = r \sin (\phi + \theta) = r \cos \phi \sin \theta + r \sin \phi \cos \theta$ ... (3.5)

Substituting equation 1 into equation 2, we get

                        $x' = x \cos \theta - y \sin \theta$

                        $y' = x \sin \theta + y \cos \theta$

So we can write the rotation equation in matrix form as

                        $P'' = R \cdot P$

Where R is $R = \begin{bmatrix} \cos \theta & \sin \theta \\ -\sin \theta & \cos \theta \end{bmatrix}$

The positive value of rotation angle define anticlockwise or counterclockwise rotation where negative value of rotation angle define clockwise rotation of an object.

Therefore for clockwise rotation, we get the matrix as

$$R = \begin{bmatrix} \cos (-\theta) & \sin (-\theta) \\ -\sin (-\theta) & \cos (-\theta) \end{bmatrix}$$

$$= \begin{bmatrix} \cos \theta & -\sin \theta \\ \sin \theta & \cos \theta \end{bmatrix}$$

Example 3.5 : 1.3 A point (5,4) is rotated anticlockwise by an angle of 45. Find rotation matrix and the resultant point.   **[Oct. 2010, 6 Marks]**

Solution :

$$R = \begin{bmatrix} \cos\theta & \sin\theta \\ -\sin\theta & \cos\theta \end{bmatrix}$$

$$\theta = 45°$$

$$R = \begin{bmatrix} 1/\sqrt{2} & 1/\sqrt{2} \\ -1/\sqrt{2} & 1/\sqrt{2} \end{bmatrix}$$

$$P' = \begin{bmatrix} 5 & 4 \end{bmatrix} \begin{bmatrix} 1/\sqrt{2} & 1/\sqrt{2} \\ -1/\sqrt{2} & 1/\sqrt{2} \end{bmatrix}$$

$$= \begin{bmatrix} \dfrac{5}{\sqrt{2}} - 2\sqrt{2} & \dfrac{5}{\sqrt{2}} + 4\sqrt{2} \end{bmatrix}$$

$$= \begin{bmatrix} 1/\sqrt{2} & 9/\sqrt{2} \end{bmatrix}$$

Example 3.6 : Consider a polygon with vertices A(10' 10)' B(15' 15) and C(20, 10). Obtain the following rotations of the polygon about the origin :

(i)   Counterclockwise π

(ii) Clockwise $\pi/2$

(iii) Counterclockwise $5\pi/4$

(iv) Clockwise $3\pi/4$.

Solution : Counterclockwise π

$$R = \begin{bmatrix} \cos\theta & \sin\theta \\ -\sin\theta & \cos\theta \end{bmatrix}$$

$$R = \begin{bmatrix} \cos\pi & \sin\pi \\ -\sin\pi & \cos\pi \end{bmatrix}$$

$$= \begin{bmatrix} \cos\pi & \sin\pi \\ -\sin\pi & \cos\pi \end{bmatrix}$$

$$= \begin{bmatrix} -1 & 0 \\ 0 & -1 \end{bmatrix}$$

$$P' = P \cdot R$$

$$P' = \begin{bmatrix} 10 & 10 \\ 15 & 10 \\ 20 & 10 \end{bmatrix} \begin{bmatrix} -1 & 0 \\ 0 & -1 \end{bmatrix} = \begin{bmatrix} -10 & -10 \\ -15 & -10 \\ -20 & -10 \end{bmatrix}$$

(ii) Clockwise $\pi/2$

$$R = \begin{bmatrix} \cos\theta & \sin\theta \\ -\sin\theta & \cos\theta \end{bmatrix}$$

$$R = \begin{bmatrix} \cos\pi/2 & \sin\pi/2 \\ -\sin\pi/2 & \cos\pi/2 \end{bmatrix}$$

$$= \begin{bmatrix} 0 & 1 \\ -1 & 0 \end{bmatrix}$$

$$P' = P \cdot R$$

$$P' = \begin{bmatrix} 10 & 10 \\ 15 & 10 \\ 20 & 10 \end{bmatrix} \begin{bmatrix} 0 & 1 \\ -1 & 0 \end{bmatrix}$$

$$= \begin{bmatrix} -10 & 10 \\ -10 & 15 \\ -10 & 20 \end{bmatrix}$$

(iii) Counterclockwise $5\pi/4$

$$R = \begin{bmatrix} \cos\theta & \sin\theta \\ -\sin\theta & \cos\theta \end{bmatrix}$$

$$R = \begin{bmatrix} \cos 5\pi/4 & \sin 5\pi/4 \\ -\sin 5\pi/4 & \cos 5\pi/4 \end{bmatrix} = \begin{bmatrix} -0.7 & -0.7 \\ 0.7 & -0.7 \end{bmatrix}$$

$$P' = P \cdot R$$

$$P' = \begin{bmatrix} 10 & 10 \\ 15 & 10 \\ 20 & 10 \end{bmatrix} \begin{bmatrix} -0.7 & -0.7 \\ 0.7 & -0.7 \end{bmatrix}$$

$$= \begin{bmatrix} 0 & -14 \\ -3.5 & -17.5 \\ -7 & -21 \end{bmatrix}$$

(iv) Clockwise $3\pi/4$

$$R = \begin{bmatrix} \cos\theta & \sin\theta \\ -\sin\theta & \cos\theta \end{bmatrix}$$

$$R = \begin{bmatrix} \cos 3\pi/4 & \sin 3\pi/4 \\ -\sin 3\pi/4 & \cos 3\pi/4 \end{bmatrix} = \begin{bmatrix} -0.7 & 0.7 \\ -0.7 & -0.7 \end{bmatrix}$$

$$P' = P \cdot R$$

$$P' = \begin{bmatrix} 10 & 10 \\ 15 & 10 \\ 20 & 10 \end{bmatrix} \begin{bmatrix} -0.7 & -0.7 \\ -0.7 & -0.7 \end{bmatrix} = \begin{bmatrix} -14 & 0 \\ -17.5 & 3.5 \\ -21 & 7 \end{bmatrix}$$

3.2 3-D TRANSFORMATION

Introduction

Some graphics applications are two-dimensional such as graphs, charts, certain maps etc. But we live in three-dimensional world and deal with many design applications which describe three-dimensional objects. In three-dimensional space we shall extend the transformations to allow translation and rotation, but the viewing surface is only two-dimensional, we must consider ways of projecting the object onto this flat surface to form the image.

The 3D co-ordinate system is divided into two types :

    (1) Right-handed system.

    (2) Left-handed system.

If the thumb of the right hand points in the positive z direction as one curls the fingers of the right hand from x into y, then the coordinates are called a right-handed system. If the thumb points in the negative z direction then it is left handed-system.

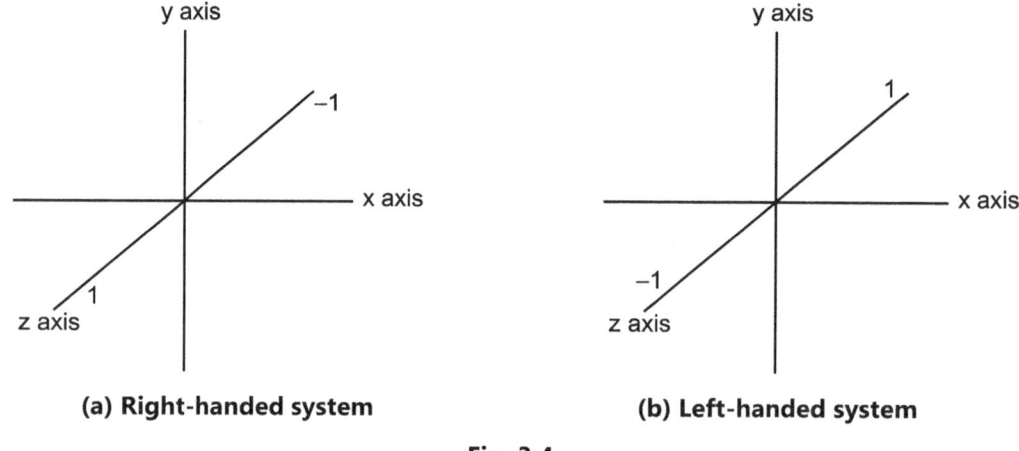

(a) Right-handed system   (b) Left-handed system

Fig. 3.4

3.2.1 Translation

Consider point p with the coordinates (x, y, z). To shift this point to new position p'(x', y', z').

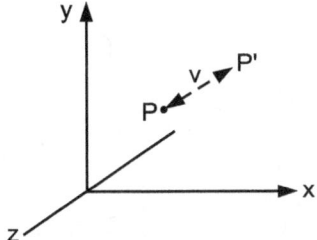

Fig. 3.5 : Translating point

As shown in above Fig. 3.5 the shifting and direction of the translation is now defined by vector $v = a_i + b_j + c_k$. Thus,

$$x' = x + a$$

$$y' = y + b$$

$$z' = z + c$$

where, a, b, c are the translation factors in x, y and z directions respectively.

The matrix representation will be,

$$T = \begin{bmatrix} 1 & 0 & 0 & 0 \\ 0 & 1 & 0 & 0 \\ 0 & 0 & 1 & 0 \\ a & b & c & 1 \end{bmatrix}$$

or

$$T = \begin{bmatrix} 1 & 0 & 0 & 0 \\ 0 & 1 & 0 & 0 \\ 0 & 0 & 1 & 0 \\ t_x & t_y & t_z & 1 \end{bmatrix}$$

$$P' = P \cdot T$$

$$[x' \, y' \, z' \, 1] = [x \, y \, z \, 1] \begin{bmatrix} 1 & 0 & 0 & 0 \\ 0 & 1 & 0 & 0 \\ 0 & 0 & 1 & 0 \\ t_x & t_y & t_z & 1 \end{bmatrix}$$

$$= [x + t_x \quad y + t_y \quad z + t_z \quad 1]$$

Like two dimensional transformation an object is translated in three-dimensions by transforming each vertex of the object.

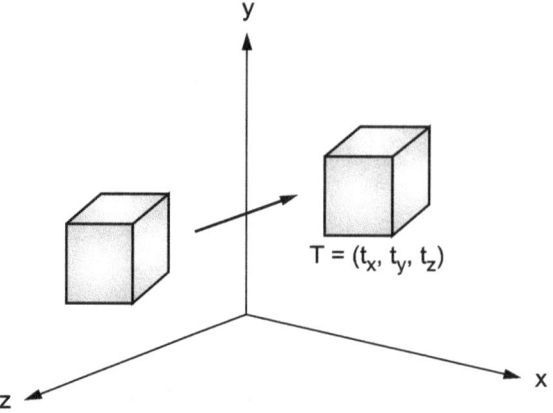

Fig. 3.6 : Translating object

3.2.2 Scaling

Scaling transformation alters the size of the object. This transformation either magnifies or reduces the size depending on the value of the scaling factor. If the scaling factor is less than 1, it reduces and if it is greater than 1 it magnifies.

Consider point P(x, y, z) which is to be scaled by S_x, S_y, S_z. Then the new coordinates will be,

$$x' = x \cdot S_x$$

$$y' = y \cdot S_y$$

$$z' = z \cdot S_z$$

The scaling matrix will be,

$$S = \begin{bmatrix} S_x & 0 & 0 & 0 \\ 0 & S_y & 0 & 0 \\ 0 & 0 & S_z & 0 \\ 0 & 0 & 0 & 1 \end{bmatrix}$$

$$[x'\ y'\ z'\ 1] = [x\ y\ z\ 1] \begin{bmatrix} S_x & 0 & 0 & 0 \\ 0 & S_y & 0 & 0 \\ 0 & 0 & S_z & 0 \\ 0 & 0 & 0 & 1 \end{bmatrix}$$

The scaling transformation is done with respect to origin i.e. the origin is kept fixed.

3.2.3 Rotation

In 2D transformation the rotation was prescribed by the angle of rotation and the point of rotation. But in case of 3D rotation, the angle of rotation as well as the axis of rotation need to be mentioned. There are three axis, so the rotation can take place about any of these axis, i.e. about x-axis, y-axis and z-axis respectively.

Three-dimensional transformation matrix for each coordinate axes rotations with homogeneous coordinates are –

Rotation About z-axis : Let P be the point object in xy plane P(x, y, 0). Rotate it by an angle θ° in counterclockwise direction. The resultant point will be P'(x', y', 0).

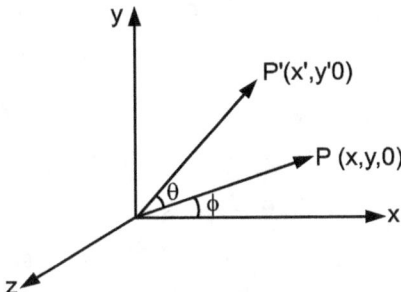

Fig. 3.7

As shown in Fig. 3.7,

$$x = r \cos \phi \qquad \qquad \text{... (3.6)}$$
$$y = r \sin \phi \qquad \qquad \text{... (3.7)}$$
$$x' = r \cos (\theta + \phi)$$
$$y' = r \sin (\theta + \phi)$$
$$x' = r \cos \theta \cos \phi - r \sin \theta \sin \phi$$
$$y' = r \sin \theta \cos \phi + r \cos \theta \sin \phi$$

Put the values of r cos φ and r sin φ from equations (3.6) and (3.7).

$$x' = x \cos \theta - y \sin \theta$$
$$y' = x \sin \theta + y \cos \theta$$

The resulting transformation will be,

$$R_z \Rightarrow x' = x \cos \theta - y \sin \theta$$
$$y' = x \sin \theta + y \cos \theta$$
$$z' = 0$$

$$[x'\ y'\ z'\ 1] = [x\ y\ z\ 1] \begin{bmatrix} \cos \theta & \sin \theta & 0 & 0 \\ -\sin \theta & \cos \theta & 0 & 0 \\ 0 & 0 & 1 & 0 \\ 0 & 0 & 0 & 1 \end{bmatrix}$$

Rotation about x-axis : This can be obtained similarly by circularly re-shuffling y and z.

$$\therefore \qquad R_x \Rightarrow x' = x$$
$$y' = y \cos \theta - z \sin \theta$$

$$z = y \sin \theta + z \cos \theta$$

$$[x' \ y' \ z' \ 1] = [x \ y \ z \ 1] \begin{bmatrix} 1 & 0 & 0 & 0 \\ 0 & \cos \theta & \sin \theta & 0 \\ 0 & -\sin \theta & \cos \theta & 0 \\ 0 & 0 & 0 & 1 \end{bmatrix}$$

Rotation About y-axis :

$$R_y \Rightarrow x' = x \cos \theta + z \sin \theta$$

$$y' = y$$

$$z = -x \sin \theta + z \cos \theta$$

$$[x' \ y' \ z' \ 1] = [x \ y \ z \ 1] \begin{bmatrix} \cos \theta & 0 & -\sin \theta & 0 \\ 0 & 1 & 0 & 0 \\ +\sin \theta & 0 & \cos \theta & 0 \\ 0 & 0 & 0 & 1 \end{bmatrix}$$

All the above rotation matrix are for rotation in counterclockwise direction. To obtain the rotation matrix in clockwise direction, change the sign of 't sin θ'.

$$\therefore \quad R_z = \begin{bmatrix} \cos \theta & -\sin \theta & 0 & 0 \\ \sin \theta & \cos \theta & 0 & 0 \\ 0 & 0 & 1 & 0 \\ 0 & 0 & 0 & 1 \end{bmatrix}$$

$$R_y = \begin{bmatrix} \cos \theta & 0 & +\sin \theta & 0 \\ 0 & 1 & 0 & 0 \\ -\sin \theta & 0 & \cos \theta & 0 \\ 0 & 0 & 0 & 1 \end{bmatrix}$$

$$R_x = \begin{bmatrix} 1 & 0 & 0 & 0 \\ 0 & \cos \theta & -\sin \theta & 0 \\ 0 & \sin \theta & \cos \theta & 0 \\ 0 & 0 & 0 & 1 \end{bmatrix}$$

3.3 ROTATION ABOUT AN ARBITRARY AXIS

Any line in a space can be used as axis of rotation. For deriving the transformation matrix for rotation by an angle θ° about any arbitrary line in a space, the following transformation must be carried out in a sequence.

- **Translation :** Perform translation, so that the line will coincide with origin.

- **Rotation :** Perform rotation to align with one of the co-ordinate axis. For example if the line is to be aligned with z-axis then first rotate it about x-axis to bring it in x-z plane and then rotate it about y-axis to align it with z-axis. Then perform rotation about z-axis.

- **Retranslation :** Then apply inverse translation to bring the line and coordinates to their original orientation.

Consider point P(x, y, z) which is to be rotated about an arbitrary line. The parametric equation for the line are –

$$x = x_1 + A_t$$

$$y = y_1 + B_t$$

$$z = z_1 + C_t$$

where, $$A = (x_2 - x_1)$$

$$B = (y_2 - y_1)$$

$$C = (z_2 - z_1)$$

$x_1, y_1, z_1 \rightarrow$ Points on the line

$A, B, C \rightarrow$ Direction vectors

The first step is to translate the line to bring it in the origin. The translation matrix will be,

$$T = \begin{bmatrix} 1 & 0 & 0 & 0 \\ 0 & 1 & 0 & 0 \\ 0 & 0 & 1 & 0 \\ -x_1 & -y_1 & -z_1 & 1 \end{bmatrix}$$

The inverse transformation will be,

$$T^{-1} = \begin{bmatrix} 1 & 0 & 0 & 0 \\ 0 & 1 & 0 & 0 \\ 0 & 0 & 1 & 0 \\ x_1 & y_1 & z_1 & 1 \end{bmatrix}$$

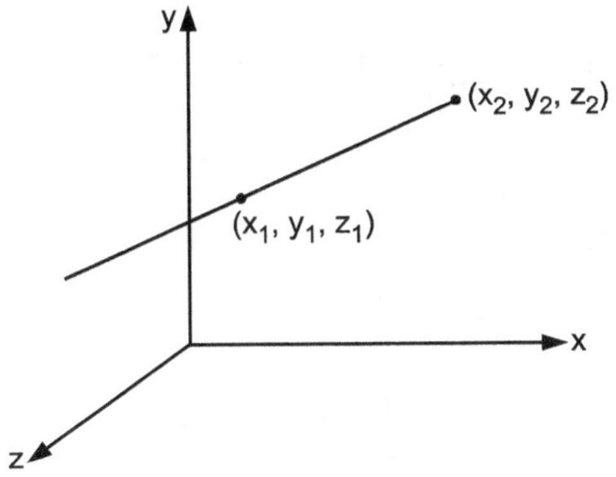

Fig. 3.8 : Before translation the position of line

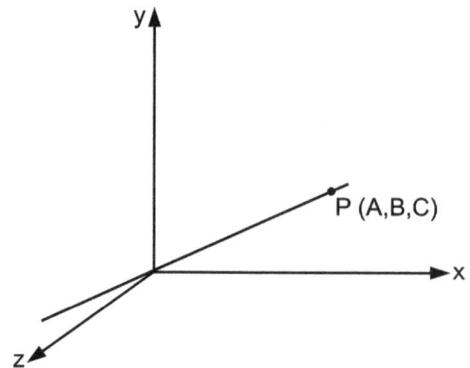

Fig. 3.9 : After translation the position of line

The second step is the rotation of line about x-axis to bring the line in x-z plane, for this the angle of rotation by which the line is to be rotated must be computed. For this, project a point P(A, B, C) in y-z plane.

Let P' be the point p in y-z plane.

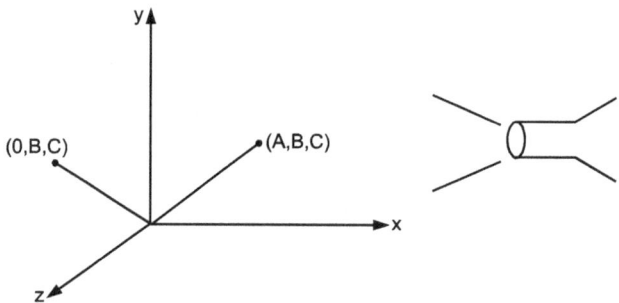

Fig. 3.10 : Projection of a line segment on yz plane

The coordinates of P' are (0, B, C). The length of segment OP' = $\sqrt{B^2 + C^2}$. The angle of rotation about x-axis is,

$$\cos I = \frac{C}{\sqrt{B^2 + C^2}} \qquad \sin I = \frac{B}{\sqrt{B^2 + C^2}}$$

Put, $\qquad \sqrt{B^2 + C^2} = V$

$\therefore \qquad \cos I = C/V \qquad\qquad \sin I = B/V$

Now rotation matrix about x-axis, so that arbitrary axis will be in xz plane, the line segment's shadow will lie in z-axis.

$$R_x = \begin{bmatrix} 1 & 0 & 0 & 0 \\ 0 & C/V & B/V & 0 \\ 0 & -B/V & C/V & 0 \\ 0 & 0 & 0 & 1 \end{bmatrix}$$

The inverse rotation will be,

$$R_X^{-1} = \begin{bmatrix} 1 & 0 & 0 & 0 \\ 0 & C/V & -B/V & 0 \\ 0 & B/V & C/V & 0 \\ 0 & 0 & 0 & 1 \end{bmatrix}$$

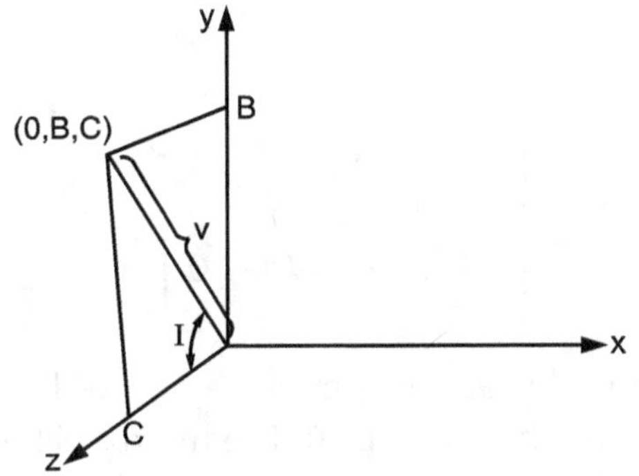

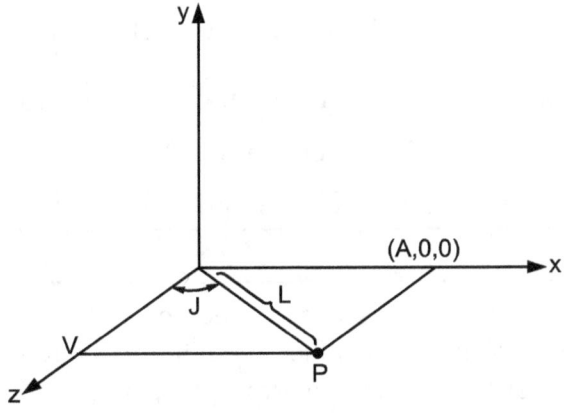

Fig. 3.11 : Parameters of line segment projection

The rotation axis lying with x-z plane is shown in Fig. 3.12.

Fig. 3.12

The parameters will remain unchanged and equal to A as it is the rotation about x-axis. The y co-ordinate becomes zero and z co-ordinate will be,

$$z = \sqrt{R^2 + C^2} = V$$

The co-ordinates of point P are P(A, 0, 0), the length OP will be $\sqrt{A^2 + B^2 + C^2}$.

　　Put,　　$\sqrt{A^2 + B^2 + C^2} = L$

∴　　　　　　(OP) = L

Now perform the rotation of line about y-axis by an angle J to make it align with z-axis.

As shown in above Fig. 3.13 is an angle between segment OP and z-axis.

$$\cos J = V/L \qquad \sin J = A/L$$

The rotation matrix about y-axis will be,

$$R_y = \begin{bmatrix} V/L & 0 & A/L & 0 \\ 0 & 1 & 0 & 0 \\ -A/L & 0 & V/L & 0 \\ 0 & 0 & 0 & 1 \end{bmatrix}$$

The inverse transformation will be,

$$R_y^{-1} = \begin{bmatrix} V/L & 0 & A/L & 0 \\ 0 & 1 & 0 & 0 \\ -A/L & 0 & V/L & 0 \\ 0 & 0 & 0 & 1 \end{bmatrix}$$

Now after performing rotation about y-axis the line will get aligned with z-axis. Then perform the rotation about z-axis by an angle θ. The matrix will be,

$$R_z = \begin{bmatrix} \cos \theta & \sin \theta & 0 & 0 \\ -\sin \theta & \cos \theta & 0 & 0 \\ 0 & 0 & 1 & 0 \\ 0 & 0 & 0 & 1 \end{bmatrix}$$

Then apply inverse transformation in sequence R_y^{-1}, R_x^{-1}, T^{-1} to rotate the axis to their original position. The resultant transformation matrix will be,

$$R_S = [T] [R_x] [R_y] [R_z] [R_y]^{-1} [R_x]^{-1} [T^{-1}]$$

3.4 REFLECTION

The reflection in 3D transformation is similar to the concept of 2D transformation. In this case the reference plane i.e. plane about which the reflection is to be taken must be known. Thus, there are three standard reflections about xy plane, xz plane and yz plane. Each plane reference implies that those co-ordinates will remain same which are constituting that plane.

3.4.1 Reflection with Respect to Any Plane

It is necessary to reflect an object through a plane other than x = 0 (yz-plane), y = 0 (xz-plane) or z = 0 (xy-plane). Procedure to achieve such a reflection i.e. reflection about any plane can be given as follows :

- Translate a known point P_0, that lies in the reflection plane to the origin of the co-ordinate system.

- Rotate the normal vector to the reflection plane at the origin until it is coincident with the z axis, this makes the reflection plane z = 0 coordinate plane i.e. xy-plane.

- Reflect the object through z = 0 (xy-plane) co-ordinate plane.

- Perform the inverse transformation to those given above to achieve the result.

Let $P_0(x_0, y_0, z_0)$ be the given known point. Translate this point to the origin by using corresponding translation matrix.

$$T = \begin{bmatrix} 1 & 0 & 0 & 0 \\ 0 & 1 & 0 & 0 \\ 0 & 0 & 1 & 0 \\ -x_0 & -y_0 & -z_0 & 1 \end{bmatrix}$$

The normal vector will be,

$$N = h_1 I + h_2 J + h_3 K$$

$$|N| = \sqrt{n_1^2 + n_2^2 + n_3^2}$$

$$\lambda = \sqrt{n_2^2 + n_3^2}$$

To match this vector with z-axis, so that the plane of reflection will be parallel to xy plane, the same procedure will be used as used in rotation.

$$R_{xy} = \begin{bmatrix} \dfrac{\lambda}{|N|} & 0 & \dfrac{n_1}{|N|} & 0 \\ \dfrac{-n_1 n_2}{\lambda |N|} & \dfrac{n_3}{\lambda} & \dfrac{n_2}{|N|} & 0 \\ \dfrac{-n_1 n_3}{\lambda |N|} & \dfrac{-n_2}{\lambda} & \dfrac{n_3}{|N|} & 0 \\ 0 & 0 & 0 & 1 \end{bmatrix}$$

For reflection about xy plane,

$$R_e = \begin{bmatrix} 1 & 0 & 0 & 0 \\ 0 & 1 & 0 & 0 \\ 0 & 0 & -1 & 0 \\ 0 & 0 & 0 & 1 \end{bmatrix}$$

The inverse translation will be,

$$T^{-1} = \begin{bmatrix} 1 & 0 & 0 & 0 \\ 0 & 1 & 0 & 0 \\ 0 & 0 & 1 & 0 \\ x_0 & y_0 & z_0 & 1 \end{bmatrix}$$

The inverse rotation will be,

$$R_{xy}^{-1} = \begin{bmatrix} \dfrac{\lambda}{|N|} & \dfrac{-n_2\,n_2}{\lambda\,|N|} & \dfrac{-n_1\,n_3}{\lambda\,|N|} & 0 \\[2mm] 0 & \dfrac{n_3}{\lambda} & \dfrac{-n_3}{\lambda} & 0 \\[2mm] \dfrac{n_1}{|N|} & \dfrac{n_2}{|N|} & \dfrac{n_3}{|N|} & 0 \\[2mm] 0 & 0 & 0 & 1 \end{bmatrix}$$

∴ Resultant transformation matrix will be,

$$R_S = [T]\,[R_{xy}]\,[R_e]\,[R_{xy}]^{-1}\,[T]^{-1}$$

3 D Clipping:

Clipping, in the context of computer graphics, is a method to selectively enable or disable rendering operations within a defined region of interest. Mathematically, clipping can be described using the terminology of constructive geometry. More informally, pixels that will not be drawn are said to be "clipped."

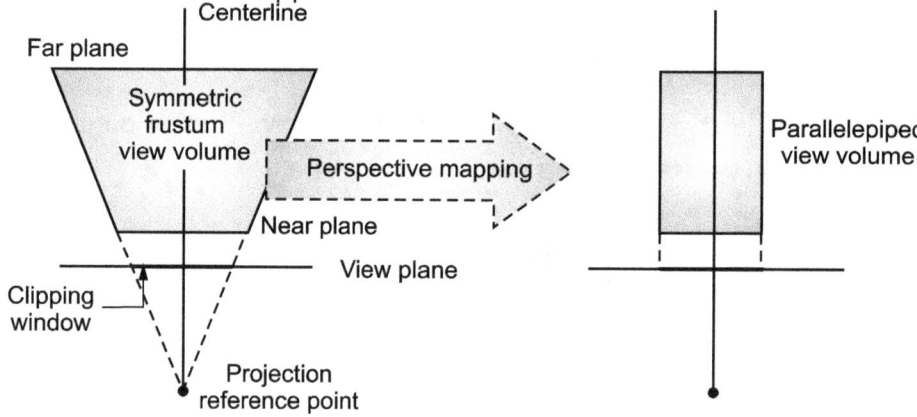

Fig. 3.13

Clipping Strategies

Two types of clipping strategies are used:

Direct Clipping: The clipping is done directly against direct view volume.

Canonical Clipping: Normalization transformations are applied which transform the original view volume into normalized (canonical) view volume. Clipping is then applied.

3-D Clipping

The purpose of 3D clipping is to identify and saveall surface segments within the view volume for display on the output device. All parts of objects that are outside the view volume are discarded. Thus the computing time is saved. 3D clipping is based on 2D clipping. To understand the basic concept we consider the following Polygon Clipping.

Polygon Clipping

Assuming the clip region is a rectangular area,

- The rectangular clip region can be represented by xmin, xmax, ymin and ymax.

- Find the bounding box for the polygon: i.e. the smallest rectangle enclosing the entire polygon.
- Compare the bounding box with the clip region (by comparing their xmin, xmax, ymin and ymax).
- If the bounding box for the polygon is completely outside the clip region , the polygon is outside the clip region and no clipping is needed.
- If the bounding box for the polygon is completely inside the clip region , the polygon is inside the clip region and no clipping is needed.
- Otherwise, the bounding box for the polygon overlaps with the clip region and the polygon is likely to be partly inside and partly outside of the clip region. In that case, we clip the polygon against each of the 4 border lines of the clip region in sequence as follows:

Using the first vertex as the current vertex. If the point is in the inside of the border line, mark it as 'inside'. If it is outside, markit as 'outside'. Check next vertex. Again mark it 'inside' or 'outside' accordingly. Compare the current and the next vertices. If one is marked 'inside' and the other 'outside', the edge joining the 2 vertices crosses the border line. In this case, we need to calculate where the edge intersects the border (ie. intersection between 2 lines). The intersection point becomes a new vertex. We mark it 'synthetic'. Now we set the next vertex as the current vertex and the followingvertex as the next vertex, and we repeat the same operations until all the edges of the polygon have been considered. After the whole polygon has been clipped by a border, we throw away all the vertices marked 'outside' while keeping those marked as 'inside' or 'synthetic' to create a new polygon.

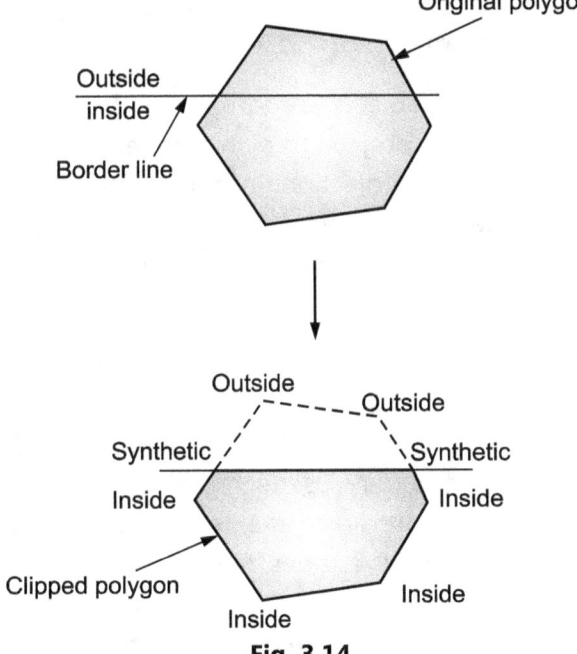

Fig. 3.14

We repeat the clipping process with the new polygon against the next border line of the clip region.

• This clipping operation results in a polygon which is totally inside the clip region.

3.5 PROJECTION

The process of representing a three dimensional object or scene into two dimensional medium is referred as projection.

Hierarchy of projection is :

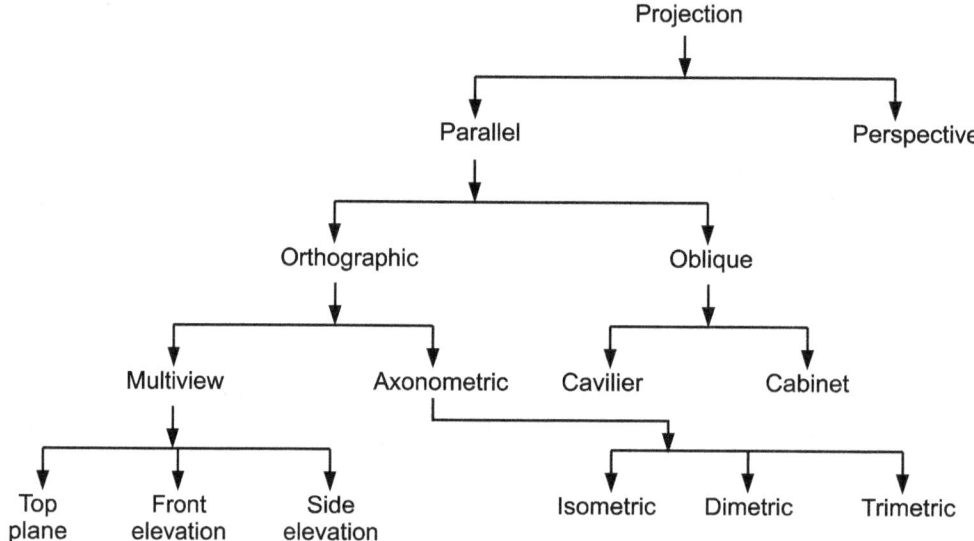

The plane geometric projections of objects are formed by the intersection of lines referred as projectors with a plane called the projection plane. Projectors are nothing but lines form an arbitrary point called as center of projection. In three dimensional space, if the center of projection is located at a finite point, then the result is a perspective projection. If the projectors are parallel and the center of projection is located at infinity then the result is a parallel projection.

3.5.1 Parallel Projection

This technique is used in drawing or drafting for producing scale drawings of three dimensional objects. This method is very useful for obtaining the accurate views of the various sides of an object. It also preserves the relative dimensions of objects. But the drawback of parallel projection is that, it does not give a realistic representation of the appearance of three dimensional object. In parallel projection, z coordinate is discarded and parallel lines from each vertex on the object are extended until they intersect the view plane.

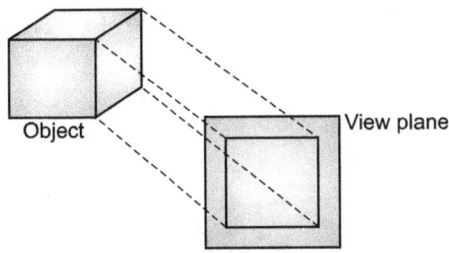

Fig. 3.15

Parallel projection is further classified into two types :

- Orthographic projection
- Oblique projection

- **Orthographic Projection :** In orthographic projection, the direction of projection is perpendicular to the projection plane. It is used in the projection of front, side and top views of the object. The orthographic top views are referred as "planes" and orthographic front, side and rear views are referred as "elevations". These projections always show the correct or true size and shape of a single face or plane of an object. Engineering drawings employ these projections because the angles and lengths are accurately depicted.

The orthographic projection is divided into following types :

(1) Mult-iview,   (2) Axonometric.

In multi-view projection, the projection plane is parallel to the principal plane. It is categorized into three types viz. Three views, Auxiliary views and Sectional views.

In Axonometric projection, the projection plane is not parallel to the principle plane. This projection can display more than one face of an object.

The axonometric projection is further classified as :

Isometric, Diametric and Trimetric projection.

Isometric : Projections are aligned in such a way that all the edges will appear shortened by same distance. Assume object as cube then form all side looks like square, but using isometric ortho projection. We can see more than one face. All principal axes are shortened equally, so that relative proportions are maintained.

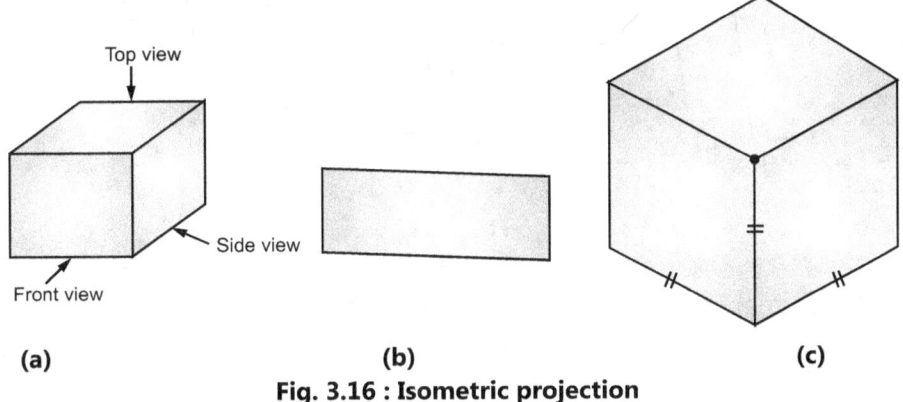

(a)   (b)   (c)

Fig. 3.16 : Isometric projection

Diametric : Edges parallel to only two axes are equally shortened.

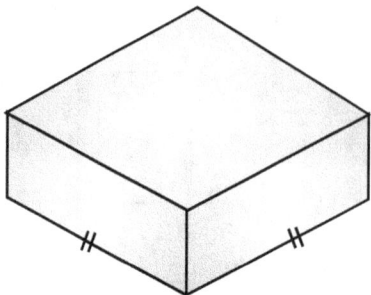

Fig. 3.17 : Diametric projection

Trimetric : None of the three edges are equally shortened.

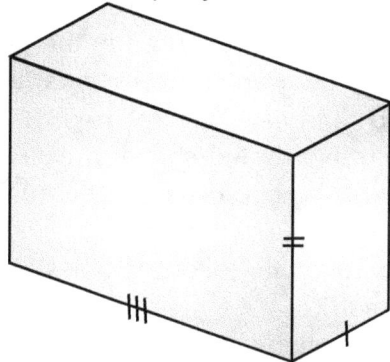

Fig. 3.18 : Trimetric projection

The most commonly used axonometric orthographic projection is the isometric projection. It can be generated by aligning the view plane so that it intersects each coordinate axis in which the object is defined at the same distance from the origin.

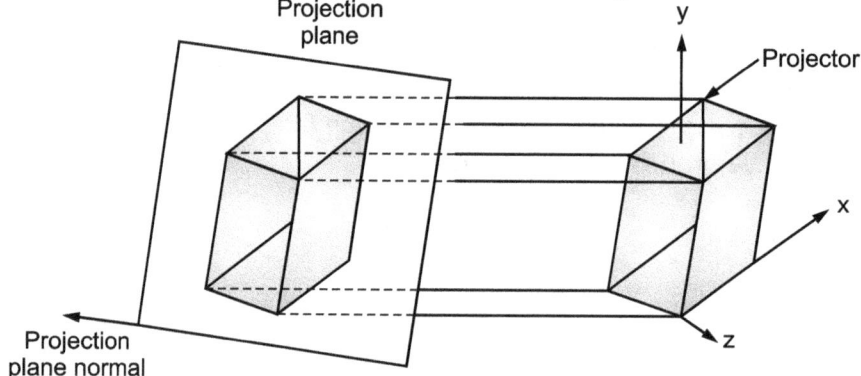

Fig. 3.19

As shown in Fig. 3.19 the isometric projection is obtained by aligning the projection vector with the cube diagonal. It uses an useful property that all the principle axes are equally foreshortened, allowing measurements along the axes to be made to the same scale hence the name iso for equal, metric for measure.

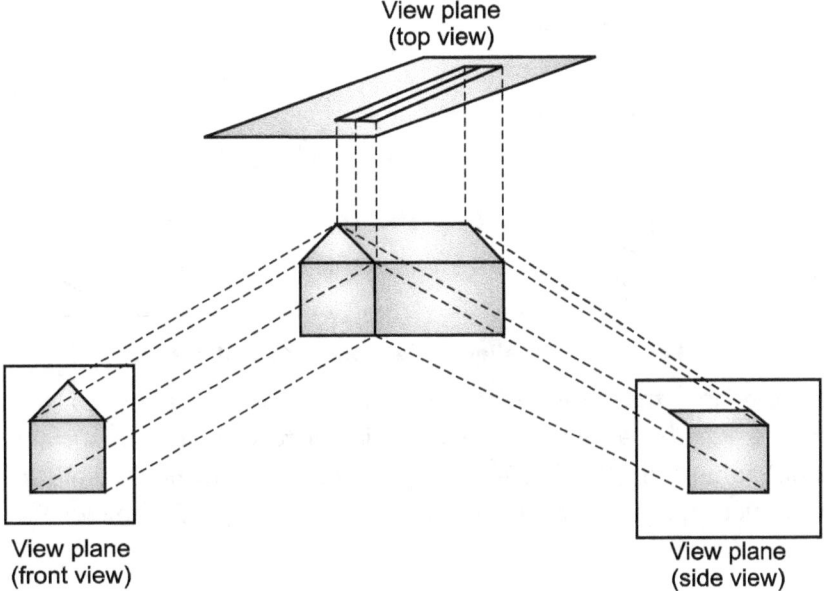

Fig. 3.20 : Orthographic parallel projection

Oblique Projection : An oblique projection is obtained by projecting points along parallel lines that are not perpendicular to the projection plane.

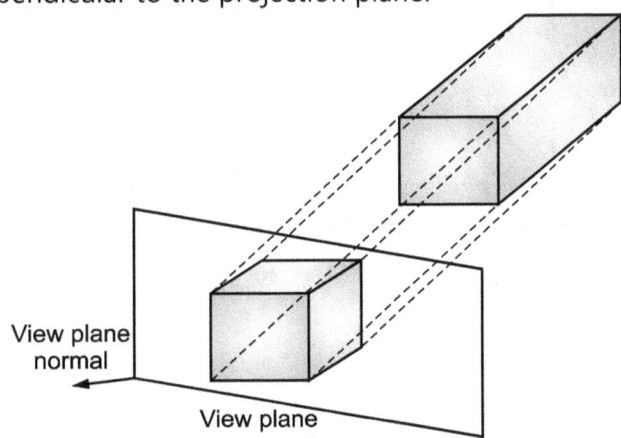

Fig. 3.21

As shown in Fig. 3.21, the view plane normal and direction of projection are not the same.

The oblique projection is further classified into :

- Cavalier projection,
- Cabinet projection.

For the cavalier projection the direction of projection makes a 45° angle with the view plane. As a result, the projection of a line perpendicular to the view plane has the same length as the line itself i.e. there is no foreshortening. Fig. 3.22 shows cavalier projection of a unit cube with α = 45° and α = 30°.

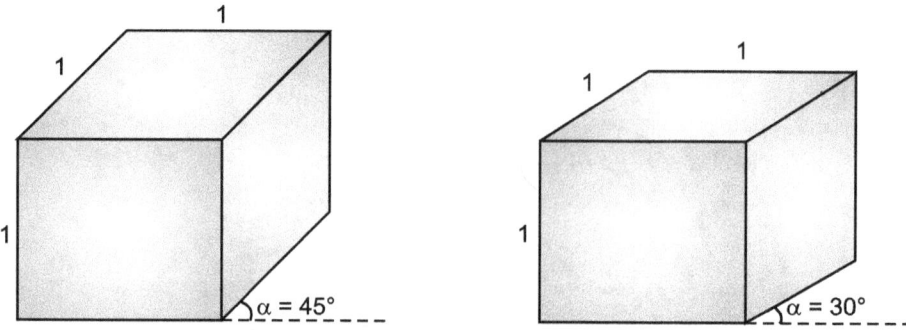

Fig. 3.22 : Cavalier projections of a unit cube

In the cabinet projection, the direction of projection makes an angle of arc tan (2) = 63.4 with the view plane. For this angle, lines perpendicular to the viewing surface are projected at one half their actual length. Cabinet projections appear more realistic than cavalier because of the reduction in the length of perpendiculars. Fig. 3.23 below shows the cabinet projections for a unit cube.

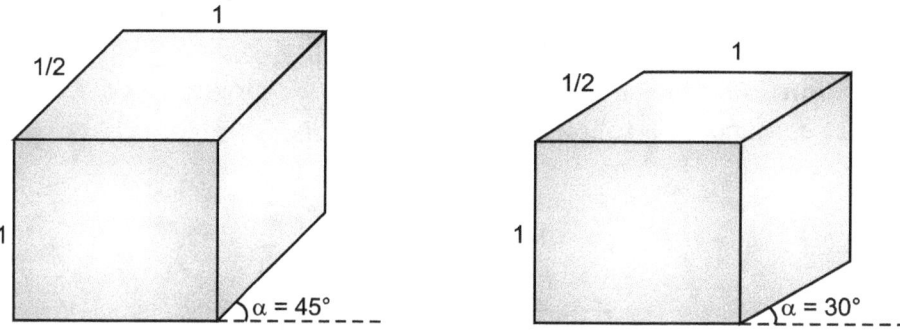

Fig. 3.23 : Cabinet projections of a unit cube

3.5.2 General Equation of Parallel Projection

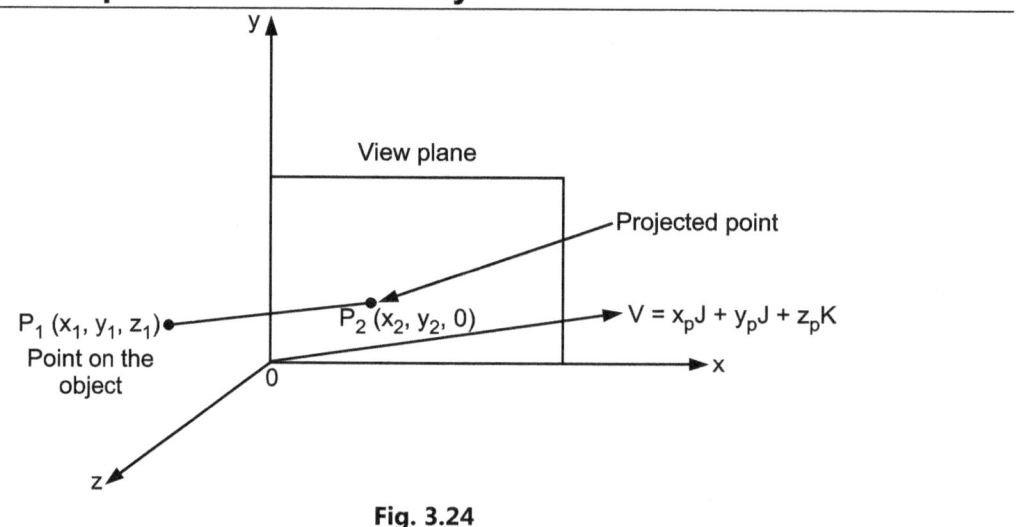

Fig. 3.24

In a general parallel projection, any direction may be selected for the lines of projection. Suppose that the direction of projection is given by the vector $[x_p, y_p, z_p]$ and that the object is to be projected onto the xy plane. If the point on the object is given as (x_1, y_1, z_1) then the projected point (x_2, y_2) can be determined as given below :

The equations in the parametric form for a line passing through the projected point (x_2, y_2, z_2) and in the direction of projection are given as –

$$x_2 = x_1 + x_p \, u$$

$$y_2 = y_1 + y_p \, u$$

$$z_2 = z_1 + z_p \, u$$

For projected point z_2 is 0, therefore the third equation can be written as,

$$0 = z_1 + z_p \, u$$

$$u = \frac{-z_1}{z_p}$$

Substituting the value of u in first two equations,

$$x_2 = x_1 + x_p \left(\frac{-z_1}{z_p} \right)$$

$$y_2 = y_1 + y_p \left(\frac{-z_1}{z_p} \right)$$

The above equation can be represented in matrix form as given below :

$$[x_2, \ y_2] = [x_1 \ y_1 \ z_1] \begin{bmatrix} 1 & 0 \\ 0 & 1 \\ \frac{-x_p}{z_p} & \frac{-y_p}{z_p} \end{bmatrix}$$

or in homogeneous co-ordinates.

$$[x_2, \ y_2, \ z_2 \ 1] = [x_1 \ y_1 \ z_1 \ 1] \begin{bmatrix} 1 & 0 & 0 & 0 \\ 0 & 1 & 0 & 0 \\ \frac{-x_p}{z_p} & \frac{-y_p}{z_p} & 0 & 0 \\ 0 & 0 & 0 & 1 \end{bmatrix}$$

i.e. $$P_2 = P_1 \cdot Par_v$$

This is the general equation of parallel projection on xy plane in matrix form.

3.6 PERSPECTIVE PROJECTION

In perspective projection, if the object is far away from the viewer then it appears smaller and it appears larger if the object is nearer to the viewer. This helps the viewer in determining depth cue. The depth cue is an indication of which portion of the image correspond to part of the object which are close or far away. In this projection the lines of projection converge at a single point which is referred as center of projection. The intersection of lines of projection with the plane of screen determines the projected image, as shown in Fig. 3.25.

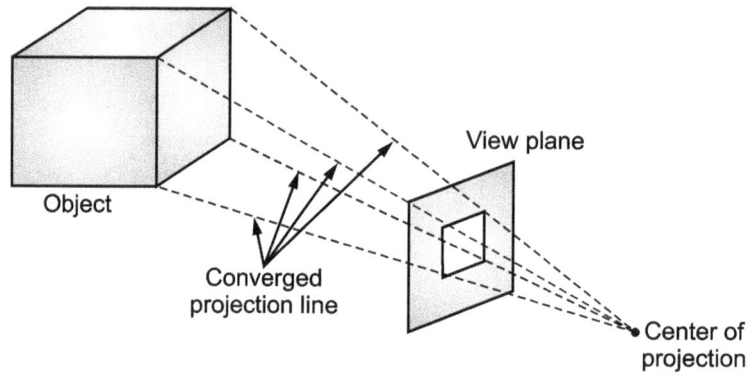

Fig. 3.25

To generate perspective projection of a three dimensional object, first of all project points along projection lines that will meet at the center of projection is selected. The center of projection is on the negative z-axis at a distance behind the projection plane.

However any position can be selected for the center of projection but for simplification of calculation it is better to choose a position along z-axis.

The transformation equation for a perspective projection can be obtained from the parametric equations which describes the projection line from point P to the center of projection.

If the center of projection is at (x_c, y_c, z_c) and point on the object is (x_1, y_1, z_1) then the projection ray will be,

$$x_1 = x_c + (x_1 - x_c) u$$
$$y = y_c + (y_1 - y_c) u$$
$$z = z_c + (z_1 - z_c) u$$

The projected point (x_2, y_2) will be the point where this line intersects the xy plane. For this intersection point z = 0,

$$z = z_c + (z_1 - z_c) u$$
$$0 = z_c + (z_1 - z_c) u$$

$$\therefore \qquad u = \frac{-z_c}{z_1 - z_c}$$

$$\therefore \qquad x_2 = x_c + (x_1 - x_c)\left(\frac{-z_c}{z_1 - z_c}\right)$$

$$x_2 = x_c - z_c \frac{x_1 - x_c}{z_1 - z_c}$$

$$y_2 = y_c - z_c \frac{y_1 - y_c}{z_1 - z_c}$$

$$x_2 = \frac{x_c z_1 - x_1 z_c}{z_1 - z_c}$$

$$y_2 = \frac{y_c z_1 - y_1 z_c}{z_1 - z_c}$$

In the matrix form :

$$P = \begin{bmatrix} -z_c & 0 & 0 & 0 \\ 0 & -z_c & 0 & 0 \\ x_c & y_c & 0 & 1 \\ 0 & 0 & 0 & -z_c \end{bmatrix}$$

Consider point (x_1, y_1, z_1), in homogeneous coordinates it is $[x_1\omega_1 \ \ y_1\omega_1 \ \ z_1\omega_1 \ \ \omega_1]$

$$[x_2\omega_2 \ \ y_2\omega_2 \ \ z_2\omega_2 \ \ \omega_2] = [x_1\omega_1 \ \ y_1\omega_1 \ \ z_1\omega_1 \ \ \omega_1] \begin{bmatrix} -z_c & 0 & 0 & 0 \\ 0 & -z_c & 0 & 0 \\ x_c & y_c & 0 & 1 \\ 0 & 0 & 0 & -z_c \end{bmatrix}$$

$$= [-x_1\omega_1 z_c + z_1\omega_1 x_c \ \ -y_1\omega_1 z_c + z_1\omega_1 y_c \ \ 0 \ \ z_1\omega_1 - z_c\omega_1]$$

$$\therefore \qquad \omega_2 = z_1\omega_1 - z_c\omega_1$$

and $\qquad z_2\omega_2 = 0$

$$\therefore \qquad z_2 = 0$$

$$x_2\omega_2 = -x_1\omega_1 z_c + z_1\omega_1 x_c$$

$$\Rightarrow \qquad x_2 = \frac{x_c z_1 - x_1 z_c}{z_1 - z_c}$$

And $\qquad y_2\omega_2 = -y_1\omega_1 z_c + z_1\omega_1 y_c$

$$\Rightarrow \qquad y_2 = \frac{y_c z_1 - y_1 z_c}{z_1 - z_c}$$

The resulting point (x_2, y_2) is then the correctly projected point.

$\therefore$ The projection transformation is,

$$P_1 = \begin{bmatrix} 1 & 0 & 0 & 0 \\ 0 & 1 & 0 & 0 \\ \dfrac{-x_c}{z_c} & \dfrac{-y_p}{z_c} & 0 & \dfrac{-1}{z_c} \\ 0 & 0 & 0 & 1 \end{bmatrix}$$

The change is the factor of $-\dfrac{1}{z_c}$. Because the first three coordinates $(x\omega, y\omega, z\omega)$ is divided by ω to obtain the actual position, changing all four co-ordinates by some common factor has no effect. The perspective projection is defined as that the center of projection is located at the origin and the view plane is positioned at z = d. Thus, the transformation matrix is given by,

$$P_2 = \begin{bmatrix} 1 & 0 & 0 & 0 \\ 0 & 1 & 0 & 0 \\ 0 & 0 & 0 & 1/d \\ 0 & 0 & 0 & 1 \end{bmatrix}$$

3.6.1 Types of Perspective Projection

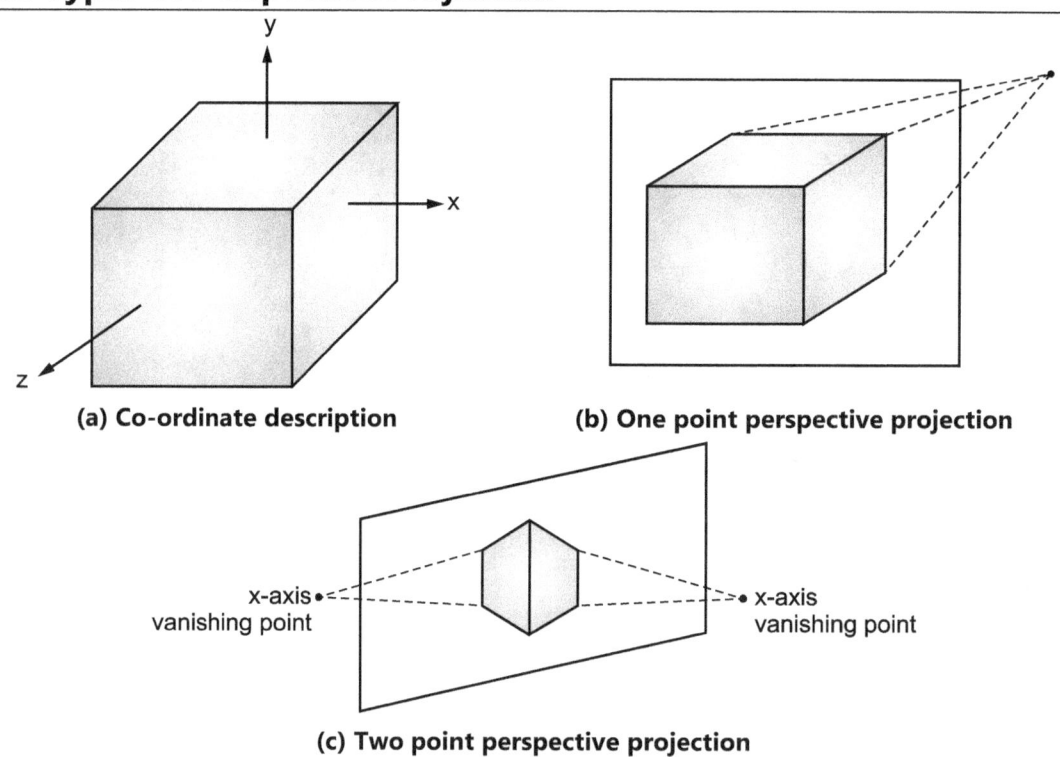

(a) Co-ordinate description   **(b) One point perspective projection**

(c) Two point perspective projection

Fig. 3.26

The perspective projections of any set of parallel lines which are not parallel to the projection plane converge to a vanishing point.

One-Point Perspective:

This projection is based on single vanishing point. Object is placed so that one of its surface is parallel to the plane of projection.

Two-point:

In this projection, two surfaces of the object have vanishing points. It is used to draw the same objects asone-point.

Three-point:

The three point perspective is achieved by positioning the object so that none of its axes are parallel to the plane of projection. It is usually used for building from top view.

EXERCISE

1. Obtain the 3-D transformation matrices for :
    (i) Translation, (ii) Scaling, (iii) Rotation about an arbitrary axis.
2. Give the classification of perspective parallel projection.
3. Explain parallel projection in detail with transformation matrix.
4. Derive the 3D primitive transformation for the following rotation :
    Rotate object about z-axis such that x-axis passes through a point $P(x_p, y_p, 0)$ in x-y plane.
5. Consider the square A(1, 0), B(0, 0), (0, 1), D(1, 1). Rotate the square ABCD by 45° anticlockwise about point A(1, 0).
6. Perform a 45° rotation of triangle A(0, 0), B(1, 1), C(5, 2).
    (i) About the origin, (ii) About P(−1, −1).
7. Explain with example, 3-D viewing transformation.
8. What is the concept of vanishing point in perspective projection.
9. Explain classification of parallel projection in detail. Discuss applications of parallel projections.
10. Consider the square A(2, 0), B(0, 0), C(0, 1), D(1, 1). Rotate the square anticlockwise direction followed by reflection about x-axis.
11. Explain the following 3-D transformation :
    (i) Rotation about all co-ordinate axis
    (ii) Rotation about any arbitrary axis.
12. Derive the general equation of parallel projection onto a given view plane in the direction of given projector.
13. Consider the square P(0, 0), Q(0, 10), R(10,10), S(10, 0). Rotate the square about fixed point. R(10, 10) by an angle 45° (anticlockwise) followed by scaling by 2 units in X direction and 2 units in Y direction.
14. What are parallel and perspective projections? Give classification of both.
15. Explain inverse transformation. Derive the matrix for inverse transformation and what is the concept of homogeneous co-ordinates.

16. Explain various steps to perform rotation about x-axis, y-axis and z-axis in 3D.

17. Explain : (i) 3-D co-ordinate system, (ii) 3-D primitives.

18. Explain the 3-D viewing process with various 3-D viewing parameters.

19. Show that the transformation matrix of reflection about a line y = x is equivalent to reflection relative to x-axis followed by anticlockwise rotation of 90°.

20. Drive transformation matrix for perspective projection.

21. Magnify the triangle with vertices A(0, 0), B(1, 1), C(5, 2) to twice its size as well as rotate it by 45°. Derive the translation matrices.

22. What is necessary for 3D clipping and windowing algorithm? Explain any one of 3D clipping algorithm.

23. A 3D cube of dimensions (length, breadth and height) 2 units each is placed in a 3D anti-clockwise axis system such that one of its vertex "A" is at origin (i.e. (0, 0, 0)) and vertex "F" in 3D space. Apply necessary transformation such that vertex F becomes the origin. Give complete mathematical formulation. Draw initial and final state of the cube.

24. Describe with respect to 2D transformation: (1) scaling (2) Rotation (3) Translation?

25. What is mean by Transformation?

26. Compate homogeneous co-ordinate system and normalized co-ordinate system?

27. What is the need of homogeneous co-ordinates system ?

27. What is composite transformation?

28. Explain the inverse transformation?

29. How can you perform homogeneous co-ordinates for scaling?

30. What are the different steps for rotation about an arbitrary axis?

31. What is mean by shear and reflection?

32. Explain reflection about line?

SEGMENT AND ANIMATION

4.1 SEGMENT INTRODUCTION

- In reality the image is made-up of several pictures or items or information. Thus, organizing the image or displaying as a single picture in display file cannot reflect this sub pictures structure.

- Thus it is very necessary to organize the display file in such a way that it will be divided into several segments, where each segment posses the portion of overall picture. Hence the segment can be defined as a logical unit, in the display file of the screen.

- In graphics, a segment is defined by the shortest possible path between two points. In a bitmap, the thinnest possible segment is the set of all pixels that lie closest to the shortest path between two points. In vector graphics, a segment is generated by specifying two end points and then executing operations that construct a straight line between and including those points. Two or more segments placed end-to-end form a polyline.

- Segmentation makes it easier to modify the picture by changing segment attributes.

4.2 SEGMENT TABLE

- Segment tables in computer graphics includes the length of corresponding segments in main memory.

- Each entry contains the length of the segment.

- Segments are the form of array like table which stored the commands in order to form the display in the screen. It has four parts.

    1. Index

    2. Size

    3. Position

    4. Visibility commands

The segment table is formed by using arrays. First array holds the segment name, second array holds the starting location for that segment, and the third array holds the segment size information while the fourth has the visibility and so on.

Segment no.	Segment start	Segment size	Scale x	Scale y	Colour	Visibility.........
0						
1						
2						
3						
.	.	.	.	.	.	.
.	.	.	.	.	.	.
.	.	.	.	.	.	.
.	.	.	.	.	.	.

Fig. 4.1 : Segment table

- For the organization of a display file, it is very necessary to give a unique name to each segment so that it can be specified. This will help to distinguish a segment from all others.
- The size of the segment measured in terms of number of display file instruction is needed. Each row in the segment table represents information of one segment including name, position, size, attributes and the image transformation parameters.
- The visibility mode checks the visibility of segment; For example to make the segment 2 visible, the visibility mode in the corresponding array is set 'ON'.
- The display file interpreter initially checks the start, size and visible attribute of the segments and it interprets only those segments which are to be made visible.
- There are other possible methods for implementing the segment table, many with the substantial advantages over array scheme. But this method allows simple accessing of segment, does not require any new data structure and its updating is straight forward.
- In display file there are some instructions which does not specify any particular segment, such instructions are placed in 'unnamed' segment.
- Generally index 0 of an array is assigned to unnamed segment.

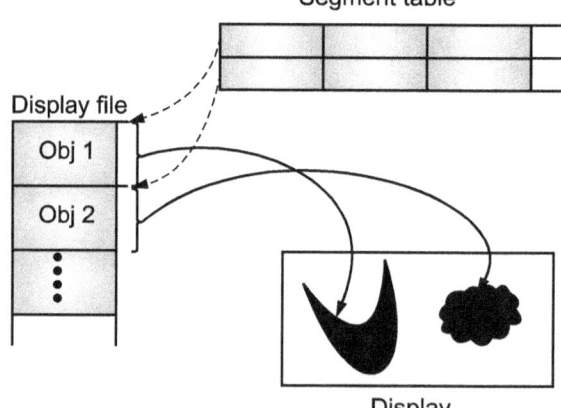

Fig. 4.2 : Segment table and display file

- An alternative method for storing segment information is the linked list.
- The linked list uses the additional field called the link or pointer which gives the location of the next segment in the segment table. As shown below Table 4.1.

Table 4.1 : Segment Table using Linked List

Segment Number	Segment Start	Segment Size	Scale x	Scale y	Color	Visibility	Link
1							4
2							3
3							2
4							5
5							Null

- Sorting of segments in segment table is quite easy task with link list structure.
- With linked list there is no such limit on the maximum number of segments like array, the growth of a linked list is dynamic.

4.3 SEGMENT OPERATIONS

There are five basic operations on display file segments

1. Create segment
2. Close segment
3. Delete segment
4. Rename segment
5. Visibility

4.3.1 Create Segment

Segment creation is the process of creating new segment, assigning name, assign size to newly created segment. Thus it is necessary to give name of the segment which is to be created.

The procedure is described in the form of an algorithm :

Step 1 : Check whether some other segment is open or not, if open then generate error message as , 'Error-segment still open' and goto step 9.

Step 2 : Read the name for new segment.

Step 3 : Check the validity of segment name, if the name is not valid then generates error message and go to step 9.

Step 4 : Check whether the new segment name has already exist; If yes then generate error message as 'duplicate segment name' and goto step 9.

Step 5 : Create segment table entry using segment name as index at segment table and by setting start for this entry to be the next free location in the display file.

Step 6 : Set segment size field for this new segment to zero, as any instruction corresponding to this new segment is not entered.

Step 7 : Initialize all other parameters attributes to some default values.

Step 8 : Indicate that the new created segment is open.

Step 9 : End.

Note : "Current open" is a global variable, which is used to keep track of currently open segment. So

4.3.2 Close Segment

- Until the segment is open we can enter the instructions in it.
- After entering all the commands the segment must be closed.
- For closing the segment simply change the value of indicator to default value i.e. zero.
- To close a currently open segment it is necessary to change the value of currently open segment. The simplest way is to change the value of current open segment to 0 i.e. unnamed segment.
- If there are two unnamed segments in display file then one has to be deleted.

Algorithm for Closing a Segment

Step 1 : Check whether any segment is open or not, if not open then return error message that no segment is open and go to step 6.

Step 2 : Change the name of currently open segment to zero.

Step 3 : Initialized the unnamed segment with no instructions.

Step 4 : Set segment size as zero.

Step 5 : Initialize open-segment as null.

Step 6 : Stop.

4.3.3 Delete Segment

When a segment is no longer needed, then the display file storage occupied by its instructions must be deleted.

To delete a segment it is very necessary to check whether the segment to be deleted is a valid segment or not, if valid then whether it is currently open or not. Because if the segment is open then it is still in use and deleting an open segment is error. Then check the size of the segment, because if the size of the segment to be deleted is zero, then there are no instructions in the display file corresponding to this segment and hence there is no need to delete the segment from display file.

For this the algorithm is as follows.

Step 1 : Read the name of segment which is to be deleted.

Step 2 : Check the validity of segment name if segment name is invalid then return error.

Step 3 : Check whether the segment is open, if yes then return error message as 'Segment is open' and goto step 8.

Step 4 : Check the size of segment if segment size = 0 then return error message as 'segment size zero, no need to delete' and goto step 8.

Step 5 : Shift the display file elements which is to be deleted by its size.

Step 6 : Recover the empty space by resetting the index of next free instruction.

Step 7 : Adjust the starting position of the shifted segment.

Step 8 : Stop.

4.3.4 Rename Segment

- The renaming of the segment is used to keep a replication of the original segment.
- In case of a display device having an independent display processor. This display processor continuously reads the display file contents and shows its contents. However in applications involving the animation there is a need to resend the sequence of images, each with slight modifications.

For instance, consider an image of a nature. In animation as we start a walkthrough, the display gets change at each instance. One way to do this is by deleting the existing segment and re-creating a new segment with corresponding modification. But this would be a slow process to avoid the delay in display the existing segment should not be deleted until the next required segment is ready. Thus two segments at a time are needed, in the display file. This can be done by building the new invisible image with temporary name. This method is called as double buffering.

The rename segment algorithm is as follows :

Step 1 : Check the validity of old name and new name. If not valid then return error message as 'name is not valid' and goto step 6.

Step 2 : Check whether any of the two segments are open, if open display error message as 'segment is open'.

Step 3 : Check new segment name does not exist in the display file already. If yes then return error message as 'name is already exist' and goto step 6.

Step 4 : Copy segment table entries from old segment name to new segment name.

Step 5 : Set segment size (old_name) = 0; i.e. deletion of old segment.

Step 6 : Stop.

4.3.5 Visibility

- Every segment is provided with a visibility attribute.
- By setting the visibility attribute of the segment we can decide whether that segment to be displayed or not.
- If the visibility attribute is set to one; then that segment is get displayed else not.
- The visibility of the segment is stored in an array, which is a part of the segment table. By scanning the array one can determine whether to display the segment or not.

4.4 ANIMATION

- Animation means giving life to any object in computer graphics. It has the power of injecting energy and emotions into the most seemingly in animate objects.
- Computer-assisted animation and computer-generated animation are two categories of computer animation.
- It can be presented via film or video.
- The basic idea behind animation is to play back the recorded images at the rates fast enough to fool the human eye into interpreting them as continuous motion. Animation can make a series of dead images come alive.
- Animation can be used in many areas like entertainment, computer aided-design, scientific visualization, training, education, e-commerce, and computer art.

4.4.1 Design of Animation Sequences

- Traditional animated films are produced as a sequence of images recorded frame-by-frame. Computer-animated films may be produced using the exact same process.
- What is different in this case is the way the frames were produced? In a traditional film, frames are drawings created by artists. In a computer-animated film, frames are produced by the computer based on the artist's directives. As we shall discuss later on, directives could vary from directly drawing each frame on a graphics tablet to just giving orders to three-dimensional characters. The results will be the same : a series of images produced by the computer.

4.4.2 Animation Languages

- A general – purpose language, such as C, LISP, Pascal or FORTRAN is often used to program the animation functions.
- Animation functions include a graphics editor, a key – frame generator, an in between generator and standrad graphics routines.
- A graphics editor allows us to design and modify object shapes.
- A typical animation specification is scene description. It includes where to position objects, light sources, camera parameters, etc.
- Another standard function is action specification that involves the layouts and motion paths for the objects and camera.
- Key – frame systems are specialized animation languages designed simply to generate the in – betweens. Also explains about degrees of freedom of an object.

4.4.3 Key-Frame

- A key-frame is a frame where we define changes in animation.
- Every frame is a key-frame when we create frame by frame animation.
- When someone creates a 3D animation on a computer, they usually don't specify the exact position of any given object on every single frame. They create key-frames.

- Key-frames are important frames during which an object changes its size, direction, shape or other properties.

- The computer then figures out all the in-between frames and saves an extreme amount of time for the animator.

- The following illustrations depict the frames drawn by user and the frames generated by computer.

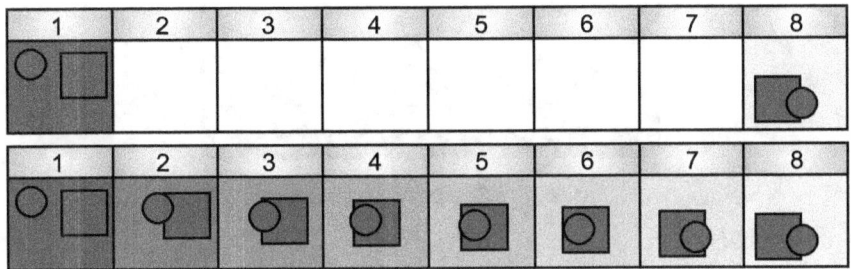

Fig. 4.3 : Key-frames

4.4.4 Morphing

- Morphing is a familiar technology to produce special effects in image or videos.

- Morphing is common in entertainment industry.

- Morphing is widely used in movies, animation games etc.

- In addition to the usage of entertainment industry, morphing can be used in computer based trainings, electronic book illustrations, presentations, education purposes etc.

- Morphing software is widely available in internet.

- Animation industry looking for advanced technology to produce special effects on their movies.

- Increasing customers of animation industry does not satisfy with the movies with simple animation. Here comes the significance of morphing.

- The Word "Morphing" comes from the word "metamorphosis" which means change shape, appearance or form. Morphing is done by coupling image wrapping with color interpolation.

- Morphing is the process in which the source image is gradually distorted and vanished while producing the target image. So earlier images in the sequence are similar to source image and last images are similar to target image. Middle image of the sequence is the average of the source image and the target image.

4.4.5 Motion Specification

There are several ways in which the motions of objects can be specified in an animation system. We can define motion in very explicit terms, or can use more abstract or more general approaches.

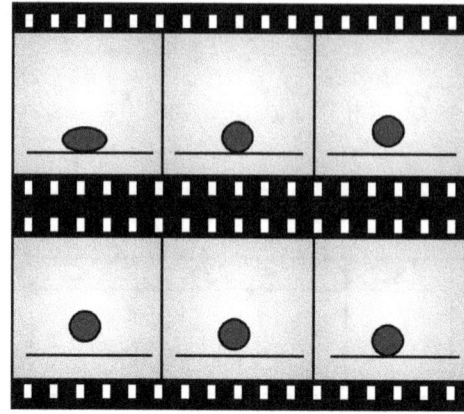

Fig. 4.4 : Motion specification

Direct Motion Specification

The most straight forward method for defining a motion sequence is direct specification of the motion parameters. Here, we explicitly give the rotation angles and translation vectors. Then the geometric transformation matrices are applied to transform co-ordinate positions. Alternatively, we could use an approximating equation to specify certain kind of motions. These methods can be used for simple user programmed animation sequence.

Goal-Directed Systems

At the opposite extreme, we can specify the motions that are to take place in general terms that abstractly describe the actions. These systems are referred to as goal directed because they determine specific motion parameters given the goals of the animation. For example, we could specify that we want an object to "walk" or to "run" to a particular destination. Or we could state that we want an object to "pick up" some other specified object. The input directive are then interpreted in term of component motions that will accomplish the selected task. Human motion, for instance, can be defined as a hierarchical structure of sub motion for the toros, limbs, and so forth.

Kinematics and Dynamics

- We can also construct animation sequences using kinematic or dynamic descriptions. With a kinematic description, we specify the animation by giving motion parameters (position, velocity, and acceleration) without reference to the forces that cause the motion.

- For constant velocity (zero acceleration), we designate the motions of rigid bodies in a scene by giving an initial position and velocity vector for each objects.

- An alternate approach is to use inverse kinematics. Here, we specify the initial and final positions of objects at specified times and the motion parameters are computed by the system. For example, assuming zero acceleration, we can determine the constant velocity that will accomplish the movement of an object from the initial position to the final position.

- Dynamic descriptions on the other hand, require the specification of the forces that produce the velocities and acceleration.

- Descriptions of object behavior under the are generally referred to as a physically based modeling. Example of forces affecting object motion include electromagnetic, gravitational, friction, and other mechanical forces.

- Object motion are obtained from the forces equations describing physical laws, such as Newton's law of motion for gravitational and friction processes, Euler or Navier-stokes equations describing fluid flow, and Maxwell's equations for electromagnetic forces.

- For example, the general form of Newton's second law for a particle of mass m is

$$F \ = \ d(mv)/dt$$

with F as the force vector, and v as the velocity vector. If mass is constant, we solve the equation F=ma, where a is the acceleration vector.

- Otherwise, mass is a function of time, as in relativistic motions of space vehicles that consume measurable amounts of fuel per unit time.

- We can also use inverse dynamics to obtain the forces, given the initial and final positions of objects and the type of motion.

- Application of physically based modeling include complex rigid-body systems and such non-rigid systems as cloth and plastic materials. Typically, numerical methods are used to obtain the motion parameters incrementally from the dynamical equations using initial conditions or boundary values.

4.5 PROPERTIES OF LIGHT

- What the human eye (or virtual camera) sees is a result of light coming off of an object or other light source and striking receptors in the eye. In order to understand and model this process, it is necessary to understand different light sources and the ways that different materials reflect those light sources.

- Trying to recreate reality is difficult.

- Lighting calculations can take a very long time.

- The techniques described here are heuristics which produce appropriate results, but they do not work in the same way reality works - because that would take too long to compute, at least for interactive graphics.

- Instead of just specifying a single color for a Ploygon we will instead specify the properties of the material that the polygon is supposed to be made out of, (i.e. how the material responds to different kinds of light) and the properties of the light or lights shining onto that material.

4.6 CIE CHROMATICITY DIAGRAM

Matching and therefore defining a colored light with a combination of three fixed primary colors is desirable approach to specify color. In 1931, the commission international de I' Eclairage (1E) defined three standard primaries called x, y and z to replace red, green and blue. Here, x, y and z represents vectors in a three-dimensional additive color space. The three standard primaries are imagination colors. They are defined mathematically with positive color-matching functions, as shown below :

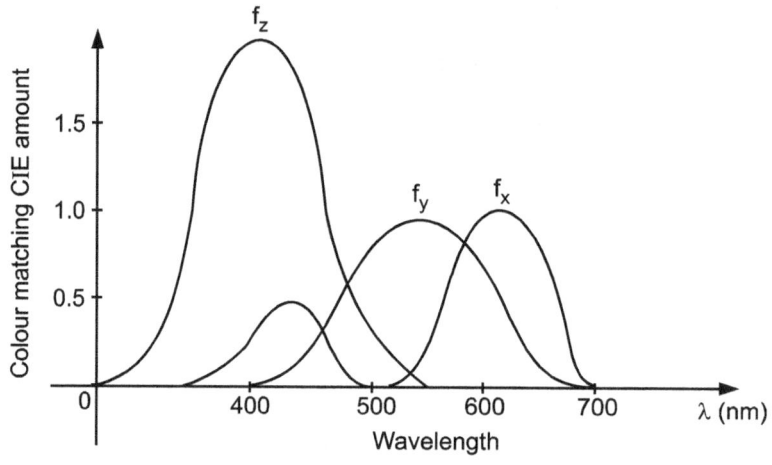

Fig. 4.5

They specify the amount of each primary needed to describe any spectral color. The advantage of using CIE primaries is that they eliminate matching of negative color values and other problems associated with selecting a set of real primaries.

Any color (λ) using CIE primaries can be expressed as,

$$C_\lambda = xX + yY + zZ$$

Where, x, y, z are the amounts of the standard primaries needed to match C_λ. X, Y and Z represent vectors in a three-dimensional additive color space.

With above expression we can define chromaticity values by normalizing against luminance (X + Y + Z). The normalizing amounts can be given as,

$$x = \frac{X}{X + Y + Z}, y = \frac{Y}{X + Y + Z}, z = \frac{Z}{X + Y + Z}$$

Notice that x + y + z = 1. That is x, y and z are on the (X + Y + Z = 1) plane. The complete description of color is typically given with the three values x, y and z. The remaining values can be calculated as follows :

$$z = 1 - x - y, X = \frac{x}{y}Y, Z = \frac{z}{y}Y$$

Chromaticity values depend only on dominant wavelength and saturation and are independent of the amount of luminous energy). Plotting x and y for all visible colors, we obtain the CIE chromaticity diagram shown below – which is the projection on to the (X, Y) plane of the (X + Y + Z = 1) plane.

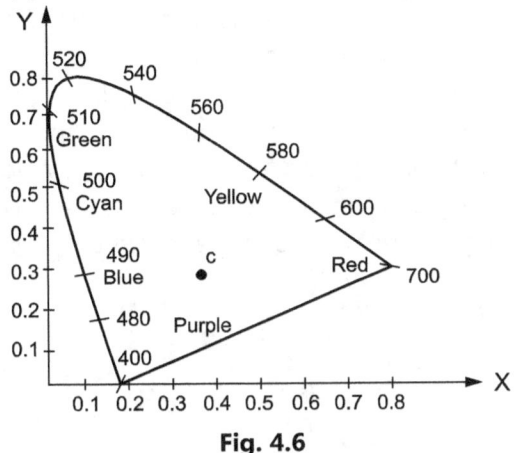

Fig. 4.6

The interior and boundary of the tongue-shaped region represent all visible chromaticity values. The points on the boundary are the pure colors in the electromagnetic spectrum, labeled according to the wavelength in nanometer from the red end to the violet end of the spectrum. A standard white light is formally defined by a light source illuminant C, marked by the center dot. The line joining the red and violet spectral points is called the purple line, which is not the part of the spectrum.

The CIE chromaticity diagram is helpful in many ways :

- It allows us to measure the dominant wavelength and the purity of any color by matching the color with a mixture of the three CIE primaries. It identifies the complementary colors. It allows to define color gamut's or color ranges, that show the effect of adding colors together.

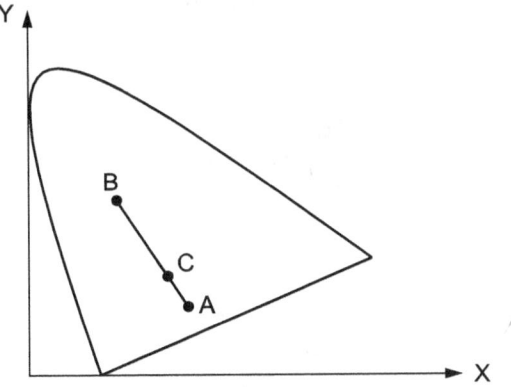

Fig. 4.7 : Complementary colors of chromaticity diagram

The Fig. 4.7 below represents the complementary colors on the chromaticity diagram. The straight line joining colors represented by points A and B pass through point C (represents white light). This means that when two colors A and B are properly mixed as shown below, white light is obtained.

Therefore, colors A and B are complementary colors and with point C on the chromaticity diagram can identify the complement of color of the known color.

• Color gamut's are represented on the chromaticity diagram as a straight line or as a polygon. Any two colors say P and Q can be added to produce any color along their connecting line by mixing their appropriate amounts. The color gamuts for three points in Fig. 4.8 below is a triangle with three color points as vertices. The triangle ABD in Fig. 4.8 shows that three primaries can only generate colors inside as on the bounding edges of the triangle.

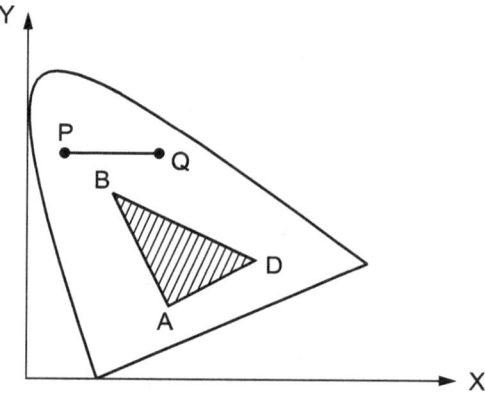

Fig. 4.8 : Definition of color gamuts

• The chromaticity diagram is also helpful to determine the dominant wavelength of a color. For color point A is drawn from C through A to intersect the spectral curve at point B. The color A can then be represented as a combination of white light C and the spectral color B. Thus, the dominant wavelength of A is P. This method for determining dominant wavelength will not work for color points that are between C and the purple line because the purple line is not part of spectrum.

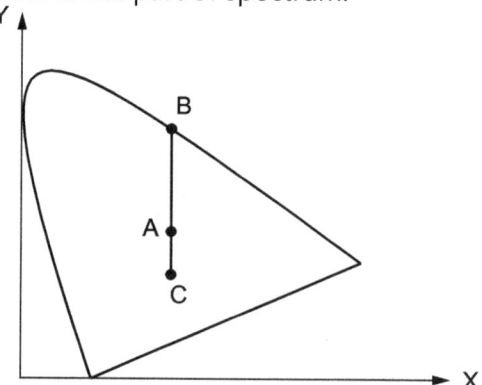

Fig. 4.9 : Determination of dominant wavelength on chromaticity diagram

4.7 COLOR MODELS

4.7.1 RGB

The red-green-blue model is formed by a color cube $\{(R, G, B) : 0 \le R, G, B \le 1\}$.

RGB Color Model

The RGB color model is an additive color model in which red, green and blue light are added together in various ways to reproduce a broad array of colors. The name of the model comes from the initials of the three additive primary colors, red, green and blue.

The main purpose of the RGB color model is for the sensing, representation and display of images in electronic systems, such as televisions and computers, though it has also been used in conventional photography. Before the electronic age, the RGB color model already had a solid theory behind it, based in human perception of colors.

RGB is a device-dependent color model: different devices detect or reproduce a given RGB value differently, since the color elements (such as phosphors or dyes) and their response to the individual R, G and B levels vary from manufacturer to manufacturer, or even in the same device over time. Thus an RGB value does not define the same color across devices without some kind of color management.

Typical RGB input devices are color TV and video cameras, image scanners, video games, and digital cameras. Typical RGB output devices are TV sets of various technologies (CRT, LCD, plasma, OLED, Quantum-Dots etc.)

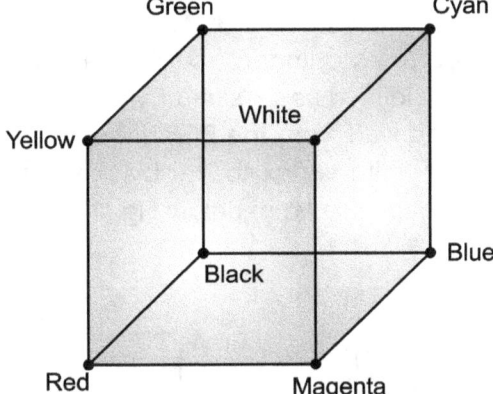

Fig. 4.10 : The RGB-cube

4.7.2 HSV

* The HSV color model is user oriented. It uses color descriptions that have a more intuitive appeal to a user.
* The color specification in HSV model can be given by selecting a spectral color and the amounts of white and black that is to be added to obtain different shades, tints and tones.
* This model uses three color parameter : hue (H), saturation (S) and value (V).
* Hue distinguishes among colors such as red, green, purple and yellow.

- Saturation refers to how far color is from a gray of equal intensity. For example, red is highly saturated whereas pink is relatively saturated.
- The value V indicates the level of brightness.
- All color models treated so far are hardware oriented. The Hue-Saturation-Value model is oriented towards the user/artist. The allowed coordinates fill a six sided pyramid the 3 top faces of the color cube as base. Note that at the same height colors of different perceived brightness are positioned. Value is given by the height; saturation is coded in the distance from the axes and hue by the position on the boundary.

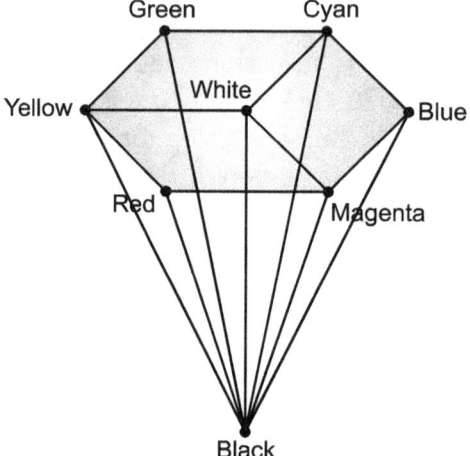

Fig. 4.11 : The HSV-model

- The model shown in Fig.4.11 uses cylindrical co-ordinate system and the subset of the space within which, model is defined as six-sided pyramid.
- The top of the hex cone is derived from the RGB. If we imagine viewing the cube along the main diagonal from the white vertex to the black vertex, we see an outline of the cube that has the hexagon shape shown in below Fig. 4.12.

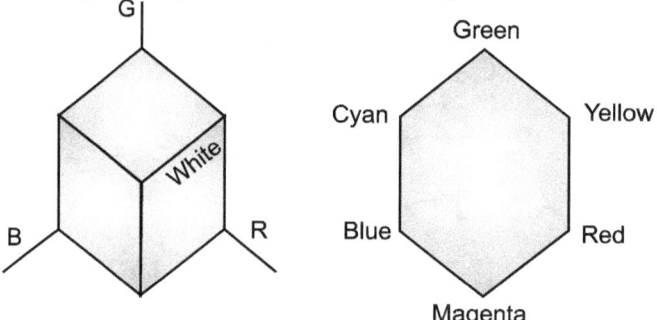

Fig. 4.12

- This boundary of cube is used as a top if hex cone and it represents various hues.
- Complementary colors in the HSV hex cone are 180° apart saturation parameter varies from 0 to 1. Its value is the ratio ranging from 0 to 1 on the triangular sides of the hex cone.

- At the top of the hex cone, colors have their maximum intensity; when V = 1 and S = 1, we have the pure hues.
- The required color can be obtained by adding either white or black to the pure hue.

HLS Color Model :

- Here the RGB-cube is deformed in such a way that a six sided double pyramid results with the same base as in the HSV-model, but with two tips at black and at white.
- The hue specifies the angle around the vertical axis of the double hex cone.
- The vertical axis in this model represents the lightness, L.
- The saturation parameters S varies from 0 to 1 and it specifies relative purity of a color.
- The colors can be made lighter by increasing the value of L and can be made darker by decreasing the value of L.

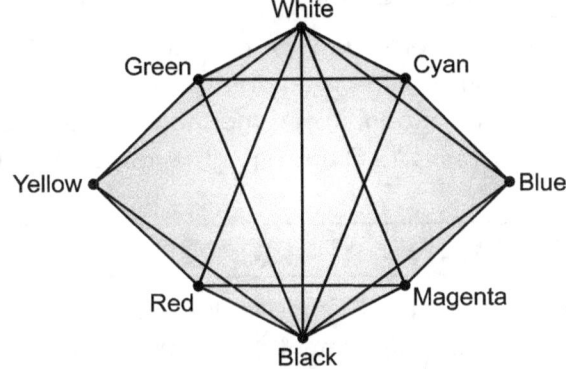

Fig. 4.13 : The HLS-model

4.7.3 CMY

- This stands for cyan-magenta-yellow and is used for hardcopy devices. In contrast to color on the monitor, the color in printing acts subtractive and not additive. A printed color that looks red absorbs the other two components G and B and reflects R. Thus its (internal) color is G+B=CYAN. Similarly R+B=MAGENTA and R+G=YELLOW. Thus the C-M-Y coordinates are just the complements of the R-G-B coordinates :

$$\begin{pmatrix} C \\ M \\ Y \end{pmatrix} = \begin{pmatrix} 1 \\ 1 \\ 1 \end{pmatrix} - \begin{pmatrix} R \\ G \\ B \end{pmatrix}$$

- If we want to print a red looking color (i.e. with R-G-B coordinates (1,0,0)) we have to use C-M-Y values of (0,1,1). Note that M absorbs G, similarly Y absorbs B and hence M + Y absorbs all but R.
- Black ((R, G, B) = (0, 0, 0)) corresponds to (C, M, Y) = (1, 1, 1) which should in principle absorb R, G and B. But in practice this will appear as some dark gray. So in order to be

able to produce better contrast printers often use black as 4th color. This is the CMYK-model. Its coordinates are obtained from that of the CMY-model by

K : = max (C, M, Y), C : C − K, M : = M − K and Y : = Y − K.

4.7.4 YIQ

* This is used for color TV. Here Y is the luminance (the only component necessary for B&W-TV). The conversion from RGB to YIQ is given by

$$\begin{pmatrix} Y \\ I \\ Q \end{pmatrix} = \begin{pmatrix} 0.30 & 0.59 & 0.11 \\ 0.60 & -0.28 & -0.32 \\ 0.21 & -0.52 & 0.31 \end{pmatrix} \cdot \begin{pmatrix} R \\ G \\ B \end{pmatrix}$$

* **Luminance (Brightness) :** The intensity of light emitted from a surface per unit area in a given direction. Hue is nothing but shade.

* In this model, luminance information is contained in Y parameter. Chromaticity information (hue and purity) is incorporated into I and Q parameters. Since Y contains luminance information, black-and-white TV monitors use only the Y signal. A color TV would take these three channels Y,I,Q and map the information back to R,G,B levels for display.

4.8 COLOR SELECTION AND APPLICATIONS

* One aspect of digital color familiar to almost all users of computer system is the color selection tool. Color is applied to documents, desktops, drawings and web pages.

* A typical desktop system might have over a dozen different tools for selecting RGB colors embedded in its applications.

* There are, however, a few ideas that consistently appear. First is the transformation of the RGB color cube into some approximation of a perceptual color space.

* The two most commonly used are the HSV and HLS systems. Second is the mapping of a 3D space to a 2D, interactive tool.

* The standard colors often represent the colors available on a display limited to 16 or 256 colors.

* There is also usually a pair of patches that show the color being changed and its new value.

Color Selection Guidelines

* The relative luminance of saturated colors follows the spectral luminous efficiency function not the spectral hue order.

* Use color consistently throughout all screens in an application.

* Use strong color in small details only, such as icons and graphical indicators.

- Avoid adjacent areas of strong blue and strong red in a display to prevent unwanted depth effects (colors appearing to lie in different planes).

- Never use the blue channel alone for fine detail such as text or graphics. Do not use, for example, blue text on a black background or yellow text on a white back-ground.

- Areas of strong color and high contrast can produce after images when the viewer looks way from the screen, resulting in visual stress from prolonged viewing.

- Do not use hue alone to encode information in applications where serious consequences might cause.

- RGB display signals are device-dependent, and the color they produce will generally differ from one display to another.

- When you need to render colors accurately, use a calibrated display and gamma correction software for best results.

- Some colors may be impossible to reproduce exactly if they lie outside the display's color gamut; so in this case use perceptual color models based on CIE uniform color spaces instead of the simplistic color models based on device-dependent RGB signals.

EXERCISE

1. What is mean by animation?
2. What are the different techniques of animation?
3. What are the different steps of conventional animation system?
4. List the different methods of controlling animation?
5. Explain fully explicit control and procedural control?
6. What are the different animation languages?
7. Explain the key frame system animation language?
8. Explain the morphing technique?
9. List the advantages of animation?
10. In which steps we use the computer in conventional animation?

UNIVERSITY QUESTIONS

1. What is a segment table? Explain the operations that can be performed on a segment table? **[Apr. 2013, 8 Marks]**

2. What is segment? How do we create it? Why do we need segments? Explain in detail the various operations of segment. **[Dec. 2013, 10 Marks]**

3. What is a segment ? Give its structure and also describe various operations carried out on the segment. **[Dec. 2014, 7 Marks]**

4.   Describe the various operations carried out on the segment.   **[June 2015, 6 Marks]**

5.   Write advantages and disadvantages of segments.   **[June 2015, 4 Marks]**

6.   What is segment? Explain segment table.   **[Dec. 2015, 5 Marks]**

7.   Explain the data structures that can be used to implement the segment table.

[Apr. 2013, 8 Marks]

8.   Write the algorithm for the following

     (i)   Change the visibility attribute of segment

     (ii) Delete a segment   **[Dec. 2015, 8 Marks]**

9.   Describe various operations carried out on the segment.   **[May 2014, 6 Marks]**

10. What is segment? Explain transformation operation on segment. **[May 2016, 3 Marks]**

11. What is segment and segment table?   **[May 2016, 3 Marks]**

12. What are the various methods of controlling animation? Explain in detail.

[Apr. 2013, 8 Marks]

13. Describe the steps required to produce real time animation.   **[Dec. 2015, 8 Marks]**

14. Define animation and explain the methods of controlling the animation. Give different
     types of animation languages.   **[Dec. 2015, 10 Marks]**

15. What is the difference between conventional and computer based animations? What
     are the various methods of controlling animation?   **[Dec. 2014, 7 Marks]**

16. Define animation. Explain the methods for controlling animations.

[May 2014, 7 Marks]

17. Write basic guidelines for animation and gaming technology.   **[May 2016, 4 Marks]**

18. What are the applications of morphing?   **[June 2015, 3 Marks]**

19. Explain morphing? What is simulating acceleration?   **[Apr. 2013, 8 Marks]**

20. Explain the following in detail

     (i)   CIE Chromaticity Diagram

     (ii) Color Models   **[Apr. 2013, 18 Marks]**

21. Explain RGB color model.   **[Dec. 2015, 4 Marks]**

22. Explain RGB, HSV, and CMY color model.   **[Dec. 2015, 8 Marks]**

23. Comapre RGB and HSV color model.   **[June 2015, 3 Marks]**

24. Explain RGB and HIS color model.   **[May 2016, 4 Marks]**

◈ ◈ ◈

SHADING AND HIDDEN SURFACES

5.1 LIGHT SOURCE

There are different types of sources of light, such as point sources (e.g, a small light at a distance), extended sources (e.g. the sky on a cloudy day), and secondary reflections (e.g. light that bounces from one surface to another).

5.2 REFLECTANCE

Different objects reflect light in different ways. For example, diffuse surfaces appear the same when viewed from different directions, whereas a mirror looks very different from different points of view.

Simple Reflection Models :

Diffuse Reflection

We begin with the diffuse reflectance model. A diffuse surface is one that appears similarly bright from all viewing directions. That is, the emitted light appears independent of the viewing location.

Let $\bar{p}$ be a point on a diffuse surface with normal $\vec{n}$, light by a point light source in direction $\vec{s}$ from the surface. The reflected intensity of light is given by:

$$L_d(\bar{p}) = r_d I \max(0, \vec{s} \cdot \vec{n}) \qquad \qquad \qquad ...(5.1)$$

where I is the intensity of the light source, r_d is the diffuse reflectance (or albedo) of the surface, and $\vec{s}$ is the direction of the light source. This equation requires the vectors to be normalized, i.e.

$$\| \vec{s} \| = 1, \| \vec{n} = 1 \|$$

The $\vec{s} \cdot \vec{n}$ term is called the *foreshortening term*. When a light source projects light obliquely at a surface, that light is spread over a large area, and less of the light hits any specific point. For example, imagine pointing a flashlight directly at a wall versus in a direction nearly parallel in the later case, the light from the flashlight will spread over a greater area, and individual points on the wall will not be as bright.

Perfect Specular Reflection

For pure specular (mirror) surfaces, the incident light from each incident direction $\vec{d}_i$ is reflected toward a unique emitting direction d_e. The emitting direction lies in the same plane as the incident direction $\vec{d}_i$ and the surface normal $\vec{n}$, and the angle between $\vec{n}$ and $\vec{d}_e$ is equal to that between $\vec{n}$ and $\vec{d}_i$. One can show that the emitting direction is given by

$$\vec{d}_e = 2(\vec{n} \cdot \vec{d}_i)\,\vec{n} - \vec{d}_i.$$

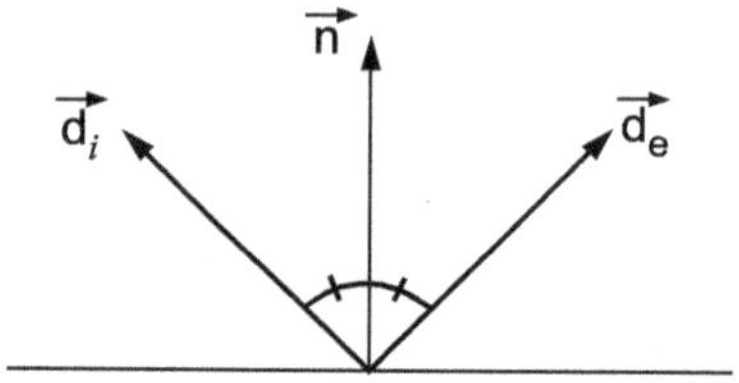

Fig. 5.1

In perfect specular reflection, the light emitted in direction $\vec{d}_e$ can be computed by reflecting $\vec{d}_e$ across the normal (as $2(\vec{n} \cdot \vec{d}_e)\,\vec{n} - \vec{d}_e$), and determining the incoming light in this direction.

General Specular Reflection :

Many materials exhibit a significant specular component in their reflectance. But few are perfect Mirrors. First, most specular surfaces do not reflect all light, and that is easily handled by introducing a scalar constant to attenuate intensity. Second, most specular surfaces exhibit some form of *off–axis specular reflection*. That is, many polished and shiny surfaces (like plastics and metals)emit light in the perfect mirror direction and in some nearby directions as well. These off–axis specularities look a little blurred. Good examples are *highlights* on plastics and metals.

More precisely, the light from a distant point source in the direction of $\vec{s}$ is reflected into a range of directions about the perfect mirror directions $\vec{m} = 2(\vec{n} \cdot \vec{s})\,\vec{n} - \vec{s}$. One common model for this is the following:

$$L_s(\vec{d}_e) = r_s\,I_{max}(0, \vec{m} \cdot \vec{d}_e)\,\alpha, \qquad\qquad ...(5.2)$$

where r_s is called the specular reflection coefficient, I is the incident power from the point source, and $\alpha \geq 0$ is a constant that determines the width of the specular highlights. As α increases, the effective width of the specular reflection decreases. In the limit as α increases, this becomes a mirror.

Ambient Illumination

The diffuse and specular shading models are easy to compute, but often appear artificial. The biggest issue is the point light source assumption, the most obvious consequence of

which is that any surface normal pointing away from the light source (i.e. for which $\bar{s} \cdot \bar{n} < 0$) will have a radiance of zero. A better approximation to the light source is a uniform *ambient* term plus a point light source. This is a still a remarkably crude model, but it's much better than the point source by itself. Ambient illumination is modeled simply by:

$$L_a(\bar{p}) = r_a I_a$$

where r_a is often called the ambient reflection coefficient, and I_a denotes the integral of the uniform illuminant.

Phong Reflectance Model

The Phong reflectance model is perhaps the simplest widely used shading model in computer graphics. It comprises a diffuse term, an ambient term and a specular term

$$L(\bar{p}, \vec{d}_e) = r_d I_d \max(0, \vec{s} \cdot \vec{n}) + r_a I_a + r_s I_s \max(0, \vec{m} \cdot \vec{d}_e)\alpha,$$

Where

- I_a, I_d, and I_r are parameters that correspond to the power of the light sources for the ambient, diffuse, and specular terms;

- r_a, r_d and r_s are scalar constants, called reflection coefficients, that determine the relative magnitudes of the three reflection terms;

- α determines the spread of the specurlar highlights;

- $\vec{n}$ is the surface normal at $\bar{p}$;

- $\vec{s}$ is the direction of the distant point source;

- $\vec{m}$ is the perfect mirror direction, given $\vec{n}$ and $\vec{s}$

- and $\vec{d}_e$ is the emittant direction of interest (usually the direction of the camera).

In effect, this is a model in which the diffuse and specular components of reflection are due to incident light from a point source. Extended light sources and the bouncing of light from one surface to another are not modeled except through the ambient term. Also, arguably this model has more parameters than the physics might suggest; for example, the model does not constrain the parameters to conserve energy. Nevertheless it is sometimes useful to give computer graphics practitioners more freedom in order to achieve the appearance they are after.

Combined Diffuse and Specular Ketctrorns with Multiple Light Sources :

For single point light source, the combined reflection from any point on illuminated surface is given as

$$I = I_{diff.} + I_{spec.}$$
$$= k_a I_a + k_d I_k (N.L) + k_s I_l (N - H)^n$$
$$I_a = \frac{\text{Intenisty of ambient light}}{\text{background light background light}}$$
$$k_a = \text{Ambient reflection coefficient}$$

$$k_s = \text{Specular reflection coefficient}$$

For multiple point light source the above equation can be modified as

$$I = k_a I_a + \sum_{i=1}^{m} I_{l_1} [k_d (N \cdot L_i) + k_s (N \cdot H_1)^n]$$

a, b, c, d are used to represent dot products.

Warn Model :

The warn model, models the light source by aiming in a certain direction instead of directions.

The intensity of light varies with direction from source. It provides method for simulating studio lighting effects.

5.3 SHADING

To create realistic images, Shading is one of the major tool used. Shaded images can create the impression that the images are real objects and not artificial ones. The advantages of using high quality shaded images are that they provide an easy, more effective and less costly way of reviewing various alternatives rather than building actual models or prototype. Once the geometric model of any object is prepared, the images are shaded and analyzed to judge how the model will look like when it is finally released.

Shading models are also called as illumination models. They are used to calculate the intensity of light at a given point on the surface of object. Although the surface shading method is different. Surface shading method is referred as surface rendering method.

5.3.1 Gourand Shading

In this method, the intensity interpolation technique developed by Gourand is used. The polygon surface is displayed by linearly interpolating intensity values across the surface. Here, intensity values for each polygon are matched with the values of adjacent polygons along the common edges. This eliminates the intensity discontinuities that can occur in flat shading.

Polygon surface with Gourand shading can be displayed as:

- Determine the average and normal vector at each polygon vertex.
- Apply an illumination model to easy polygon vertex to determine the vertex intensity.
- Linearly interpolate the vertex intensities over the surface of the polygon.

We can obtain a normal vector at each polygon vertex by averaging the surface normals and all polygons sharing that vertex. This is illustrated in Fig. 5.2 shown below.

Fig. 5.2 : Calculation of normal vector at polygon vertex, V

As such in above Fig. 5.2 there are three surface normals N_1, N_2 and N_3 for polygon sharing vertex V. Therefore, normal vector at vertex V is given as,

$$N_V = \frac{N_1 + N_2 + N_3}{|N_1 + N_2 + N_3|}$$

In general, for any vertex position V, we can obtain the unit vertex normal by equation,

$$N_V = \frac{\sum\limits_{i=1}^{n} N_i}{\left| \sum\limits_{i=1}^{n} N_i \right|}$$

where n is the number of surface normals of polygons sharing that vertex.

5.3.2 Halftoning Shading

- **Halftone** is the reprographic technique that simulates continuous tone imagery through the use of dots, varying either in size, in shape or in spacing.

- "Halftone" can also be used to refer specifically to the image that is produced by this process, where continuous tone imagery contains an infinite range of colors or greys.

- The halftone process reduces visual reproductions to an image that is printed with only one color of ink, in dots of differing size.

- This reproduction relies on a basic optical illusion—that these tiny halftone dots are blended into smooth tones by the human eye. At a microscopic level, developed black–and–white photographic film also consists of only two colors, and not an infinite range of continuous tones

- A technique used in newspaper printing. Only two intensities are possible, blob of ink and no blob of ink.

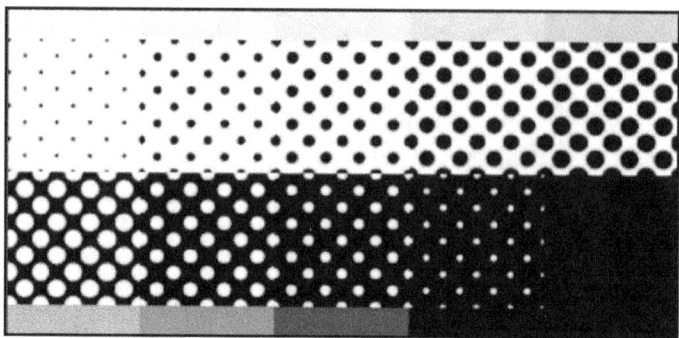

Fig. 5.3

- But, the size of the blob can be varied. Also, the dither patterns of small dots can be used

Fig. 5.4 : Halftoning – Dot Size

5.3.3 Phong Shading

- Phong shading also known as normal–vector interpolation shading interpolates the surface normal vector N, instead of the intensity. By performing following steps, we can display polygon surface using Phong shading:

- Determine the average unit normal vector at each polygon vertex.
- Linearly interpolate the vertex normal over the surface of the polygon.
- Apply an illumination model along each scan line to determine projected pixel intensities for the surface points.

- The first steps in the phong shading is same as first step in this Gourand shading. In the second step the vertex normals are linearly interpolated over the surface of the polygon. This is illustrated in Fig. 5.5 as follows.

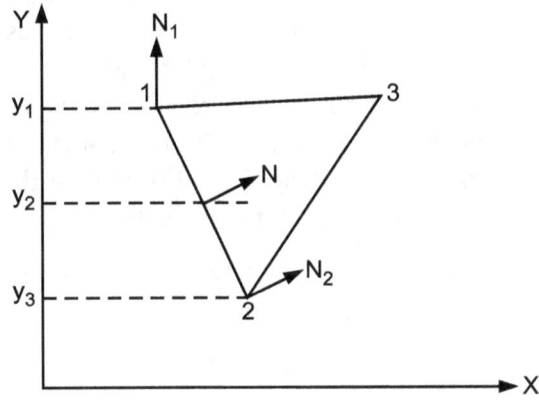

Fig. 5.5

- As shown in above Fig. 5.5, the normal vector N for the scan line intersection point along the edge between vertices 1 and 2 can be obtained by vertically interpolating between edge end points normal:

$$N = \frac{Y - Y_2}{Y_1 - Y_2} N_1 + \frac{Y_1 - Y}{Y_1 - Y_2} N_2$$

- Like, Gourand shading, here also we can use incremental method to evaluate normal between scan lines and along each individual scan line. Once the surface normals are evaluated the surface intensity at that point is determined by applying the illumination method.

5.4 HIDDEN SURFACES

When objects are to be displayed with color or shaded surface, we apply surface– rendering procedures to the visible surfaces so that the hidden surfaces are obscured. Some visible surface algorithms establish visibility pixel by pixel across the viewing plane, other determine visibility for object surface as a whole. By removing the hidden lines we also remove information about the shape of the back surfaces of an object.

5.4.1 Types of Surfaces

- Bilinear surfaces
- Ruled surfaces
- Developable surfaces

- Coon patch
- Sweep surfaces
- Surface of revolution
- Quadratic surfaces

- **Bilinear Surfaces**

A flat polygon is the simplest type of surface. The bilinear surface is the simplest non flat (curved) surface because it is fully defined by means of its four corner points. It is discussed here because its four boundary curves are straight lines and because the coordinates of any point on this surface are derived by linear interpolations. Since this patch is completely defined by its four corner points, it cannot have a very complex shape. Nevertheless it may be highly curved. If the four corners are coplanar, the bilinear patch defined by them is flat. Let the corner points be the four distinct points P00, P01, P10, and P11. The top and bottom boundary curves are straight lines and are easy to calculate.

They are $P(u, 0) = (P10 - P00)u + P00$ and $P(u, 1) = (P11 - P01)u + P01$.

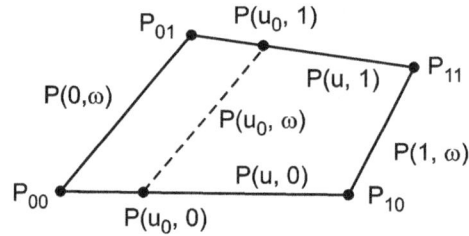

Fig. 5.6

To linearly interpolate between these boundary curves, we first calculate two corresponding points $P(u0, 0)$ and $P(u0, 1)$, one on each curve, then connect them with a straight line $P(u0, w)$. The two points are $P(u0, 0) = (P10 - P00)u0 + P00$ and $P(u0,1) = (P11 - P01)u0 + P01$, and the straight segment connecting them is $P(u0, w) = (P(u0, 1) - P(u0, 0))w + P(u0, 0)$ $= [(P11 - P01)u0 + P01 - (P10 - P00)u0 + P00]w + (P10 - P00)u0 + P00$.

- **Bezier Surfaces**

To create a Bezier surface, we blend a mesh of Bezier curves using the blending function

$$P(u, v) = \sum_{j=0}^{m} \sum_{k=0}^{n} P_{j,k} \, BEZ_{j,m}(v) \, BEZ_{k,n}(u)$$

where j and k are points in parametric space and $P_{x,y}$ represents the location of the knots in real space. The Bezier functions specify the weighting of a particular knot. They are the Bernstein coefficients.

By controlling light intensity in different directions.

The directionality is provided by $\cos^n p$, p is angle from central direction warn model can be used for spot lighting.

Back Face Defection and Removal

The picture of polygon is drawn as one side pointed light and other painted dark. To find which surface is light and which is dark is the question.

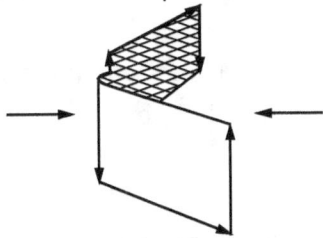

Fig. 5.7

When we look at light surface, polygon appear to be drawn with counter clockwise. When we look at dark surface the polygon appear to be drawn with clockwise.

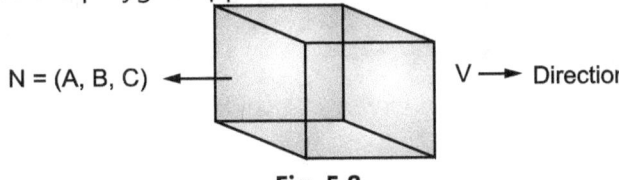

Fig. 5.8

The direction of light face is

$$NV > 0$$

N – Normal vector to polygon surface with Cartesian components (A, B, C)

V – Vector in the viewing direction

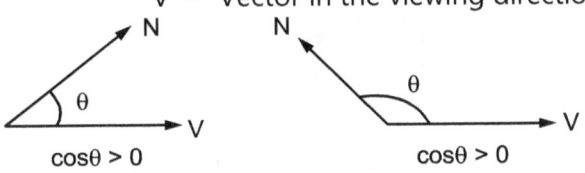

Fig. 5.9

Cosine angle between to rectors

If the dot product is positive, polygon faces towards viewer. Otherwise it faces away.

5.4.2 Painter's Algorithm

- Sort polygons by farthest depth.
- Check if polygon is in front of any other.
- If no, render it.
- If yes, has its order already changed backward?

    (a) If no, render it.

    (b) If yes, break it apart.

    Which polygon is in front? Our strategy: apply a series of tests.

    (a) First tests are cheapest

(b) Each test says poly1 is behind poly2, or maybe.
- If min z of poly1 > max z poly2 ———1 in back.
- The plane of the polygon with smaller z is closer to viewer than other polygon.
  (a,b,c,)*(x,y,z) > = d.
- The plane of polygon with larger z is completely behind other polygon.
- Check whether they overlap in image
  a. Use axial rectangle test.
  b. Use complete test.

Problem Cases: Cyclic and Intersecting Objects
- Solution : split polygons

Advantages of Painter's Algorithm
- Simple
- Easy transparency

Disadvantages
- Have to sort first.
- Need to split polygons to solve cyclic and intersecting objects.

5.4.3 Z–Buffer Algorithm

Here, the depth of the surface is given by the coordinates. Algorithm compares the depth of each pixel position. We use the normalized coordinates. So that the range of depth(z) values vary from 0 to 1.

$$Z = 0 \text{ denotes the back clipping plane.}$$
$$Z = 1 \text{ denotes the front clipping plane.}$$

We use two types of memories.
- Frame buffer: which stores the intensity values for each pixel position and
- Z–buffer: which stores the depth of each pixel (x,y) position.
  Algorithm keeps track of the minimum depth value.

Algorithm
- Initialize depth (x,y)=0
  Framebuffer (x,y) = I background for all (x,y)
- Compute the z–Buffer values by using the equation of the plane.
  $$Ax + By + Cz + D = 0$$
  [here, we store information about all the polygonal surface included in the picture.]
  The pixels are scanned by the scaline incremental method.
  $$Z = -1/C \, (Ax+By+D) \text{ i.e. for any pixel position } (X_k,Y_k) \text{ the depth}$$
  $$(X_k,Y_k) = Z_k$$

$$Z_k = -1/C(Ax_k+By_k+C) \text{ The next pixel position is at } (X_k+1, Y_k) \text{ or } (X_k, Y_k-1)$$

$$Z_{k+1} = -1/C(A(x_k+1)+By_k+D)$$

$$Z_{k+1} = -1/C(A(x_k+1)+By_k+D) -A/C$$

$$Z_{k+1} = -Z_k-A/C \text{ calculates the values of depth recursively.}$$

Similarly, the depth values down the edges of intersection of the polygon surface and the scanline are given as calculated as follows:

Let $y = mx+c$ is the example of the left most intersecting edge then from $(X_k, Y_k) \rightarrow (X', Y_k-1)$ along the edge gives,

$$Y_k = mX_k+C \; 1= m(X_k-X')$$

$$Y_k-1 = mX'+C \; X'= X_k -1/m$$

The depth value then becomes,

$$Z_{k+1} = -1/C (A (X_k-1/m) + By_k-1 + D)$$

$$Z_{k+1} = -1/C(AX_k + By_k - B+D)+ (A/M)/C$$

$$Z_{k+1} = -1/C(AX_k + By_k +D)+B/C+ (A/M)/C$$

$$Z_{k+1} = Z_k+ ((A/M)+B)/C$$

- If the calculated depth value is Z_{k+1} and if at (x,y) pixel position

$$Z > \text{calculated depth } (x,y) \text{ Then,}$$

Set the depth value as $depth(x,y) = z$ and frame buffer $(x,y)= I$ surface.

- Repeat steps 2 and 3, till all the polygonal surfaces are processed.

5.4.4 Binary Space Partitioning

- Suitable for a static group of 3D polygon to be viewed from a number of view points.

- Based on the observation that hidden surface elimination of a polygon is guaranteed if all polygons on the other side of it as the viewer is painted first, then itself, then all polygons on the same side of it as the viewer.

1. The algorithm first build the BSP tree:

  - A root polygon is chosen (arbitrarily) which divides the region into 2 half–spaces (2 nodes => front and back).

  - A polygon in the front half–space is chosen which divides the half–space into another 2 halfspaces.

  - The subdivision is repeated until the half–space contains a single polygon (leaf node of the tree).

  - The same is done for the back space of the polygon.

2. To display a BSP tree:
    *   See whether the viewer is in the front or the back half–space of the root polygon.
    *   If front half–space then first display back child (subtree) then itself, followed by its front child / subtree.
    *   The algorithm is applied recursively to the BSP tree.

BSP Algorithm

Procedure DisplayBSP(tree: BSP_tree)

```
Begin
If tree is not empty then
If viewer is in front of the root then
Begin
DisplayBSP(tree.back_child)
displayPolygon(tree.root)
DisplayBSP(tree.front_child)
End
Else
Begin
DisplayBSP(tree.front_child)
displayPolygon(tree.root)
DisplayBSP(tree.back_child)
End
End
```

Discussion

*   Back face removal is achieved by not displaying a polygon if the viewer is located in its back half–space.
*   It is an object space algorithm (sorting and intersection calculations are done in object space precision).
*   If the view point changes, the BSP needs only minor re–arrangement.
*   A new BSP tree is built if the scene changes.
*   The algorithm displays polygon back to front (Depth–sort).

5.4.6 Area Subdivision Algorithms

The area–subdivision method takes advantage of area coherence in a scene by locating those view areas that represent part of a single surface. The total viewing area is successively divided into smaller and smaller rectangles until each small area is simple, i.e. it is a single pixel, or is covered wholly by a part of a single visible surface or no surface at all.

The procedure to determine whether we should subdivide an area into smaller rectangle is:

1. We first classify each of the surfaces, according to their relations with the area:

- Surrounding surface – a single surface completely encloses the area.

- Overlapping surface – a single surface that is partly inside and partly outside the area.

- Inside surface – a single surface that is completely inside the area.

- Outside surface – a single surface that is completely outside the area. To improve the speed of classification, we can make use of the bounding rectangles of surfaces for early confirmation or rejection that the surfaces should be belong to that type.

2. Check the result from 1, that, if any of the following condition is true, then, no subdivision of this area is needed.

   - All surfaces are outside the area.

   - Only one surface is inside, overlapping or surrounding surface is in the area.

   - A surrounding surface obscures all other surfaces within the area boundaries.

For cases b and c, the color of the area can be determined from that single surface.

Fig. shows scanline method for surface removal

Active edge list for scanline 1 – AD, BC, EH, FG edges.

Active edge list for scanline 2 – AD, EH, BC, FG

S_1 is ON – Along the scanlines between edges AD and BC.

S_2 is ON – EH and FG

Along scaline 2 : S_1 is ON AD and EH edge

Flag for both surfaces – EH and DC edge ON.

Hence, depth of S_1 is less than S_2 so, intensities of surface S_1 are loaded into frame buffer.

Scan–line :

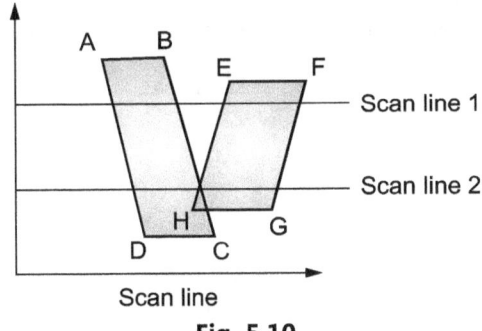

Fig. 5.10

Fig. 5.10 shows scanline method for surface removal.

Active edge list for scanline 1.

   AD, BC, EH, FG edges

Active edge list for scanline 2.

   AD, EH, BS, FG

S_1 is ON – along the scanlines between edges AD and BC.

S_2 is ON – EH and FG.

S_1 is ON AD and EH edge

Flag for both surfaces ON – EH and DC.

Hence, depth of S_1 is less than S_2 so, intensities of surface S_1 are loaded into frame buffer.

EXERCISE

1. Explain :

    (i)   Back face Detection method

    (ii) Depth buffer method for detection

2. Explain :

    (a) Depth Cueing

    (b) Surface Rendering

3. Explain the classification of Visible surface Detection methods with example.

4. Explain boundary fill algorithm in Detail. Explain the term seed pixel.

5. What is windowing and clipping? Explain the viewing transformation.

6. Explain polygon clipping algorithm for polygon clipping.

7. Final polygon coordinates are A(0,0), B(1,0), C(0,1) and D(1,1) perform scaling on X = 2, perform rotation by 90 degree and perform x shear by 4.

8. Explain the term homogeneous coordinate system and the use of homogeneous coordinate system.

9. List the steps for finding the inverse matrix and write the matrix for inverse.

10. What is the need of projection? Explain ways of projection 3D objects onto 2D screen in detail.

CURVES AND FRACTALS

6.1 INTRODUCTION

Straight lines have a simple mathematical form, which makes them easy to deal with operations such as transformations or clipping. However, the real world many of things consist of curves. We might need to plot a mathematical function or the path of a rocket, or to design the hood of a sports car or wing of an airplane. Natural objects are neither perfectly flat nor smoothly curved but have rough, jagged contours. Thus, it is important to learn methods for getting curve lined.

6.2 TRUE CURVE GENERATION

Two approaches can be used to draw curved lines.

- To use a curve generation algorithm such as DDA.
- To use interpolation techniques.

In the first approach, a true curve is created. In the second approach, the curve is approximated by a number of small straight lines.

Circular Arc Generation using DDA Algorithm :

DDA i.e. Digital differential analyzer algorithm uses the differential equation of the curve. The differential equations for simple curve such as circle is fairly easy to solve. The equation for an arc in the angle parameter can be given as,

$$x = R \cos \theta + x_0$$
$$y = R \sin \theta + y_0 \qquad \qquad \ldots (6.1)$$

where, (x_0, y_0) is the center of curvature and R is the radius of arc.

Differentiating equation (6.1), we get,

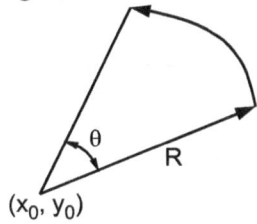

Fig. 6.1

$$dx = - R \sin \theta \, d\theta$$
$$dy = R \cos \theta \, d\theta \qquad \qquad \ldots (6.2)$$

From equation (6.1), we can solve for $R \cos \theta$ and $R \sin \theta$ as follows :

$$x = R \cos \theta + x_0$$

$$R \cos \theta = x - x_0 \text{ and}$$

$$R \sin \theta = y - y_0 \qquad \qquad \ldots (6.3)$$

Substituting values for $R \cos \theta$ and $R \sin \theta$ from equation (6.3) in equation (6.2), we get,

$$dx = -(y - y_0) \, d\theta \text{ and}$$

$$dy = (x - x_0) \, d\theta \qquad \qquad \ldots (6.4)$$

The values of dx and dy indicate the increment in x and y respectively, to be added in the current point on the arc to get the next point on the arc. Therefore, we can write,

$$x_2 = x_1 + dx$$

$$= x_1 - (y_1 - y_0) \, d\theta$$

$$y_2 = y_1 + dy$$

$$= y_1 + (x_2 - x_0) \, d\theta \qquad \qquad \ldots (6.5)$$

The equation (6.5) forms the basis for arc generation algorithm. From equation (6.5), we can see that the next point on the arc is the function of $d\theta$. To have a smooth curve, the neighboring points on the arc should be close to each other. To get this, the value of $d\theta$ should be small and not to leave gaps in the arc. Usually, the value of $d\theta$ can be determined from the following equation :

$$d\theta = \min (0.01, 1/(3.2 \times (|x - x_0| + |y - y_0|)))$$

1. Read the center of curvature say (x_0, y_0).

2. Read the arc angle, say θ.

3. Read the starting point of the arc, say (x, y).

4. Calculate $d\theta$.

$$d\theta = \min (0.01, 1/(3.2 \times (|x - x_0| + |y - y_0|)))$$

5. Initialize, Angle = 0.

6. While (Angle < θ).

    do

    {   Plot (x, y)

         $x = x - (y - y_0) \times d\theta$

         $y = y + (x - x_0) \times d\theta$

            Angle = Angle + $d\theta$

    }

7. STOP

6.3 INTERPOLATION

In this technique the curve is approximated by a number of small straight line segments. It is possible to draw an approximation to a curve, if an array of sample points are known. Then it can be guessed what the curve should look like between the sample points. If the curve is smooth and the sample points are close together, then a pretty good guess can be made to determine the missing portion of the curve. The guess will probably not be exactly right, but it will be close enough for appearances.

The process is :

• Fill in the portions of the unknown curve with pieces of known curve which pass through the nearby sample points. Since the known and unknown curves share these sample points in a local region, it is assumed that in this region, the two curves look pretty much alike.

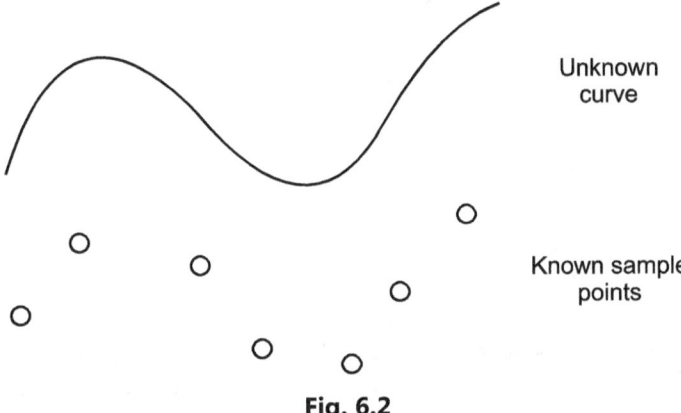

Fig. 6.2

• Fit a portion of the unknown curve with a curve that is known.

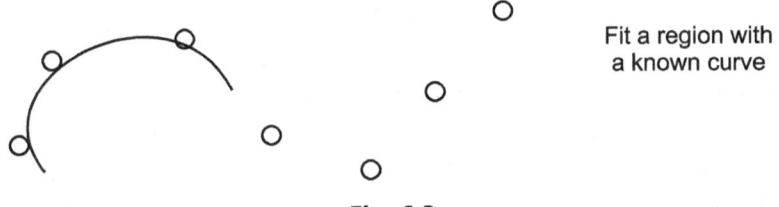

Fig. 6.3

• Now, fill in a gap between the sample points by finding the co-ordinates of point along the known approximating curve.

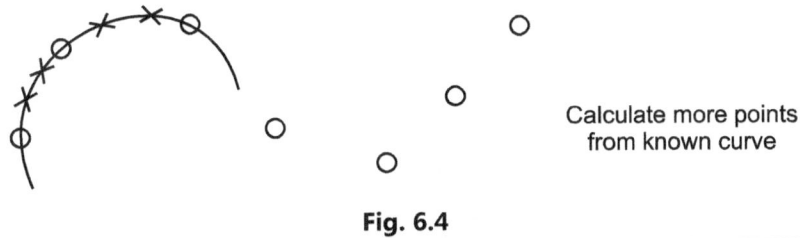

Fig. 6.4

- Connect these points with line segments.

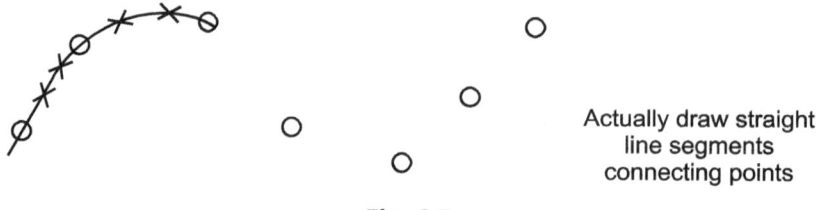

Actually draw straight
line segments
connecting points

Fig. 6.5

To invent a function which can be used for interpolation, consider a polynomial curve that will pass through n sample points.

$$(x_1, y_1, z_1), (x_2, y_2, z_2), \ldots\ldots, (x_n, y_n, z_n)$$

We will construct the function as the sum of terms, one term for each sample point. These functions can be given as,

$$f_x(u) \; = \; \sum_{i=1}^{n} x_i B_i(u)$$

$$f_y(u) \; = \; \sum_{i=1}^{n} y_i B_i(u)$$

$$f_z(u) \; = \; \sum_{i=1}^{n} z_i B_i(u)$$

The function $B_i(u)$ is called '**bending function**'. For each value of parameter u, blending function determines how much the ith sample point affects the position of curve. In other words, we can say that each sample points tries to pull the curve in its direction and the function $B_i(u)$ gives the strength of the pull. If for some value of u, $B_i(u) = 1$ for unique value of i (i.e. $B_i(u) = 0$ for other values of i), then i^{th} sample point has complete control of the curve and the curve will pass through i^{th} sample point. For different value of u, some other sample point may have complete control of the curve. In such case, the curve will pass through that point as well. In general, the blending functions control to each of the sample points in turn for different value of u. Let's assume that the first sample point (x_1, y_1, z_1) has complete control when u = −1, the second when u = 0, the third when u = 1 and so on i.e. when u = −1 $\Rightarrow$ $B_1(u) = 1$ and 0 for u = 0, 1, 2, ..., n − 2.

When u = 0 $\Rightarrow$ $B_2(u) = 1$ and 0 for u = −1, 1, ..., n − 2

$\vdots$

$\vdots$

$\vdots$

When u = (n − 2) $\Rightarrow$ $B_n(u) = 1$ and 0 for u = −1, 0, ..., (n − 1)

To get $B_1(u) = 1$ at $u = -1$ and 0 for $u = 0, 1, 2, ..., n - 2$, the expression for $B_i(u)$ can be given as,

$$B_1(u) = \frac{u(u - 1)(u - 2) \ldots [u - (n - 2)]}{(-1)(-2) \ldots (1 - n)}$$

where denominator term is a constant used. In general form i^{th} bending function which is 1 at $u = i - 2$ and 0 for other integers can be given as,

$$B_i(u) = \frac{(u + 1)(u)(u - 1) \ldots [u - (i - 3)][u - (i - 1)] \ldots [u - (i - 2)]}{(i - 1)(i - 2)(i - 3) \ldots (1)(-1)(i - n)}$$

The approximation of the curve using above expression is called **Lagrange interpolation**.

From the above expression blending functions for four sample points can be given as,

$$B_1(u) = \frac{u(u - 1)(u - 2)}{(-1)(-2)(-3)}$$

$$B_2(u) = \frac{(u + 1)(u - 1)(u - 2)}{1(-1)(-2)}$$

$$B_3(u) = \frac{(u + 1)u(u - 2)}{(2)(1)(-1)}$$

$$B_4(u) = \frac{(u + 1)u(u - 1)}{(3)(2)(1)}$$

Using above blending functions, the expression for the curve passing through sampling points can be realized as follows :

$$x = x_1 B_1(u) + x_2 B_2(u) + x_3 B_3(u) + x_4 B_4(u)$$

$$y = y_1 B_1(u) + y_2 B_2(u) + y_3 B_3(u) + y_4 B_4(u)$$

$$z = z_1 B_1(u) + z_2 B_2(u) + z_3 B_3(u) + z_4 B_4(u)$$

It is possible to get intermediate points between two sampling points between two sampling points by taking values of u between the values of u related to the two sample points under consideration. For example, we can find the intermediate points between second and third sample points for which values of u are 0 and 1 respectively; by taking value of u between 0 and 1, this is shown below.

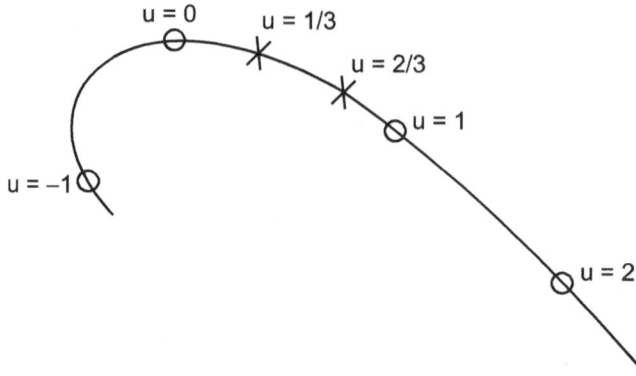

Fig. 6.6

The subsequent intermediate points can be obtained by repeating the same procedure. Finally, the points obtained by this procedure are joined by small straight line segments to get the approximated curve.

6.4 INTERPOLATING ALGORITHMS

To implement the curve-drawing program, the same blending function values are needed for each section of the curve that is drawn. If each section is approximated by three straight-line segments then each section will require the blending function values for u at 0, 1/3, 2/3 and 1 as shown below.

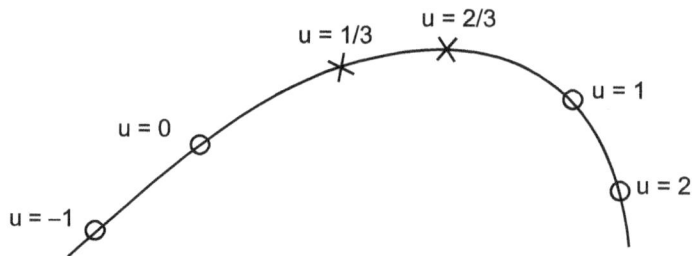

Fig. 6.7

These values are calculated once and saved in an array for use in drawing each curve section.

The first algorithm SET-SMOOTH allows the user to specify how many straight-line segments should be used to complete a section of the curve. This number will tell the u values at which to calculate and save the blending function values. The blending function values needed for the first and last sections of the curve are also calculated and stored in arrays.

The second algorithm MAKE-CURVE multiplies the sample points and blending function which generates points on the approximation curve. These points are then connected by line segments. After a section of the curve has been drawn, the sample points are shifted so that the blending functions can be applied to the next section, which is accomplished by third algorithm NEXT-SECTION.

To start drawing the algorithm, we require the first four sample points. With these sample points and arrays the first two curve sections can be drawn using the next routine START-CURVE. It expects an arguments array containing the first four sample points. It loads these points into another array and then the pen is positioned at the first sample point and then algorithm is used to draw the first two sections of the curve. The sample points are then shifted to prepare for drawing the next curve section.

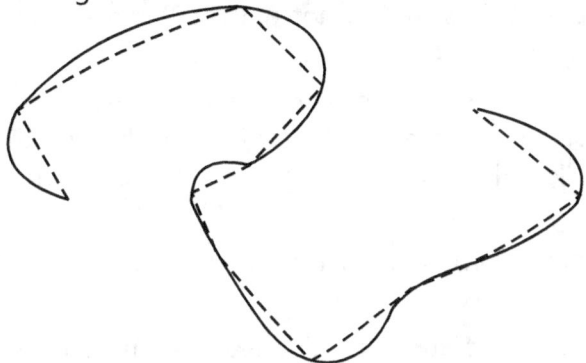

Fig. 6.8 : Interpolation smoothing

Once the curve has been started new sections can be added one at a time. For each new sample point, a new section of the curve can be drawn. Since we are adding the fourth sample point while interpolating between the second and third sample points, the section of the curve being drawn always lags one sample point behind the points entered. The routine PUT-IN-SM is used to place sample points in arrays. The curve may be extended as desired by repeated calls to a routine CURVE-ABS but when we are ready to end it, we must process the last section. This can be done by using the END-CURVE routine, which takes as an argument the last point on the curve.

6.5 INTERPOLATING POLYGONS

The blending function can be used to round the sides of a polygon. It is easier to deal with a polygon since no special initial or final section occurs. We just step around the polygon, smooth out each side by replacing it with several small line segments. We start with a polygon that has only few sides and end up with a polygon which has many more sides and appears smoother as shown below.

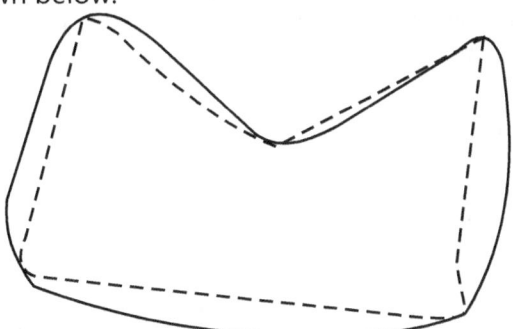

Fig. 6.9 : Smoothing of a polygon

6.6 B-SPLINE

The language interpolation program produces various inadequacies. In this method the sum of the blending function is not 1 at every value of u. The blending functions were designed to sum at 1 for integer values of u and not a fractional value. Each section of the curve is connected to the next section at a sample point. It is not necessary that the slope of two sections match at this point. Thus, we do not get a completely smooth curve, if there are corners at the sample points. The control of curve depends on u.

To get the smooth control over the curve, the curves must be pulled onto the neighbourhood of sample point rather than force it to go through the point. Then the result will be a curve which follow the general contours indicated by the sample points but may not actually pass through the points.

A set of blending function which follows the above approach and always sum to 1 are referred as B-splines.

For most of the applications the cubic B-spline are adequate. The cubic B-spline blending functions interpolate over four sample points and are cubic polynomials in u.

The B-spine generate curve sections which have continuous slopes so that they fit together smoothly.

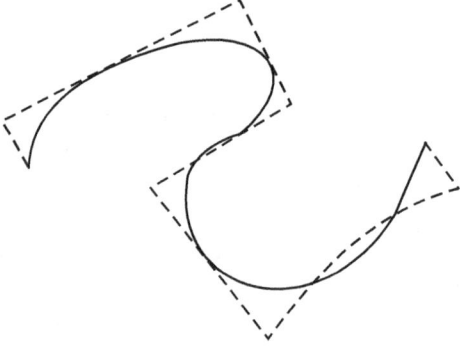

Fig. 6.10

The following is an example of a five-segment B-spline curve (although this is simply a hand-drawn example). The points which indicate the ends of the individual curve segments and thus the joined points are known as the knots.

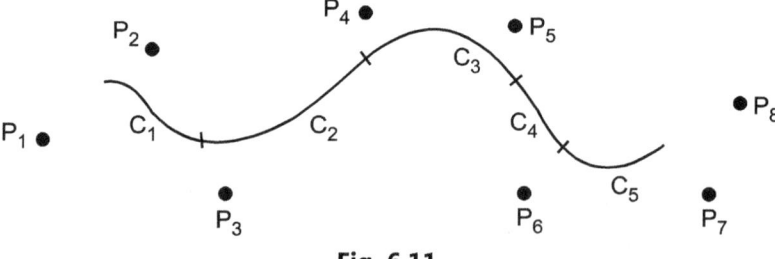

Fig. 6.11

Each curve segment is determined by four control points, as follows.

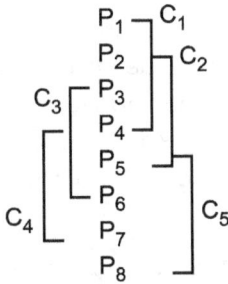

Fig. 6.12

6.6.1 Properties of B-spline Curve

- The sum of the B-spline basis functions for any parameter value u is 1.

    i.e. $$\sum_{i=1}^{n+1} N_{i,k}(u) = 1$$

- Each basis function is positive or zero for all parameter values i.e. $N_{i,k} \geq 0$.

- Except for k = 1 each basis function has precisely one maximum value.

- The maximum order of the curve is equal to the number of vertices of defining polygon.

- The degree of B-spline polynomial is independent of the number of vertices of defining polygon (with certain limitations).

- B-spline allows local control over surface because each vertex affects the shape of a curve only over a range of parameter values where its associated basis function is non-zero.

- The curve exhibits the variation diminishing property. Thus, the curve does not oscillate about any straight line move often than its defining polygon.

- The curve generally follows the shape of defining polygon.

- Any transformation can be applied to the curve by applying it to the vertices of defining polygon.

- The curve line within the convex hull of its defining polygon.

6.6.2 Triadic Curves

There are two triadic curves :

1.   B-spline curve

2.   Bezier curve

B-spline Curve Functions :

The B-spline basis is non-global because each vertex B_i is associated with a unique basis function. Thus, each vertex affects the shape of the curve only over a range of parameter values where its associated basis function is non-zero. This function allows the degree of the resulting curve to be independent of the number of vertices. It is possible to change the degree of the resulting curve without changing the numbers of vertices of the defining polygon.

If P(u) be the position vectors along the curve as a function of the parameter u, a B-spline curve is given by,

$$P(u) = \sum_{i=1}^{n+1} B_i \, N_{i,k}(u) \quad u_{min} \le u < u_{max}; \; 2 \le k \le n + 1$$

where, B_i are the position vectors of the n + 1 defining polygon vertices and the $N_{i,k}$ are the normalized B-spline basis functions.

For the ith normalized B-spline basis function of order k, the basis function $N_{i,k}(u)$ are defined as,

$$N_{i,1}(u) = \begin{cases} 1 & \text{if } x_i \le u < x_i + 1 \\ 0 & \text{Otherwise} \end{cases}$$

and

$$N_{i,k}(u) = \frac{(u - x_1) \, N_{i,k-1}(u)}{x_{i+k-1} - x_i} + \frac{(x_{i+k} - u) \, N_{i+1,k-1}(u)}{x_{i+k} - x_{i+1}}$$

The values of x_i are the elements of a knot vector, satisfying the relation $x_i \le x_{i+1}$. The parameter u varies from u_{min} to u_{max} along the curve P(u). The choice of knot vector has a significant influence on the B-spline basis functions $N_{i,k}(u)$ and hence on the resulting B-spline curve.

6.6.3 Techniques of Smoothing Curve using B-spline

To ensure a smooth transition from one section of a piecewise parametric curve to the next, we can impose various continuity conditions at the connection points.

In geometric continuity we require parametric derivatives of two sections to be proportional to each other at their common boundary instead of equal to each other. Parametric continuity is set by matching the parametric derivatives of adjoining two curve sections at their common boundary. In zero order parametric continuity, given as c^0, it means simply the curve meet and same is for zero order geometric continuity. In first order parametric continuity called as c^1 means that first parametric derivatives of the co-ordinate functions for two successive curve sections are equal to the joining proportional at the intersection of two successive sections. Second order parametric continuity or c^2 continuity means that both the first and second parametric derivatives of the two curve sections are same at the intersection and for second order geometric continuity or c^2 continuity means that both the first and second parametric derivatives of the two curve sections are proportional at their boundary. Under c^2 continuity curvature of the two curve sections match at the joining positions.

Two curves

$$r(t) = (t^2 - 2t, t)$$

$$n(t) = (t^2 + 1, t + 1)$$

Fig. 6.13 (a) : Zero order continuity

Derivative

$$r(t) = 2t - 2, 1$$

$$r(1) = 2 - 2, 1$$

$$= 0, 1$$

Fig. 6.13 (b) : First order continuity

Derivative

$$n(t) = 2t, 1$$

$$n(0) = 0, 1$$

Fig. 6.13 (c) : Second order continuity

6.6.4 B-spline and Corners

The B-spline blending functions were designed to eliminate sharp corners in the curve and the curve does not usually pass through sample points. However, a sharp corner and passage through a sample point can be produced in a B-spline curve.

The B-spline function is non-global because each vertex B_i is associated with a unique basis function. Thus, each vertex affects the shape of the curve only over a range of parameter values where its associated basis function is non-zero. The degree of resulting curve is independent of the number of vertices. It is possible to change the degree of the resulting curve without changing the number of vertices of the defining polygon.

The call,

CURVE – ABS – 3 (x_0, y_0, z_0) produces one sample point at (x_0, y_0, z_0) pulling the curve in that direction as shown below.

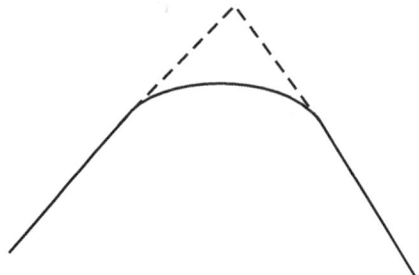

Fig. 6.14 : One point

The two calls,

CURVE – ABS – 3 (x_0, y_0, z_0)

CURVE – ABS – 3 (x_0, y_0, z_0)

produces two sample points, both will pull the curve to the same place. Thus, the curve will be pulled closer to this point (x_0, y_0, z_0) and the corner will look little shaper.

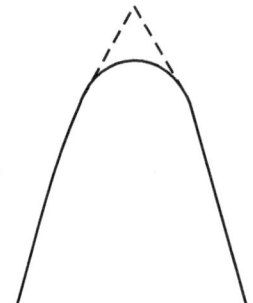

Fig. 6.15 : Two points

If three identical calls are made,

CURVE – ABS – 3 (x_0, y_0, z_0)

CURVE – ABS – 3 (x_0, y_0, z_0)

CURVE – ABS – 3 (x_0, y_0, z_0)

The curve will be pulled at the point (x_0, y_0, z_0) as shown below.

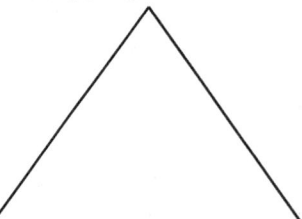

Fig. 6.16 : Three points

The disadvantages of blending function are as follows :

- Requires very complicated mathematical form.
- Large amount of display-file storage is required.

6.7 BEZIER CURVE

Bezier curve is an another approach for the construction of the curve. These curves are widely available in various CAD systems and in general graphic packages.

Consider cubic Bezier curve, as it is adequate for most graphics applications. It needs four control points. These four points completely specify the Bezier curve. But the addition of extra point is not possible in this curve. The Bezier curve and its control points are shown below.

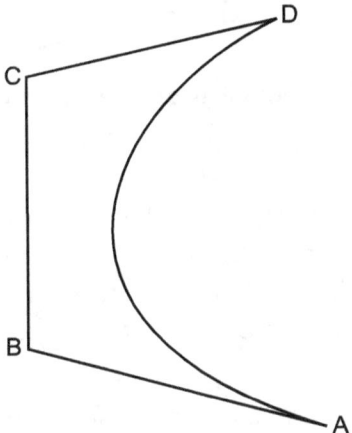

Fig. 6.17 : Bezier curve

The curve begins at the first control point and ends on the fourth point. Thus, to connect two Bezier curve join the first control point of the second curve to the last control point of the first curve. As shown in above Fig. 6.17 at the start of the curve, it is tangent to the line connecting first and second control points, similarly at the other end, it is tangent to the connecting the third and fourth control points. Thus, to join two Bezier curves smoothly, the third and fourth control points of the first curve must be arranged on the same line as the first and second control points of the second curve. The Bezier curve can be better described by the equations given below :

$$X = x_4u^3 + 3x_3u^2 (1 - u) + 3x_2 u (1 - u)^2 + x_1 (1 - u)^3$$
$$Y = y_4u^3 + 3y_3u^2 (1 - u) + 3y_2u (1 - u)^2 + y_1 (1 - u)^3$$
$$Z = z_4u^3 + 3z_3u^2 (1 - u) + 3z_2 u (1 - u)^2 + z_1 (1 - u)^3$$

In the above expression, as u increases from 0 to 1, the curve moves from the first to the fourth control points.

The another way to construct Bezier curve is by taking the mid-points. In this method, the above equations are not needed.

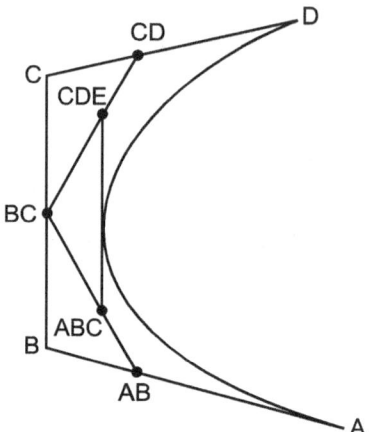

Fig. 6.18 : Subdivision of a bezier curve

As shown in the above diagram, the points A, B, C, D are the original Bezier curve control points. Here, we are having three lines AB, BC and CD then we have to find the mid-points of these lines as 'P', 'Q' and 'R' respectively. After that we have to join PQ and QR. Then again find the mid-point of these newly generated lines as 'S' and 'U'. Then form a line segment between 'S' and 'U'. And find mid-point of this line as 'T'. Now point 'T' will be on Bezier curve. This point 'T' divides the curve into two sections one is (A, P, S and T) and second will be (D, R, U and T).

Thus, by taking mid-points, we can find a point on the curve and also split the curve into two sections. We can continue to split the curve into smaller sections, until we have sections so short that they can be replaced by straight lines or till the size of section is not greater than the size of pixel.

6.7.1 Basic Properties of Bezier Curve

- **Control Points :** The Bezier curve are hard to use because not all the control points lie on the curve. The control points also satisfy two important mathematics properties : the curve does pass through two end points (P_0 and P_n) and the curve is tangent at the end points to the corresponding edge of the polygon of control points.

- **Multiple Values :** The parametric formulation of the Bezier curve allows it to represent multiple valued shapes. In fact, if the first and last control points coincide, the curve is closed.

- **Axis Independence :** A Bezier curve is independent of the co-ordinate system used to measure the locations of the control points.

- **Global or Local Control Points :** These curves do not provide localized control. Moving any control point will change the shape of every part of the curve.

- **Variation Diminishing Property :** Bezier curves are variation diminishing; a curve is guaranteed to lie within the convex null of the control points that define it. Thus, the Bezier curve never oscillates wildly away from its defining control points.

- **Versatility :** The versatility of Bezier curve is governed by the number of control points used.

- **Order of Continuity :** Bezier curve of modest order can be pieced together to describe a more complex curve. In these cases, the joints between the curves must be smooth. To achieve zero order continuity at a joint, it is necessary only to make the end control points of the two curves coincide.

6.7.2 Comparison of Bezier and B-spline Curve

Bezier Curve	B-spline Curve
1. Basis functions are real.	1. Basis function is positive or zero for all parameter values.
2. Degree of the polynomial defining the curve segment is one less than the number of defining polygon points.	2. Degree of B-spline polynomial is independent on the number of vertices of defining polygon.
3. Curve generally does not follow the shape of the defining polygon.	3. Curve generally follows the shape of the defining polygon.
4. Curve is invariant under an affine transformation.	4. Any affine transformation can be applied to the curve by applying it to the vertices of polygon.

6.7.3 Examples on Bezier Curve

Example 6.1 : Obtain the curve parameters for drawing a smooth Bezier curve for the following control points :

A (0, 0); B (10, 40); C (70, 30); D (60, −20)

Solution :

Equation of the Bezier curve is,

$$P(u) = (1 - u)^3 P_1 + 3u (1 - u)^2 + 3u^2 (1 - u) P_3 + u^3 P_4$$

Let us take $u = 0, \dfrac{1}{4}, \dfrac{1}{2}, \dfrac{3}{4}$

$$P(0) = P_1 = (0, 0)$$

$$P\left(\frac{1}{4}\right) = \left(1 - \frac{1}{4}\right)^3 P_1 + 3\frac{1}{4}\left(1 - \frac{1}{4}\right)^2 P_2 + 3\left(\frac{1}{4}\right)^2 P_3 + \left(\frac{1}{4}\right)^3 P_4$$

$$= \frac{27}{64}(0, 0) + \frac{27}{64}(10, 40) + \frac{9}{64}(70, 30) + \frac{1}{64}(60, -20)$$

$$= \left[\frac{27}{64} \times 0 + \frac{27}{64} \times 10 + \frac{9}{64} \times 70 + \frac{1}{64} \times 60\right.$$

$$\left.\frac{27}{64} \times 0 + \frac{27}{64} \times 40 + \frac{9}{64} \times 30 + \frac{1}{64} \times (-20)\right]$$

$$= \left[\frac{0 + 270 + 630 + 60}{64}, \frac{0 + 1040 + 270 - 20}{64}\right]$$

$$= (15, 20.15)$$

$$P\left(\frac{1}{2}\right) = \left(1 - \frac{1}{2}\right)^3 P_1 + 3\frac{1}{2}\left(1 - \frac{1}{2}\right)^2 P_2 + 3\left(\frac{1}{2}\right)^2\left(1 - \frac{1}{2}\right) P_3 + \left(\frac{1}{2}\right)^3 P_4$$

$$= \frac{1}{8}(0, 0) + \frac{3}{8}(10, 40) + \frac{3}{8}(70, 30) + \frac{1}{8}(60, -10)$$

$$= \left[\frac{1}{8} \times 0 + \frac{3}{8} \times 10 + \frac{3}{8} \times 70 + \frac{1}{8} \times 60, \times\frac{1}{8} \times 0 + \right.$$

$$\left.\frac{3}{8} \times 40 + \frac{3}{8} \times 30 + \frac{1}{8} \times (-10)\right]$$

$$= \left(\frac{30 + 210 + 60}{8}, \frac{120 + 90 - 20}{8}\right)$$

$$= (37.5, 23.75)$$

$$P\left(\frac{3}{4}\right) = \frac{1}{64} P_1 + \frac{9}{64} P_2 + \frac{27}{64} P_3 + \frac{27}{64} P_4$$

$$= \frac{1}{64}(0, 0) + \frac{9}{64}(10, 40) + \frac{27}{64}(70, 30) + \frac{27}{64}(60, -20)$$

$$= \left(\frac{90 + 1890 + 1620}{64}, \frac{360 + 810 - 540}{64}\right)$$

$$= (56.25, 9.8)$$

Example 6.2 : Obtain the curve parameters for drawing a smooth Bezier curve for the following control points : A (1, 1); B (2, 3); C (4, 3) and D (6, 4).

Solution :

The equation of the Bezier curve is given as,

$$P(u) = (1 - 4)^3 P_1 + 3u (1 - 4)^2 P_2 + 3u_2 (1 - 4) P_3 + u^3 P_4$$

$$\text{for } 0 \leq u \leq 1$$

where, P(u) is the point on the curve P_1, P_2, P_3, P_4.

$$\text{Consider } u = 0, \frac{1}{4}, \frac{1}{2}, \frac{3}{4}$$

$\therefore$

$$P(0) = P_1 = (1, 1)$$

$$P\left(\frac{1}{4}\right) = \left(1 - \frac{1}{4}\right)^3 P_1 + 3\frac{1}{4}\left(1 - \frac{1}{4}\right)^2 P_2 \left(\frac{1}{4}\right)^2$$

$$+ 3\left(1 - \frac{1}{4}\right) P_3 + \left(\frac{1}{4}\right)^3 P_4$$

$$= \frac{27}{64}(1, 1) + \frac{27}{64}(2, 3) + \frac{9}{64}(4, 3) + \frac{1}{64}(6, 4)$$

$$= \left[\frac{27}{64} \times 1 + \frac{27}{64} \times 2 + \frac{9}{64} \times 4 + \frac{1}{64} \times 6, \right.$$

$$\left. \frac{27}{64} \times 1 + \frac{27}{64} \times 3 + \frac{9}{64} \times 3 + \frac{1}{64} \times 4\right]$$

$$= \left(\frac{123}{64}, \frac{134}{64}\right)$$

$$= (1.9218, 2.1718)$$

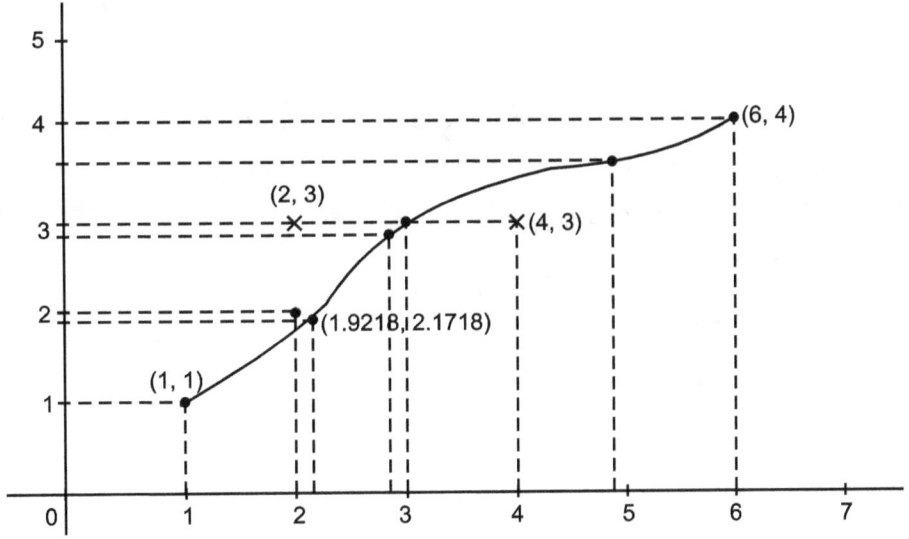

Fig. 6.19

6.8 FRACTALS

The objects which are having smooth surfaces and regular shapes are generally described by using equations. But natural objects such as mountains, trees, oceans, waves and clouds have irregular shapes. It will be very difficult to draw these shapes by using normal equations. There are many methods of modeling these natural objects, but one of the most interesting from a mathematical perspective is that of fractals. So we can describe natural objects by using fractals, where procedures rather than equations are used to model the objects. Procedurally defined objects have characteristics quite different from objects described with equations.

One of the basic properties that characterize fractals is self-similarity. The self similarity property of an object can take different forms, depending on the choice of fractal representation. Self-similarity means we zoom into a piece of a fractal, we will keep seeing the same structure repeated over and over.

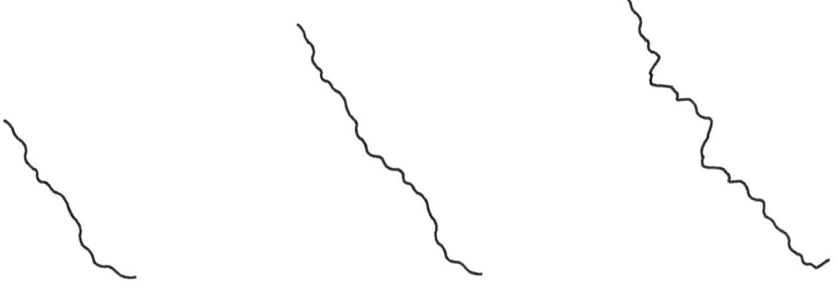

Fig. 6.20

For a certain distance we will see a coastline as a simple, quite smooth line see above Fig. 6.20. But as we go near to that line, it will appear more rough. If we take a more closer view we will see the whole line as jaggy and rough. There is no limit for the times we can zoom in.

6.8.1 Classification of Fractals

The fractals can be classified as,

- Self similar

- Self affine and

- Invariant.

- **Self Similar Fractals :**

These fractals have parts those are scaled down versions of the entire object. In these fractals, objects subparts are constructed by applying a scaling parameter s to the overall initial shape. It is a choice of user to use the same scaling factor s for all subparts, or use different scaling factors for different scaled-down parts of the object. Another subclass of self similar fractals is a statistically self-similar fractals, in which user can also apply random variations to the scaled-down subparts. These fractals are commonly used to model-trees, shrubs and other plants.

- **Self-Affine Fractals :**

These fractals have parts those are formed with different scaling parameter, s_x, s_y, z_z in different co-ordinate directions. In these fractals, we can also apply random variations to obtain statistically self-affine fractals. These fractals are commonly used to model water, clouds and terrain.

- **Invarient Fractals :**

In these fractals, non-linear transformation is used. It includes self-squaring fractals such as the Mandelbrot set, which are formed with squaring functions in complex space, and self-inverse fractals, form with inversion procedures.

6.8.2 Fractal Dimension

It is the second measure of an object dimension. Imagine that a line segment of length L is divided into N identical pieces. The length of each line segment l can be given as,

$$l = \frac{L}{N}$$

The ratio of length of original line segment and the length of each part of the line segment is referred to as scaling factor and is given as,

$$s = \frac{L}{l}$$

From above two equations, we can write,

$$N = s$$

i.e. $$N = s^1$$

In other words, we can say that if we scale a line segment by a factor 1/s then we have to add N pieces together to get the original line segment. If we scale square object by a factor 1/s, we will get a small square. In case of s = 2, we require 4 pieces of square to get original square.

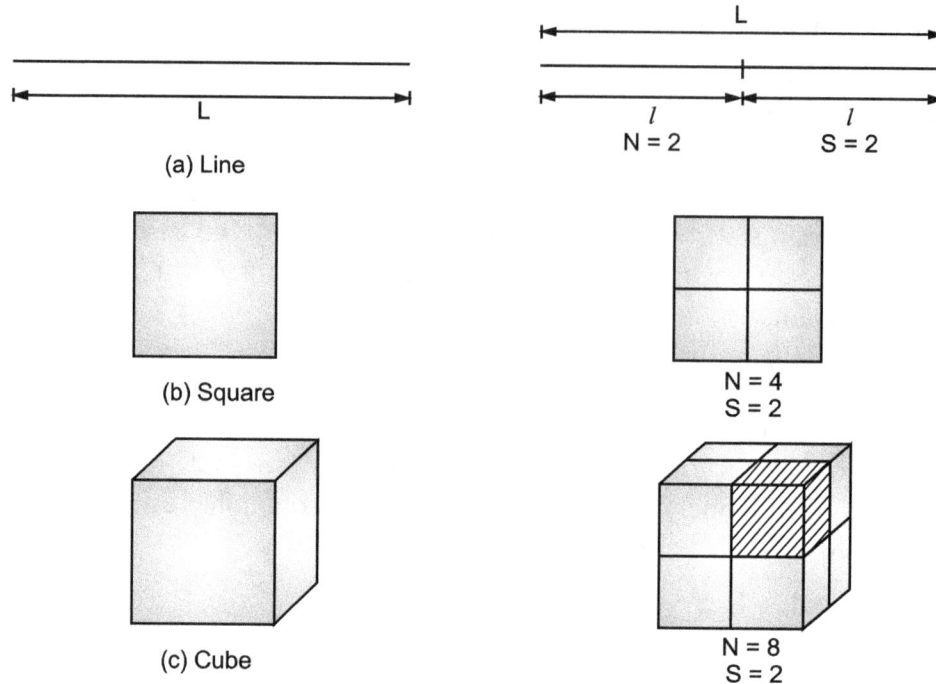

Fig. 6.21 : Scaling of objects in various dimensions

In general, we can write,

$$N = s^2$$

Similarly, for cubical object, we have,

$$N = s^3$$

We have seen that we can specify the dimension of the object by variable D. Here, the exponent of s is a measure of object dimension. Thus, we can write,

$$N = s^D$$

Solving for D, we get,

$$D = \log N / \log s$$

This D is called as **Fractal dimension**.

6.8.3 Fractal Lines

The computer can easily generate self-similar fractal curves. The self-similar drawing can be done by calling a recursive procedure. Consider a curve consist of N self-similar pieces, each scaled by 1/s. This can be drawn by a routine which calls itself N times with arguments scaled by 1/s. In the computer routine each recursive call has smaller arguments i.e. smaller length. There will be some point where the length becomes smaller than the size of a pixel.

Since the wiggles will be smaller than a pixel and cannot be displayed, hence there is no need to continue the recursion beyond this, so the computer procedure can terminate when lengths become less than a pixel and still provide the computer's best approximation to the fractal.

Thus, using computer the user can easily generate realistic coastlines or mountain peaks or lightning bolts without concern for all the small bends and wiggles. The computer can generate the wiggles. The user needs only to provide the end points.

6.8.4 Fractal Surfaces

A fractal line is suitable for the path of a lightning bolt but for something like a three-dimensional mountain range, there is a need of fractal surface. There are several ways to generate fractal surface. The one method is based on triangles given three vertex points in space, we shall generate a fractal surface for the area between them. There are methods for decomposing arbitrary polygons into triangles, hence the method can be used to cover more general shapes. The method is as follows :

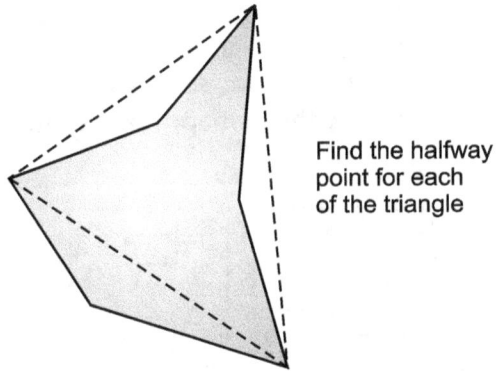

Find the halfway point for each of the triangle

Fig. 6.22 : Find the halfway point for each of the triangle

Diagram considers each edge of the triangle. A fractal line can be imagined along each line and then compute its halfway point by the same means as used for fractal lines.

Now by connecting these halfway points with line segments, we can subdivide the surface into four smaller triangles as shown below.

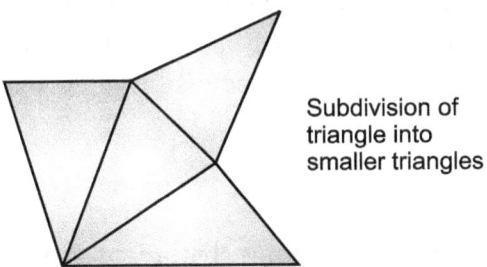

Subdivision of triangle into smaller triangles

Fig. 6.23 : Subdivision of triangle into smaller triangles

Koch – Snowflake Curve : This curve is drawn by dividing line into 4 equal segments are adjusted so that they form adjacent sides of an equilateral triangle.

Fig. 6.24 : First Approximation

The above process is repeater for each of four segments so as to get second approximation.

Fig. 6.25 : Second approximation

This curve is also known as triadic curve as the middle third of line segments are modified. Length of this curve is infinite. It doesnot deviate from its original shape.

Hilbert curve

A Hilbert curve (also known as a Hilbert space-filling curve) is a continuousfractalspace-filling curve. It can be constructed by following successive approximations. If the square is divided into four quadrants we can draw the first approximation by connecting center points of each quadrant.

Fig. 6.26 : Third Approximation to Hilberts Curve

The second approximation to this curve can be drawn by dividing each of quadrants and connecting their centers. The above figure shows third approximation which is gained by subdividing the quadrants again.

Advances in Gaming:

- **Facial Recognition:**

3D camera allows developers to create games that adapt to the emotions of the gamer by scanning different points on persons face.

- **Gesture Control:**

It allow users to connect with their gaming experience.

- **High-Defination Display:**

Now a days, televisions with higher features are available to watch or play the game. Pixel capacity is increased.

- **Wearable Gaming:**

It is direct or indirect view of physical, real-world environment whose elements are augmented by computer input such as graphics card.

Gaming Platforms:

NVIDIA Workstation:

The NVIDIA Tesla K10 graphics processing unit (GPU) accelerator is a PCI Express, double-wide, full height (4.376 inches by 10.5 inches by 1.52 inches) form factor computing module comprising two NVIDIA GK104 GPUs. The Tesla K10 offers a total of 8 GB of GDDR5 on-board memory (4 GB per GPU) and supports PCI Express Gen3. The Tesla K10 can be configured by the OEM or by the end user to enable or disable ECC or error correcting codes that can fix single-bit errors and detect double-bit errors. Enabling ECC will cause some of the memory to be used for the ECC bits, so the user available memory will decrease by 10%. On the Tesla K10 the ECC protection is for DRAM only

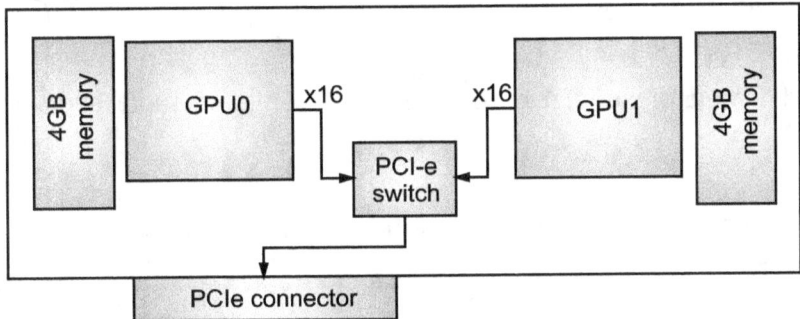

Fig. 6.27 : Block Diagram for Tesla K10 GPU accelerator

Above figure is the block diagram for Tesla K10 GPU accelerator. It comprises two identical GK104 GPUs, each with 4 GB of GDDR5 memory. The GPUs are connected via a PCI Express switch. The board supports PCI Express Gen3.

I860

The Intel i860 Microprocessor architecture balances integer, floating-point and graphics performance. The applications of i860 include scientific computing, 3D graphics workstation, and multiprocessor systems. On a single chip it includes: Integer Operations, Floating-point operations, Graphics operations, Management of memory and Data and instruction catches. It includes RISC integer core processing unit with one clock instruction execution.

It supports vector floating point operations without special vector instructions by using on-chip data cache and a variety of parallel techniques.

6.9 COMPUTER GRAPHICS TOOLS

6.9.1 Introduction

Autodesk Maya commonly shortened to Maya, is 3D computer graphics software that runs on Windows, Mac OS and Linux, originally developed by Alias Systems Corporation (formerly Alias|Wavefront) and currently owned and developed by Autodesk, Inc. It is used to create interactive 3D applications, including video games, animated film, TV series, or visual .Maya is an application used to generate 3D assets for use in film, television, game development and architecture. Users define a virtual workspace (scene) to implement and edit media of a particular project. Scenes can be saved in a variety of formats, the default being .mb (Maya Binary). Maya exposes a node graph architecture. Scene elements are node-based, each node having its own attributes and customization. As a result, the visual representation of a scene is based entirely on a network of interconnecting nodes, depending on each other's information. For the convenience of viewing these networks, there is a dependency and a directed acyclic graph.

6.9.2 Components

Since its consolidation from two distinct packages, Maya and later contain all the features of the now defunct Unlimited suites.

Fluid Effects

A realistic fluid simulator (effective for smoke, fire, clouds and explosions, added in Maya 4.5)

Classic Cloth

Cloth simulation to automatically simulate clothing and fabrics moving realistically over an animated character.

Fur

Animal fur simulation similar to Maya Hair. It can be used to simulate other fur-like objects, such as grass.

nHair

A simulator for realistic-looking human hair implemented using curves and Paint Effects. These are also known as dynamic curves.

Maya Live

A set of motion tracking tools for CG matching to clean plate footage.

nCloth

Added in version 8.5, nCloth is the first implementation of Maya Nucleus, Autodesk's simulation framework. nCloth gives the artist further control of cloth and material simulations.

nParticle

Added in version 2009, nParticle is addendum to Maya Nucleus toolset. nParticle is for simulating a wide range of complex 3D effects, including liquids, clouds, smoke, spray, and dust.

MatchMover

Added to Maya 2010, this enables compositing of CGI elements with motion data from video and film sequences.

Camera Sequencer

Added in Autodesk Maya 2011, Camera Sequencer is used to layout multiple camera shots and manage them in one animation sequence.

6.9.3 Maya Embedded Language

Alongside its more recognized visual workflow, Maya is equipped with a cross-platform scripting language, called Maya Embedded Language. MEL is provided for scripting and a means to customize the core functionality of the software, since many of the tools and commands used are written in it. Code can be used to engineer modifications, plug-ins or be injected into runtime.

6.9.4 System Requirements

Operating Systems

Autodesk supports the Windows (XP SP3 or later), Mac, and Linux platforms. As of Maya 2011, the software is 64-bit under Mac OS X. On Linux, the supported distributions are Red Hat and Fedora, 64-bit.

6.9.5 3D Studio Max

Introduction

- Autodesk 3ds Max, formerly 3D Studio Max, is 3D computer graphics software for making 3D animations, models, and images.

- It was developed and produced by Autodesk Media and Entertainment.

- It has modeling capabilities, a flexible plugin architecture and can be used on the Microsoft Windows platform. I

- It is frequently used by video game developers, TV commercial studios and architectural visualization studios. It is also used for movie effects and movie pre-visualization.

- In addition to its modeling and animation tools, the latest version of 3ds Max also features shaders (such as ambient occlusion and subsurface scattering), dynamic simulation, particle systems, radiosity, normal map creation and rendering, global illumination, a customizable user interface, and its own scripting language.

Features:

- **MAXScript**

  MAXScript is a built-in scripting language that can be used to automate repetitive tasks, combine existing functionality in new ways, develop new tools and user interfaces, and much more. Plugin modules can be created entirely within MAXScript.

- **Character Studio**

  Character Studio was a plugin which since version 4 of Max is now integrated in 3D Studio Max, helping users to animate virtual characters.

- **Scene Explorer**

  Scene Explorer, a tool that provides a hierarchical view of scene data and analysis, facilitates working with more complex scenes.

- **DWG Import**

  3ds Max supports both import and linking of DWG files. Improved memory management in 3ds Max 2008 enables larger scenes to be imported with multiple objects.

- **Texture Assignment/Editing**

  3ds Max offers operations for creative texture and planar mapping, including tiling, mirroring, decals, angle, rotate, blur, UV stretching, and relaxation; Remove Distortion; Preserve UV; and UV template image export.

- **General Keyframing**

  Two keying modes — set key and auto key — offer support for different keyframing workflows.

  Fast and intuitive controls for keyframing — including cut, copy, and paste — let the user create animations with ease. Animation trajectories may be viewed and edited directly in the viewport.

- **Constrained Animation**

  Objects can be animated along curves with controls for alignment, banking, velocity, smoothness, and looping, and along surfaces with controls for alignment.

- **Skinning**

  Either the Skin or Physique modifier may be used to achieve precise control of skeletal deformation, so the character deforms smoothly as joints are moved, even in the most challenging areas, such as shoulders.

- **Skeletons and Inverse Kinematics (IK)**

  Characters can be rigged with custom skeletons using 3ds Max bones, IK solvers, and rigging tools powered by Motion Capture Data.

All animation tools — including expressions, scripts, list controllers, and wiring — can be used along with a set of utilities specific to bones to build rigs of any structure and with custom controls, so animators see only the UI necessary to get their characters animated.

- **Integrated Cloth Solver**

  It enables the user to turn almost any 3D object into clothing, or build garments from scratch. Collision solving is fast and accurate even in complex simulations

- **Integration with Autodesk Vault**

  Autodesk Vault plug-in, which ships with 3ds Max, consolidates users' 3ds Max assets in a single location, enabling them to automatically track files and manage work in progress. Users can easily and safely share, find, and reuse 3ds Max (and design) assets in a large-scale production or visualization environment.

Use:

- Many recent films have made use of 3ds Max, or previous versions of the program under previous names, in CGI animation, such as Avatar and 2012, which contain computer generated graphics from 3ds Max alongside live-action acting.

- 3ds Max has also been used in the development of 3D computer graphics for a number of video games.

- Architectural and engineering design firms use 3ds Max for developing concept art and previsualization.

Standard Primitives:

Box :	Produces a rectangular prism. An alternative variation of box, called Cube, proportionally constrains the length, width and height of the box.
Cylinder :	Produces a cylinder.
Torus :	Produces a torus – or a ring – with a circular cross section, sometimes referred to as a doughnut.
Teapot :	Produces a Utah teapot. Since the teapot is a parametric object, the user can choose which parts of the teapot to display after creation. These parts include the body, handle, spout and lid.
Cone :	Produces upright or inverted cones.
Sphere :	Produces a full sphere, hemisphere, or other portion of a

	sphere.
Tube :	Produces round or prismatic tubes. The tube is similar to the cylinder with a hole in it.
Pyramid :	Produces a pyramid with a square or rectangular base and triangular sides.
Plane :	Produces a special type of flat polygon mesh that can be enlarged by any amount at render time. The user can specify factors to magnify the size or number of segments, or both. Modifiers such as displace can be added to a plane to simulate a hilly terrain.
Geosphere :	Produces spheres and hemispheres based on three classes of regular polyhedrons.

6.9.6 Introduction to OpenGL ES:

Open GL is used to develop modern graphics applications. Before drawing things, we need to initialize OpenGL. This is done by creating an OpenGL context, which is essentially a state machine that stores all data related to the rendering of your application.

The first thing to do when starting a new OpenGL project is to dynamically link with OpenGL.

Windows: Add opengl32.lib to your linker input

Linux: Include -lGL in your compiler options

OS X: Add -framework OpenGL to your compiler options

OpenGL ES is a royalty-free, cross-platform API for full-function 2D and 3D graphics on embedded systems - including consoles, phones, appliances and vehicles. It consists of well-defined subsets of desktop OpenGL, creating a flexible and powerful low-level interface between software and graphics acceleration. OpenGL ES includes profiles for floating-point and fixed-point systems and the EGL™ specification for portably binding to native windowing systems. OpenGL ES 1.X is for fixed function hardware and offers acceleration, image quality and performance. OpenGL ES 2.X enables full programmable 3D graphics. OpenGL SC is tuned for the safety critical market.

Specifications:

Because extensions vary from platform to platform and driver to driver, OpenGL ES segregates headers for each API version into a header for the core API (OpenGL ES 1.0, 1.1, 2.0, 3.0, 3.1 and 3.2) and a separate header defining extension interfaces for that core API. These header files are supplied here for developers and platform vendors. They define interfaces including enumerates, prototypes, and for platforms supporting dynamic runtime extension queries, such as Linux and Microsoft Windows, function pointer typedefs.

For Programmable Hardware: OpenGL ES 2.0 is defined relative to the OpenGL 2.0 specification and emphasizes a programmable 3D graphics pipeline with the ability to create shader and program objects and the ability to write vertex and fragment shaders in the OpenGL ES Shading Language. OpenGL ES 2.0 does not support the fixed function transformation and fragment pipeline of OpenGL ES.

EXERCISE

1. Explain the following polygon filling algorithms:

   (i)   Seed Fill   (ii) Edge Fill

2. Explain Sutherland-Hodgman algorithm for clipping.

3. Describe Scan Line algorithm to generate solid area on the screen.

4. Explain View Transmission with an example.

5. What are the different types of polygon? How to find whether given point is inside the polygon or not.

6. Explain with respect to 2D transformation

   (i) Scaling   (ii)   Rotations   (iii) Translations

7. Perform a 450 rotation of triangle A(0,0), B(1,1), C(5,2) :

   (i) about the origin   (ii)   about(-1,-1)

8. Explain the following character generation methods

   (i) Stroke Method   (ii) Starburst Method   (iii) Bitmap Method

9. Consider the line from (1,1) to (6,4). Use Bresenham's line drawing algorithm to rasterize this line and give output pixels.

UNIVERSITY QUESTIONS

1. What are the properties of Bezier curve ? Describe the procedure to generate Bezier curve ?

2. What do you mean by topological and fractal dimensions ?

   [May 2005, May 2006, Dec. 2007, Dec. 08]

3. Why is cubic form chosen for representing curves ?   **[May 2005, Dec. 2006]**

4. Explain the techniques of smoothing of curves using B-spline.   **[May 2005, 2007]**

5. Derive blending function of Bezier curve.   **[May 2005]**

6. Explain how fractals are used to generate fractal surfaces.

   [May 2005, 2006, 2007, Dec. 2006, 2007, 2009]

7. Explain curve generation method with example.   **[Dec. 2005]**

8.   What is fractal dimension ? Explain Koch curve in detail, giving fractal dimension.

[Dec. 2005, 2009, May 2008, 2009]

9.   Explain Bezier curve and B-spline curve functions for generating curves. **[Dec. 2005]**

10. Explain interpolation for curve generation.   **[Dec. 2005, May 2008, 2009]**

11. Compare Bezier and B-spline techniques for curve generation and discuss properties.   **[May 2006, Dec. 2009]**

12. Explain Hilbert's curve in detail.   **[May 2006, Dec. 2009]**

13. What is true curve generation ? Write a pseudo code to implement DDA arc generation.   **[May 2006, Dec. 2006, 2007, 2009, Nov. 2011]**

14. Write short notes on :

     (i)   Interpolating algorithm   **[Dec. 2006, May 2008]**

     (ii) Fractal geometry ?   **[Dec. 2006]**

15. State advantages of B-spline over Bezier for generating curve.   **[Dec. 2006]**

16. Write short note on : Curve generating by using approximation.   **[May 2007]**

17. Write short note on : B-spline and Corners.   **[Dec. 2007]**

18. Define fractals and give any two examples of fractals.   **[May 2008, 2009]**

19. Explain algorithm to draw fractal lines.   **[Dec. 2008]**

20. What is spline ? Give the various methods for specifying spline curve.   **[Dec. 2008]**

21. Write short note on fractal lines and fractal surfaces. State at least two applications.

[May 2011]

22. Write short note on B-splines. Draw necessary diagrams.

[May 2011, Nov. 2011]

23. Explain the term control points and order of connectivity in curve drawing.

[May 2011]

24. List various methods for drawing curved lines. Write a short note (with diagram) on Bezier curve. Write necessary blending function.   **[May 2011]**

25. Explain Lagrangian interpolation method.   **[Nov. 2011]**

26. Explain B-spline technique for generating curves with an example.   **[Nov. 2011]**

End-Sem. Theory Examination

Time : 2 Hours   **Max. Marks : 50**

Instructions to the candidates :

  (1) Answer Q. 1 or Q.2, Q. 3 or Q. 4, Q. 5 or Q. 6, Q. 7 or Q. 8.

  (2) Neat diagrams must be drawn wherever necessary.

  (3) Figures to the right side indicate full marks.

  (4) Assume suitable data if necessary.

---

1. **(a)** Define following terms:

    (i)   Persistence

    (ii)   Resolution

    (iii) Aspect Ratio

    (iv) Raster Scan Display.   **[6]**

  (b) Explain Cohen-Sutherland Line Clipping method with suitable example.   **[6]**

OR

2. **(a)** Write C code for Bresenham's line drawing algorithm.   **[6]**

  (b) Explain with example Windowing and clipping   **[6]**

3. **(a)** Explain Sutherland hodman polygon clipping.   **[6]**

  (b) Describe the 2-D transformation matrix for rotation about arbitrary point.   **[6]**

OR

4. **(a)** Explain seed fill algorithm in detail.   **[6]**

(b) Explain parallel and perspective projection with diagram.   **[6]**

5. (a) Write short note on Animation sequences   **[6]**

(b) Write short note on openGL ES.   **[7]**

OR

6. (a) What is shading ? What steps are required to shade an object using Gourand shading.   **[6]**

(b) Differentiate between Diffuse reflection and Specular Reflection   **[7]**

7. (a) Explain blending function in detail.   **[6]**

(b) Explain how fractals are used to generate fractal surfaces. Give two examples of fractal surfaces.   **[7]**

OR

8. (a) Explain the technique of smoothing of curves using B-Spline.   **[6]**

(b) Explain algorithm for fractal lines.   **[7]**

❋ ❋ ❋

Time : 2 Hours   **Max. Marks : 50**

N.B. :-

(1) Neat diagrams must be drawn wherever necessary.

(2) Figures to the right side indicate full marks.

(3) Use of calculator is allowed.

(4) Assume suitable data if necessary.

(5) Attempt Q. 1 or Q. 2, Q. 3 or Q. 4, Q. 5 or Q. 6, Q. 7 or Q. 8.

---

1. (a) Define Persistence, Random scan and Raster scan displays? Explain functioning of flat panel display. **[6]**

   (b) Write Bresenham's line algorithm and find out which pixel would be turned on for the line with end points (2,2) to (6, 5) using the same. **[6]**

OR

2. (a) Explain the TIFF image file format with block diagram. **[6]**

   (b) Explain Bresenham's circle drawing algorithm with mathematical derivation. **[6]**

3. (a) Write 2D transformation matrices of translation, scaling and shearing. Give the derivation of 2D rotation matrix. **[6]**

   (b) Explain Sutherland-Hodgeman clipping algorithm with example. **[6]**

OR

4. (a) How to perform rotation about an arbitrary axis in 3-D. **[6]**

   (b) Explain scan line algorithm with example. **[6]**

5. (a) Explain Bezier curve with properties. **[6]**

   (b) Enlist hidden face removal algorithm and explain any two. **[7]**

OR

6. (a) Explain and compare shading algorithms. **[6]**

   (b) Define Fractals? Explain Hilbert Curve and Koch curve. **[7]**

7. (a) Explain BITBLT operation of raster technique. **[4]**

   (b) What is OpenGL ES? Explain in brief the libraries supported by OpenGL ES. **[5]**

   (c) Draw block diagram of i860. **[4]**

OR

8. (a) Define animation. Explain the methods for controlling animations. **[7]**

   (b) Describe various operations carried out on the segment. **[6]**

DECEMBER 2014

Time : 2 Hours   **Max. Marks : 50**

N.B. :-

(1) Answer question Nos. Q. 1 or Q. 2, Q. 3 or Q. 4, Q. 5 or Q. 6, Q. 7 or Q. 8.

(2) Neat diagrams must be drawn whenever necessary.

(3) Assume suitable data, if necessary.

1. **(a)** What is computer graphics? State the applications of computer graphics. **[6]**

    (b) Explain Bresenham's line algorithm and find out which pixels would be turned on for the line with end points (5, 2) to (8, 4) using the same. **[6]**

OR

2. **(a)** Explain TIFF file organization with block diagram. **[6]**

    (b) What is aliasing and anti-aliasing? List and explain 2 anti-aliasing techniques. **[6]**

3. **(a)** Explain the different methods for testing a pixel inside a polygon. **[5]**

    (b) Explain the concept of 3D rotation about an arbitrary axis with an example. **[7]**

OR

4. **(a)** Write transformation matrix for Scaling and Rotation and scale the polygon with co-ordinates A(4, 5), B(8, 10) and C(8, 2) by 2 units in x-direction and 3 units in y-direction. Find the transformed A, B and C points. **[6]**

    (b) Explain Sutherland-Hodgeman clipping algorithm with example. **[6]**

5. **(a)** Explain the light, reflectively, color and shading in computer graphics. **[5]**

    (b) Define Bezier curve. State its properties. Derive blending function of Bezier curve. **[8]**

OR

6. **(a)** Explain and compare shading algorithms. **[6]**

    (b) Describe any two hidden face removal algorithm with diagram. **[7]**

7. **(a)** What is a segment? Give its structure and also describe various operations carried out on the segment. **[7]**

    (b) Write a short note on 3D MaxStudio or Maya. **[6]**

OR

8. **(a)** Draw block diagram of i860. **[6]**

    (b) What is the difference between conventional and computer based animations? What are the various methods of controlling animation? **[7]**

MAY 2015

Time : 2 Hours   **Max. Marks : 50**

N.B. :-

(1) Neat diagrams must be drawn wherever necessary.

(2) Assume suitable data, if necessary.

(3) Attempt Q. 1 or Q. 2, Q. 3 or Q. 4, Q. 5 or Q. 6, Q. 7 or Q. 8.

1. **(a)** Describe Frame buffer display in computer graphics.   **[4]**

    (b) Explain display file and its structure.   **[4]**

    (c) Explain Bresenham's Line drawing algorithm.   **[4]**

OR

2. **(a)** Write short notes on : Persistence, Resolution, Aspect ratio.   **[4]**

    (b) Write the properties of video display devices.   **[4]**

    (c) Using DDA algorithm find out which pixels would be turned on for the line with end points (1, 1) to (5, 3).   **[4]**

3. **(a)** Write Cohen-Sutherland line clipping algorithm.   **[4]**

    (b) Explain concept of viewing parameters with an example.   **[4]**

    (c) What is meant by coherence and how it can increase the efficiency of scan line polygon filling.   **[4]**

OR

4. **(a)** Write the transformation matrix for translation and scaling.   **[2]**

    (b) Write algorithm to fill the polygon area using flood fill method.   **[4]**

    (c) Explain the concept of 2D rotation about an arbitrary point with matrix representation.   **[6]**

5. **(a)** Compare RGB and HSV color model.   **[3]**

    (b) Explain the procedure to generate B-spline curve.   **[4]**

    (c) What is surface shading algorithm? Explain phong shading.   **[6]**

OR

6. **(a)** What are the advantages of Warnock's algorithm?   **[3]**

    (b) Explain the concept of reflection, shadows and ray tracing.   **[4]**

    (c) Explain Hillbert's curve with an example.   **[6]**

7. **(a)** What are the applications of morphing?   **[3]**

    (b) Write a short note on 3D maxstudio or Maya.   **[4]**

    (c) Describe the various operations carried out on the segment.   **[6]**

OR

8. **(a)** Explain image transformations with example.   **[3]**

    (b) Write advantages and disadvantages of segments.   **[4]**

    (c) Draw block diagram of i860.   **[6]**

DECEMBER 2015

Time : 2 Hours   **Max. Marks : 50**

N.B. :-

(1) Neat diagrams must be drawn wherever necessary.

(2) Figures to the right indicate full marks.

(3) Assume suitable data, if necessary.

1. **(a)** Explain the following :   **[6]**

    (i)   Frame buffer

    (ii)   Resolution

    (iii) Aspect ratio

    (b) Find out points for line segment having end points (0, 0) (–8, –4) using DDA line drawing algorithm.   **[6]**

OR

2. **(a)** What is error factor in Bresenham's circle drawing algorithm? Write Bresenham's circle drawing algorithm.   **[8]**

    (b) Explain in brief :   **[4]**

    (i)   Raster scan display

    (ii)   TIFF file format

3. **(a)** Explain Even-odd inside test with example.   **[3]**

    (b) Write flood fill algorithm.   **[3]**

    (c) Explain rotation about arbitrary point. Generate transformation matrix for same.   **[6]**

OR

4. **(a)** Explain parallel and perspective projection with example.   **[4]**

    (b) Write and explain Cohen-Sutherland line clipping algorithm.   **[8]**

5. **(a)** Explain point source illumination.   **[3]**

    (b) Explain fractals with example.   **[3]**

    (c) Write painters algorithm.   **[3]**

    (d) Explain Bezier curve in detail.   **[4]**

OR

6. (a) Explain diffused illumination.   **[3]**

    (b) Explain RGB color model.   **[4]**

    (c) Explain fractal lines with example.   **[3]**

    (d) Explain painter's algorithm.   **[3]**

7. (a) Give any four basic guidelines for animation.   **[4]**

    (b) Explain need of NVIDIA workstation in gaming.   **[5]**

    (c) Write a short note on OpenGL ES.   **[4]**

OR

8. (a) Explain role of Maya/equivalent open source tool in graphics design.   **[4]**

    (b) What is segment? Explain segment table.   **[5]**

    (c) Explain architecture of any NVIDIA processor.   **[4]**

MAY 2016

Time : 2 Hours   **Max. Marks : 50**

Instructions to the candidates :

(1) Attempt Q. 1 or Q.2, Q. 3 or Q. 4, Q. 5 or Q. 6, Q. 7 or Q. 8.

(2) Neat diagrams must be drawn wherever necessary.

(3) Figures to the right side indicate full marks.

(4) Assume suitable data if necessary.

1. (a) Write and explain any four state of the applications of Computer Graphics   **[4]**

    (b) Explain significance of error term in Bresenham's circle drawing algorithm. Explain its mathematical derivations.   **[8] OR**

2. (a) A write Bresenham's line drawing algorithm. Compare pixel values for line P(0, 0) Q. (6, 6)   **[6]**

    (b) Write short notes on: **[6]**

      (i)   Frame Buffer

      (ii)   Display Devices

      (iii)   Character Generation Methods

3. (a) What is inside test ? Explain even odd method in detail.   **[6]**

   (b) Write and explain with an example Cohen-Sutherland line clipping algorithm.   **[6] OR**

4. (a) What is homogenous coordinate system? Derive transformation matrix for rotation about arbitrary point.   **[8]**

   (b) Write matrices in homogenous coordinate system for the following transformations: **[4]**

   (i)   3-D rotation with respect to Y-axis

   (ii)   3-D scaling

   (iii) 2-D reflection with respect to origin

   (iv)   2-D Y-shear.

5. (a) Explain RGB and HIS color mode.   **[4]**

   (b) Explain diffused illumination and point source illumination.   **[3]**

   (c) Explain reflections, shadows, ray tracing.   **[6] OR**

6. (a) Explain interpolation and B-splines for curve generation.   **[4]**

   (b) Write short note on: **[6]**

   (i)   Painter's algorithm

   (ii)   Warnock algorithm

   (iii) Z-buffer.

   (c) Explain fractal lines with an example.   **[3]**

7. (a) What is segment ? Explain transformation operation on segment.   **[3]**

   (b) Explain in brief :   **[8]**

   (i)   NVIDIA workstation

   (ii)   Methods for controlling animation.

   (c) Explain significance of Open GLES.   **[2] OR**

8. (a) Write basic guidelines for animation and gaming technology.   **[4]**

   (b) What is segment and segment table ?   **[3]**

   (c) Explain i860 with a block diagram.   **[6]**

NOVEMBER 2016

Time : 2 Hours   **Max. Marks : 50**

Instructions to the candidates :

(1) Answer Q. 1 or Q.2, Q. 3 or Q. 4, Q. 5 or Q. 6, Q. 7 or Q. 8.

(2) Neat diagrams must be drawn wherever necessary.

(3) Figures to the right side indicate full marks.

(4) Assume suitable data if necessary.

---

1. (a) Explain the functioning of the following interactive computer devices: **[6]**

    (i) Joysticks

    (ii) Touch Panels

    (iii) Light Pen

(b) What is scan conversion ? Using DDA algorithm rasterize a line from (0, 0) to (6, 7).   **[6]**

OR

2. (a) Enlist any four graphics file formats. Explain tiff image file format in detail.   **[6]**

(b) Scan convert the line from (5, 5) to (13, 9) using Bresenham's line drawing Algorithm.   **[6]**

3. (a) Which algorithm is suitable for filling polygon with different pattern? Explain.   **[4]**

(b) Write materices for 3-D object scaling, rotation about X-axis, Y-axis, Z-axis.   **[8]**

OR

4. (a) Explain boundary fill algorithm using recursive approach for 4-connected and 8-Connected pixels.   **[8]**

(b) Derive matrix for rotation about arbitrary point. Also rotate point (3 3) with respect to (1, 1) by 90 degree.   **[4]**

5. (a) Explain B- spline curve. What are its advantages over the Bezier curve?   **[8]**

(b) What is fractals ? Explain any two applications of the fractals.   **[5]**

OR

6. (a) Explain RGB and HIS color model   **[6]**

(b) Write a short note on the following back face removal algorithm: **[4]**

    (i)   Painter algorithm

    (ii) Z-Buffer.

(c) Explain point source illumination and diffused illumination.   **[3]**

7. (a) What is an Animation? Explain different animation techniques.   **[6]**

    (b) Explain block diagram of i860 processor.   **[7]**

OR

8. (a) Explain the significance of NVIDIA workstation in gaming.   **[4]**

    (b) Explain the features of computer graphics and animation software.   **[4]**

    (c) Explain a segment table with an example along with data structure used to implement the segment table.   **[5]**

www.ingramcontent.com/pod-product-compliance
Lightning Source LLC
Chambersburg PA
CBHW080822020726
47501CB00009B/2381